KT-148-097

VIOLETA AMONG
THE STARS

Also by Dulce Maria Cardoso in English translation
The Return

DULCE MARIA CARDOSO

VIOLETA AMONG THE STARS

Translated from the Portuguese by
Ángel Gurría-Quintana

MACLEHOSE PRESS
QUERCUS · LONDON

First published as *Os Meus Sentimentos*
by Tinta da China, Lisbon, in 2005
First published in Great Britain in 2021 by

MacLehose Press
An imprint of Quercus Publishing Ltd
Carmelite House
50 Victoria Embankment
London EC4Y 0DZ
An Hachette UK company

 Co-funded by the
Creative Europe Programme
of the European Union

This publication has been funded with support from the European Commission. This
publication reflects the views only of the author, and the Commission cannot be held
responsible for any use which may be made of the information contained within.

A CIP catalogue record for this book is available from the British Library.

ISBN (HB) 978 1 52940 244 5
ISBN (TPB) 978 1 52941 513 1
ISBN (Ebook) 978 1 52940 245 2

Designed and typeset in Haarlemmer by Libanus Press Ltd
Printed and bound in Great Britain by Clays Ltd, Elcograf S.p.A.

 MIX
Paper from
responsible sources
FSC® C104740

Papers used by MacLehose Press are from well-managed forests
and other responsible sources.

For Luís, always
For my sister, for Coca and Paulo

It is the garden of Death that seeks you and always finds
you . . .
It is the garden that, without knowing it, you irrigate
with your blood

Dulce María Loynaz, Jardín, Novela Lírica

suddenly

I should have stayed at home, I should have stayed at home, I should have stayed at home, for some time, seconds, hours, I can do nothing,

suddenly I stop

the position I'm in, head down, hanging by the seatbelt, not uncomfortable, strangely my body does not weigh me down, it must have been a hard crash, I opened my eyes and found myself like this, head down, arms resting on the car's ceiling, legs dangling, the awkwardness of a ragdoll, eyes fixed, listless, on a drop of water that clings to a vertical shard of glass, I can't make out the noises around me, I start again, I should have stayed at home, I should have stayed at home,

refrains are so tedious

for some time, seconds, hours, I can do nothing, I must have landed very far from the road, rain beating on the car's plate metal, wheels spinning in the air, chirp, chirp, crickets, no, no, it can't be crickets, tick tock, indicators blinking, inside the water drop, only my eyes unable to look away, only my eyes, my car overturned on empty ground, my travel bag tangled in a bush, the waxing products, the free samples for my customers and my account books strewn in the mud, further away a shoe in a distant puddle, the headlamps still on, the rain, the trails of fireflies flitting until they die on the ground, chirp, it cannot be crickets, everywhere splinters of glass shimmering brightly, shards chasing the night away,

I should have stayed at home

the hot liquid dripping from my mouth is blood, I recognise the taste, my mouth is a pulp, hot, too hot, disgusting, I want to move, to free myself from the seatbelt, my hands do not obey me, two lifeless limbs, my legs, two absences, and my eyes fixed, inert, on the light-filled drop of water, a light-flooded drop, almost catching me, defeating me, I resist, I start again, I should have stayed at home, I should have stayed at home,

suddenly

I feel no pain, I am not afraid, my eyes drowning in the drop of light, my ears ringing with the sound of crickets,

I might no longer exist here at this moment

this moment might no longer exist for me

I drive through the darkness

gently, I glide along the road that is always the same, leaving
it behind even as it renews itself ahead of me, a generous
tongue swallowing me, black, infinite, I move on, guided
by the cats' eyes at the side of the road, the steel crash-
barriers, the wind twisting the leafless trees into sad
skeletons, lines sketched in charcoal against the sky, the
electricity pylons, scarecrows holding hands in a line that
goes nowhere

gently

I move on towards the place where the infinite unfolds, my
head in a pleasant spin, earlier this afternoon I sold the
house, I signed away the deeds with the silver pen, my hand
did not tremble, I did not hesitate, if I expected it to be easy
it was terrifyingly easier, I am travelling on the night of the
storm, people have talked about nothing else over the past
few days, the weather forecasts, civil protection authorities,
in cafés, my customers, a single subject,

a storm was announced

the only topic of conversation, so much fuss and it might all come to nothing, they always get it wrong, who can foresee nature's whims, words exchanged, it will be worse by the seaside, my head in a spin that feels good, I stretch a hand out blindly to the right, I am feeling around for my cassette tape, from today everything will be different, I say it again, from today everything will be different, the rain beats down on the car roof with a noise that should scare me, it thickens the car windows, doubles them, thousands of burst drops against the glass, watery webs torn apart by the wind, gusts of wind reaching speeds of up to, I defy the stormy night,

I drive through the darkness

my hand blindly seeking a voice that will calm the storm, lightning, a trace of light from the beginning, in the beginning there was only light, in the beginning there was only light and we were already blinded forever,

bêtises, ma chérie, bêtises

I find it hard to breathe, a pain in my chest, a single subject, you always drink too much, my heavy body following the hand, the same difficulty in the simplest of gestures,

freak, freak

another lightning bolt, a pretty neon cleaving the dark, I find the cassette tape, thunder, the darkness roaring, it would not be hard to believe that the sea has replaced the sky and is pouring down over the earth, I move forward, as if over the sky, a road that goes on and on into the darkness, I put the cassette into the tape player, I press rewind, scratching the silence, a single subject at the service station,

look at that fat lady falling over drunk

an exchange of words, some of the things you see out there are disgraceful, not even a conversation, the things you see out there, my boot is filled with different types of wax, handouts, samples, brochures, my account books, my customers are expecting me early tomorrow morning, they have been doing so for years, not these ones, not in this place, others, in other places, an understanding, I am a good salesperson, the best, I know exactly what the various waxes are made from, the temperature at which they melt, the types of skin they suit, my life is a battle against millions of hairs, there is nothing I am prouder of, perhaps Dora, perhaps, I know my enemies, I know their tricks, they can't deceive me, not even when they split to become stronger, or when they become ingrown, or when the cowards grow beneath the skin, hidden, I know my enemies and I never miss a chance to expose them, I don't let them pretend, or buy time, it's all-out war, when I look at a stranger's legs I can immediately tell my enemies' strength, how to combat them, other professionals might have a look and see nothing, I can take wagers, about what weapons to deploy, wax, cream, razor blade, those electric shavers buzzing annoyingly like flies, when I look at a stranger's legs I can immediately measure my enemies' strength, I can make out scars, ingrown hairs, even when I want to think about something else, especially if I want to think about something else, I'm a good sales-person, the best, I'll travel a hundred, two hundred kilo-metres, as many as are needed to sell my wax, I don't know how to do anything else, I pursue my enemies, millions of enemies everywhere, an unequal fight, lost, from today everything will be different, despite feeling so tired, I chase from my mind any thought that, from today, from tomor-row, not a thing will be different, not a single thing, I cannot accept an endless sea of days ahead of me, my life frittered away in a repetition of days, of gestures, of words, Ângelo saying,

nobody can correct the past, full stop

why do I hear Ângelo the spoilsport, whatever you do you cannot get rid of yourself, of what you were, what you still are, whatever you do, why do I hear Ângelo the spoilsport instead of the songs on my tape, from today everything will be different, I sold the house, it's true that it hasn't been long, at the service station I went back to my old ways, another man and the same old trick, the same lie, or, to be more precise, another lie, perhaps a more serious one, to all those men I had been with and who asked my name I answered with a riddle and

I share my name with a flower and also a colour

not a single one guessed correctly, perhaps it would have been strange, perhaps I would have found it very strange if I had given it any thought, I did not give it any thought, before him all the men who tried to guess replied Rose, most of them did not take their chances, smiled and walked away, they didn't really want to know my name, it was only a question, the most basic question, they were in a hurry, only a question, the most common question, to chase away the silence, the embarrassment, the shame of having been inside a woman like me, I never knew anything as merciless as satisfied flesh, the fact is that until this night, until him, all men had guessed Rose, I liked that, to have another name and it was not me who was there but someone called Rose, a creature I sometimes felt sorry for, so when that man asked I went through the charade in the knowledge that he would reply Rose or just smile, I was so sure of it that I was shocked to hear my name, I am very frightened, anyone who hunts as I do is always afraid, all prey learn quickly about the fear that can save them, there is something on the road, the rain won't let me see, the windscreen wipers are going at full speed, there is something up ahead, I brake hard, the car is not responding, lurches, zigzags, I'm not even scared, I get it back in gear, squint, too big to be a dead dog or cat, I move on with caution, only when I am very close do I see it is a fallen tree, its branches flailing in the wind, a whirlwind of leaves, I swerve, away from the leaves spiralling in the dark, from the branches thrashing, at least this tree did not die standing, I am always saddened by trees that die standing, they are still dreaming of future Springs when someone sticks a notice onto their trunks, this tree will be cut down, they can still feel the weight of nests and the flapping of sparrows, I am saddened by dead trees waiting for travellers who never arrive, nobody likes the shadow of death, they wait until the chainsaw cuts them to the ground, the trunk in wooden slices, the canopy a pile of branches that someone will collect to light a fireplace or, a leaf sticks to the windscreen, I am bringing it with me, from today everything will be different, I cannot correct what happened, I have no say in what happens next, an emergency exit sign on the right, the leaf blows away, it did not want to come with me, it does not want me as company, I am drunk, a leaf cannot want anything, I am drunk, leaves know everything about us, I am drunk, my heart is hurting me, my body stranger to me than those strangers who take it, I can hardly recognise it with the pain, the drink left my head spinning pleasantly, I rub my eyes in vain, they are still bleary, I begin to cry, the leaf did not want to come with me, I am so ridiculous, I feel the man's hands on my skin, I run my fingers over the small grooves that his fingernails left on my body, trails, I don't know what to do with the smell of a stranger now embedded in my flesh, I'm scared, what if I am no longer myself, what if I never belong to myself again, why do I let myself die,

why does life kill me

I speed up towards the infinite that is now my destination, one way, from today everything will be different, the night scares me, six blasts of darkness lurking beyond the car windows, it is very late, 4:37 on the dashboard's digital clock, actually 4:32, I always gave myself a five minute head-start, it's true they never did me any good, I never arrived in the future, always some small delay, some holdup, excuses I can no longer remember, I see a car up ahead, the first I've seen since I left the service station, I accelerate to catch up with the two red taillights reflected by the water on the road, the car is moving slowly, I decide to overtake, I am driving past an unknown woman on the night of the storm, I turn my face to her, round, overly round, my body, fat, sadly fat, my job, salesperson, my house, on Travessa do Paraíso, Paradise Street, my daughter, Dora, I leave the stranger behind in my car's spray, a coil twisting in the air, instead of the red taillights reflected on the road two white headlamps in my rear-view mirror, magic, if I could really do magic I would disappear from myself, I speed up, I move away from the white lights as they diminish in the distance, I steal their faces, their bodies, their jobs, their families, a drunken woman is easily entertained, even by a dumb game such as this one, the headlamps of the car I over-took disappear in my rear-view mirror, once again there is just the night, a road sign, a yellow rectangle on the hard shoulder, which

drive with caution

I read out loud, drive with caution, the voice bouncing against the windows, another rectangle, this one is hanging, advertising a junction, four appropriately numbered roads, four destinations, I can finally change my direction, reverse my progress, give up, it is tempting to think that I can choose, and what if from today everything really were different, I know the junction from my maps, I always collected maps, I mean, I have been collecting maps for a long time, hundreds of maps at home, used, brand new, who cares, on maps I can choose my route without fear, I can go round and round in my paper worlds, I go everywhere, places I cannot relate to any landscape, or face, or flower, nothing, places that only exist to satisfy my wish to escape on those very warm afternoons, I open the maps on my bedroom floor, I don't want to know anything about the world, I never wanted to, those very warm afternoons, I pull down the shutters and my body is covered in luminous ovals, clusters of geometrically arranged points of light, I spend whole afternoons travelling, I approach the junction, the four numbered destinations, rain falls translucent at the feet of the concrete streetlamps, drops scintillating, a shower of fireflies, what if I changed my destination, what if I gave up

bêtises, ma chérie, bêtises

on Denise and Betty, what if for once I went to a place where no-one is expecting me, I never travelled anywhere without someone expecting me, I continue my journey, I cannot give up my fight, every day my enemies defeat me on my own body, on other people's bodies, my enemies who will be the last to die, my heart stopped, my lungs flooded, my flesh cold and my enemies still growing for a few hours, one day, I shouldn't think about that, I am a good salesperson, the best, tomorrow I'll be back, I asked Dora to buy bread, I left her a message on one of those little yellow papers that you can stick anywhere, please buy bread, I must not have heard what Dora said as she left the restaurant,

I'm leaving home tomorrow

how foolish to think I heard Dora say she was abandoning me, I left the message in the usual place, tomorrow Dora will buy bread and leave it on the kitchen table, never upturned because it's bad luck, Dora knows that upturned bread brings bad luck, my Dora knows so many things, it worries me that she can learn them with the same apathy with which she scans the barcodes for hundreds of products at the hypermarket checkout, the same apathy with which she posed nude for fine arts students, a slim body, almost a child's, whatever angle you view it from, without anyone discovering the dimples that appear when she smiles, the funny way she tightens her fists, a bundle of fingers, dozens of life drawings of a stranger, not my daughter, the same apathy that made her quit school, declaring, I never learned anything there anyway, an apathy that grows in her chest and overflows and hits me in the heart, I put my foot down on the pedal, the road opaque, the gestures softened,

if you want to smash yourself to pieces on the road
that's up to you

I burst out laughing, why are my laughs dying against the
windows, why am I surrounded by this silence, Ângelo is
wrong, again

laughter is the best thing we can offer others

bloody Ângelo is wrong, he does not understand life, I keep
on laughing, at Denise, at Betty, at Dora, at Ângelo, at the
handouts I give away to my customers, a stainless steel salt
and pepper holder and a porcelain toothpick holder, wax
for sensitive skin, for black skin, for women who are prone
to varicose veins, I laugh out loud, my screeches fluttering
in the car, I am so tired, it was a long day, very long, and
the night is a black blanket that smothers me

tell me a secret
keep me awake
until this night is over

instead of revealing its secrets, instead of saving me, a
blanket that suffocates me, and if I went back home, to the
bread that Dora will buy, the four destinations, the junction,
if I could choose, it is late, I give in to my fate, I move on,
the wind blows about the oleanders planted in the central
reservation, tiny points of light at the junction now dis-
appearing in the rear-view mirror, the shower of fireflies

around the tall streetlights, another sign at the roadside, this one bright yellow, a sun in the middle of the night, don't drink and drive, I laugh, laughter bouncing around in the car until it crashes into the silence that kills it, I could kill for a cigarette, I feel around for a pack, a succession of slow gestures, listless, I have a lot of time, I put a cigarette to my mouth, a caress on my dormant lips, silence,

tell me a secret

silence everywhere, I drive past a factory, seen in the distance the lit-up rectangle looks pretty, I am unconcerned about my heart slowing down to an ever sleepier beat, I close my eyes for just a moment, I am tired, in a few hours I will be telling Denise that my wax does not cause bruising, scarring or swelling, that she just won't find any other wax that so efficiently destroys the hair's germinal matrix, I am the best at delivering the spiel, no question, I am the best salesperson, I know what wax to recommend for sensitive skin, the road is always the same, the white markings form a continuous line, moving faster, I am tired, I close my eyes for just a moment, just a moment like weeds growing in empty lots

do what I have to even if later I feel ashamed, I never really feel shame, perhaps a slight discomfort, a knot in my throat that loosens as I drive away, a slight unease, the vague sense of a sin I have no intention of being redeemed for, I take the exit to the service station, I am hungry, I go past the café, I stop in front of the large windows, the rain does not let me see inside, I switch on my high beams, a waiter turns in surprise, a rabbit caught in the headlamps, the café is almost empty, a huge room with empty tables and chairs, a lone couple at the back and on the left a group of boys, few people travel on a night like this, it is so late, I turn off the headlamps, kill the engine,

always do what I have to even if later I feel ashamed

I exit the car unhurriedly, open the umbrella, pull the raincoat tight, all my movements are strangely slow, at odds with the rain falling violently, two small puddles on the asphalt, the glass doors open automatically as I approach, I like doors that open on their own, and vending machines that dispense cigarettes or stamps and give back the exact change, I enter the café and go to the counter, the boys fall silent for a moment when they see me and then one of them, who cares which one, they all look the same, says, large, extra extra-large, they all laugh, the laughter isn't over yet and they are already speculating, must eat three times as much as a normal person, must be a disease, the bed, can you imagine the bed,

there once was a woman who was so fat, so fat, that when she fell out of bed she fell out on both sides

more laughter, at least they're young and, perhaps because of that, merciless, I am even less fond of older people who hide the pleasure they get from witnessing someone else's disgrace, at least they're young and, perhaps because of that, indifferent, maybe in a minute one of the boys will say, the other day I saw an even fatter one and that will be enough for them to forget about me, move onto something else, youth does not stop, it is consumed by senseless haste, a server takes my order, I ask for two pastries and a coffee, pay up-front, the clanking of the cash register, my hands fumbling in my handbag,

the *porte monnaie, ma chérie*, the *porte monnaie*

the small tasks always seem so difficult for me, a coin falls out of my hand, I bend over to pick it up, how difficult to do even the simplest things, I point at the pastries I've paid for, not that I need to point, I know their actual names, I can even pronounce them properly, a lady must be *chic, très chic*, under all circumstances, an *éclair* and a *millefeuille*, please

the server does not understand, the world's most beautiful language wasted on an ignorant server, I ask again, a cream puff and a custard slice, right, he says, right, so a cream puff and a custard slice, and moving his metal tongs in circles he searches for my order in the glass cabinets where I can see yesterday's creamy pastries, and the ones from the day before, here they are, the satisfied air of someone who has just solved a mystery, the metal tongs picking up the pastries and dropping them onto a plate, the server is not worried about one pastry ruining the other, or their creams mixing, both pastries on a plate that the server puts onto the counter before heading for the coffee machine, he fills the filter with ground coffee, a brisk gesture, places the cup underneath, the server imagines he is a good employee but he isn't, he is let down by his haste, his carelessness, the cup is not in the right position so coffee drips down the side, the server hands me the plate with one pastry on top of the other and a cup stained with spilled coffee that

where's your head at, Maria da Guia, where's your head at

I accept, I step away from the counter carrying the plate with two pastries in one hand and the coffee in another, I hesitate, I feel the server's mocking smile on my back, the more insignificant the choice the longer I take, I choose a table from which I can see the car, one condition met, it is irrelevant but at least I have one condition, I sit, I place the pastries and coffee on the table, all my movements are slow,

do what I have to even if later

Denise and Betty are expecting me early tomorrow morning, if Ângelo had come with me as we agreed my movements would be different, hurried, very hurried, I can never spend too much time in someone's company, I could never get used to other people's presence, I still can't understand those people who can't eat or sleep alone, those who complain about loneliness, perhaps those who can tolerate others are happy, and even happier are those who need others, the couple at the table at the back get up and leave, the glass doors open, competent, unlike the employee, a bad employee, sloppy, scratches his head and yawns, outside the couple takes shelter beneath an umbrella, the man kisses the woman's face before getting into the car, illicit lovers saying goodbye after an evening tryst, I correct myself immediately, so obvious, it cannot all be so monotonous, I cannot allow tedium to seep into life, I think of other theories, they all seem unlikely and tedious, I give up, reality is always frightful, my imagination, my imagination counts for nothing when compared to reality, the woman says something that makes the man laugh, I avoid looking towards the boys' table, I cut into the *millefeuille*, it wasn't baked today, maybe yesterday, the day before yesterday, who knows, the puff pastry is hard, I don't care, the sickly sweet mush in my mouth gives me pleasure, I gobble the *millefeuille* and then move on to the *éclair*, the sugar icing sticks to my teeth, I run my tongue repeatedly over the stickiness, the boredom that suits me so well showing on my face, my mother's card-playing companions looking at me,

sometimes it seems like she doesn't regulate her appetites very well

while Maria da Guia twisted her apron, more distressed than the birds my father chased around in their cages,

don't pull that face, menina, your poor mother gets annoyed

don't eat cakes, menina, your poor mother gets so upset

the menina is a naughty girl, menina is a very naughty girl

and Maria da Guia who is languishing in a rented room, no more than five square metres, having thrown away her chances of having another life with her communist boyfriend,

when we are given one life we don't know how to live another, menina

the *éclair* crumbles in my mouth, one of the boys tells the others off, raises his voice, it's bad luck to take the piss

the boy is not being kind, it is fear that makes him tell off the others, one of the boys, not the scared one, is wearing a T-shirt that says smile, another has a man skiing and a name, some ski resort, I was here, or, someone I know was here, I concentrate on my plan to offload the eco-friendly wax I have in the car boot, a good salesperson must develop a persuasive pitch, it is not easy to persuade Denise,

the environment can go fuck itself

perhaps I will ask Denise's Ukrainian fellow for some help, what's his name, Serguei, or maybe the previous one was called Serguei and this one is called Alexandre, who knows, they are all so similar, Serguei, I think this one is Serguei, anyway it might not be such a good idea to try to make friends with the Ukrainian fellow that Denise treats like a dog, no-one listens to a dog's opinion, I must think of another way, persuading Betty is easy, all I have to do is talk about the world we are leaving behind for our children, Betty is always worrying about the two pale children she brought into this world, the boys' laughter interrupts my thoughts, I drink my coffee, I am satisfied, I sold the house, I will no longer belong to it, free at last, from today every-thing will be different, I don't know why I took Ângelo and Dora to that restaurant, I knew that my child

this restaurant is so sad

and Ângelo do not like that restaurant, Ângelo got it into his head that he is allergic to spices, and Dora, well, Dora is always a special case, they both think I did it on purpose to spite them, whereas what I had in mind was to propose a truce, tell them that I hope that in the future, when I get back I will take them out again, I will make them understand my intention, my wish for peace, I try to find the pack of cigarettes in my handbag, smoking kills, in huge letters, on one side, while on the other, smoking makes skin look older, if I happen not to die, if I turn out to be eternal, I will be able to claim compensation because I was assured that smoking kills, since when did everything start talking, the road says, drive carefully, keep your distance, don't drink and drive, any day now it will be the hall in a building saying, if you have a hot neighbour keep your hands off her, or even, feeling up the hot neighbour requires the permission of the building's residents who may reserve the right to this or that, or another, if you step in dog shit don't wipe your shoes on your neighbour's door mat, try to wipe them on another building's door mats, I light a cigarette, earlier this afternoon at the bank, sign up for one of our help-to-buy accounts, retirement savings accounts, any day now the bank will be saying, sign up for one of our daylight robbery plans, get the add-ons, extreme perversity, or escape to a tropical country, at the pharmacy I visited yesterday to get some nose drops, don't die for love, use a condom, watch your cholesterol, measure your blood pressure, drink a litre and a half of water every day, avoid fatty foods, exercise, the pharmacy remains strangely quiet when I tell it to get lost, the pharmacy and all its advice, I don't think it's right that roads, banks, pharmacies, clothes are incessantly talking, the nonsense spouted by good old fashioned speakers was already enough, I get up to go to the counter, I will order a drink, there is not much choice at service stations, I ask for a gin, I don't like it much, it tastes like perfume, again I have to pay in advance, find coins, again the little tasks that always seem so difficult to me, now the cash register is doing the talking, under the terms of the food safety act all food sold on these premises, I stop listening when the server pours me a gin with a barely disguised look that says,

looking like that and drunk on top of it

unbelievable, I get back to the table, I am still thinking about how to pitch the wax made with one hundred per cent natural products, the eco symbol guarantees that it is environment-friendly, none of this will interest Denise, even the worst salesperson knows that you mustn't waste a good spiel, I have to persuade her to pay twice as much for the eco wax, I must give it more thought, every now and then the boys punch and kick each other and let out guffaws, what are these boys doing here at a time like this, the servers laugh with the boys, they know about me, I can't imagine a reason why the boys would be here at this time on a night like this, they must live locally, the children of the service station's employees, employees doing other shifts, the lives of others no matter how vulgar are always a mystery, do what I have to even if

I knock back the gin and leave the café, the boys and the servers stare at me, they must also be wondering what I'm doing here at this time, where I'm going, or perhaps they know about me, they know what I do, I don't think so, so many people pass through the service station, unless they remember me from how I look, I don't care, I open the umbrella, quick steps towards the car, my slow ambling from earlier gone, it's been proven that fat people are inconstant beings, perhaps it's a self-esteem issue, I follow two lorry drivers towards the car park, journeys are long and bodies are always voracious in their desire for other bodies,

do what I have to even if later I feel shame

I have always found what I need in lorry parks, I can't complain, nor am I proud of it, it is just the gluttony of bodies, I park in a strategic spot, if Ângelo had come along with me this journey would have been different, another journey, one small detail and reality changes, almost nothing, in fact nothing is essential, if Ângelo had come along this journey would have been different, if he had not stayed at home spread out on the sofa watching endless television repeats all night, he finishes off a beer and gets up to throw out the bottle, he is incapable of leaving empty beer bottles or dirty ashtrays on a table, he cannot go to bed without doing a round of the house and if he finds anything out of place he fixes it immediately, he won't go to sleep until he knows everything is in its place, bathroom towels folded three times and tea towels stretched across the oven door handle, only one proper way of turning down the bed, folding back the frilly bedspread along the creases, the slippers are always by the carpet's left corner, the alarm clock always the same distance from the bedside lamp and the battery powered radio, Ângelo says everything has its place, and one place only, in order to live in peace, Ângelo who every day dusts the objects cluttering the two rooms, he is especially careful with the jade elephant by the entrance with its trunk pointing towards the door for good luck,

it's bad luck to take the piss

with the porcelain dancers on top of the cabinet and the fruit bowl with the swans in the middle of the table polished with cedar oil, I can't imagine what would happen if Ângelo lost his elephant, his dancers and his swans, I don't find it too hard to believe that he would lose his mind, I have seen it happen for much less, the first thing Ângelo does as soon as he gets up is open the windows so the clean morning air fills the house, two or three rays of sun on a nice day, never more than that because the flat is at ground level on a street where the sun can hardly squeeze in, next he scrubs the kitchen and toilet with bleach and when necessary waxes the living room and bedroom floors, if he didn't have to clean the house Ângelo's life would be much sadder or would not be a life, that is how much the house means to him, he doesn't mind being heckled when he performs at social clubs, or children throwing cake at him when he is dressed as a clown at children's parties over the weekend, or pensioners on a daytrip complaining about the comedian not being funny, he doesn't care as long as he can get back to the house and find the figurines dusted and in the right place, the furniture oiled and the bedspread stretched out with the frills hanging just so, the bathtub immaculately white and the toilet lid shut, nothing matters more, which is why I don't find it hard to believe that Ângelo would lose his mind if he lost his house, if Ângelo had come with me I wouldn't be

when we lead one life we cannot have another

parked in this lorry park, with my high-beams on, waiting for tonight's prey, a curious lorry driver, someone restless, once I've identified my prey I act according to the rules that my hunting experience has helped me establish, I'm always cautious, and on a night like this I can't afford to scare off the prey, men are the biggest scaredy-cats I know, my first rule is to allow a switching of roles, I become the perfect prey for any hunter, even the most inexperienced, once I have sated my flesh I don't mind them finding out the truth, it amuses me when that happens, and if they happen to say, there's more to you than you let on, or worse, I mean, things they judge to be worse, for instance, you're quite the whore, aren't you, I don't care, once my flesh is sated I don't care in the least whether they insult or flatter me,

do what I have to

it would be easier if it weren't bucketing down, I would walk around the lorry park, for this sort of thing I always wear high heels so it will be obvious that there's a woman walking around, on normal nights, after a dozen steps, my prey start looking out for me, as I walk I usually repeat a tongue-twister or proverb under my breath, curiosity killed the cat but satisfaction brought him back, curiosity killed the cat but satisfaction brought him back, on normal nights I have the luxury of choosing and for that too I have my own rules, with this storm happening I'll have to make do with the first man to show up, I keep my headlamps on, I pull a map out of the glove compartment and put it on my lap, for all intents and purposes I turn into a woman who is lost, as I arrange the map I say in a high-pitched voice, my hero, you are here to save me, I will kill you with a dagger with an emerald-studded handle that I keep close to my heart, oh my hero, come get a taste of death, Maria da Guia was always telling me the same story,

when we are told one story we always hear another

a boring story not featuring princesses and fairies but a woman who got rid of her children, a story so annoying that it wasn't even sad, or maybe it was just that Maria da Guia could not tell it well enough, you need some talent for everything, I got distracted, someone might be observing me, I go back to playing my role, on a night like this any mistake can be fatal, I go back to pretending to be worried and put my anxious hands on the map, I took the time to change the cassette and the earworm now playing will become yet another fact on this dark night as it lies in wait of its meaning, I wait, and in the moment that precedes the discovery of a prey I feel an indescribable pleasure, I light a cigarette, no man can resist the seductive power of a cigarette in a woman's hands, even if I do not have long fingers and my smoke does not form into curls that hide my face as it does in those black and white films I used to watch on television, I let the cigarette burn between my fingers, I am an obese woman on the border between being a type I or a type II, according to the chart so helpfully created by health professionals, were it not for that chart I would be lost in life, whereas now, even if I swing between type I and type II, I know what chart I belong in and what categories I am between, this sort of information is important for me, it is always the simplest of questions that make me most indecisive, I put on my frightened face, it is so authentic that I can almost feel the fear I am faking, the map open on my lap, the earworms playing and the cigarette forgotten in my hand, I am perfect in my role, I enjoy the pleasure of waiting with the certainty that I will be successful, I was never disappointed by the hunger bodies feel for other bodies, flesh is always filled with the desire that brings me here, that pushes me, if necessary, into the narrow lorry cabins reeking of sweat, rosaries hanging from rear-view mirrors and photos of the wife and children in magnetic photo frames made of plastic, I always struggled to climb the steps into the cabins and I can hardly move in such a tight space, but I follow them readily, with obedience so blind that it unnerves me, it frightens me, I mustn't forget to be frightened, for the men it must seem like this is the first time I climb into a lorry, I justify the ease with which I accept their invitation alleging curiosity, curiosity killed the cat, which makes me even more credible, victims are naturally curious, and should the men lock their doors, which they often do, I remember to show my fright, I must always act in character, no professional actress ever played her role so convincingly,

the shame you make me feel

most lorry drivers want to talk so I have to keep up the conversation no matter how boring it gets, another of my rules, make these men feel it was they who persuaded me to follow them, if they weren't so apprehensive it wouldn't take us as long, I wouldn't have to fake my amazement, oh, I had never been so high up, the road looks so far away, cars must seem like ants from up here, I would not have to fake an interest in trivial things like mirrors, so big, the buttons on the dashboard, I almost always say the same things in those tight cabins, I speak until the men, growing in confidence, start getting closer, the more nervous ones lock the lorry doors, what I want is about to happen and even then, despite the sting of desire tormenting my flesh, I continue talking, I play my part so well

the shame you make your father feel, Violeta

that I have sometimes come across some men who, taking pity on me, have let me know of their intentions, of the danger I was in, I would immediately change my strategy, good hunters must always have alternative plans, to those charitable men I would speak about the sadness of being unloved, I would become a beggar hungry for any crumbs they might offer and the result was the same, the charitable ones would take my body to satisfy their own, the only difference was that they believed themselves to be acting out of kindness for someone who was in need of it, luckily there are fewer of the charitable ones as I like them the least, but it may be unfair to describe all men like that, I never came across one man who I might mistake for another, diversity is the one thing that amazes me about humanity, though it is only an apparent diversity, perhaps I am not being unfair about their essence, when I think about the many men I have met over the years what comes to mind is the solitude, an unease in their eyes, in the force with which they grab me and, perhaps more importantly, in the fact that they needed my body, a body like mine, as men gain confidence, and I don't get tired of saying it, men's fear is truly frightening, they come close and

the cats in the garden always ran away from me

I can smell their nauseating breath, of sleep and cigarettes, decaying teeth, their cooked dinner, after a while men's breath also becomes repetitive, but even that won't stop me from

instead of running away from my father who poisoned
their milk

seeking them out, these men who trust me more the more
defenceless they are, absurd, the cats also trusted the man
who killed them and collected their stiffened bodies with
their green glass eyes to burn them, they ran away from
me, they always ran away from me, they had the punishment they deserved, if they hadn't run away from me
perhaps they would have been saved, years later my father
found a justification,

if I don't kill them they'll get into the cages

the cruellest act can always be justified, the most insignificant too, we are so hung up on understanding everything,
on avoiding, frightened, the mystery of death, the final
mystery, the men I meet at service stations have for a long
time now not held any mysteries, I can guess their answers
to the questions I ask them, how long have you been on
the road, they like questions that allow them to do some
calculations, I did my first trip when I was twenty-three,
now I'm fifty-two, so it's been, others prefer dates, I started
driving in nineteen so-and-so, others reply without hesitation, it's been seventeen years and two months, it's always
good to be certain of anything even if it is something as
pointless as that, another question these men like, how
many kilometres have you put in, just last week, for instance, thousands and thousands, if I had an escudo for

every kilometre I'd be a millionaire, or a cent, there are no more escudos, cents or escudos, same difference, it's just as hard to earn them both, and the one before him, or was it some other week, if the road was always going upwards I would have made it to heaven by now, he seemed a sensitive type, he told me he cries when he drives past burnt woodland, the truth is that sensitive types bore me hugely, of course I don't let on, luckily most men are not like that, in any case they are all the same in the way they approach me, first their breath, then the hands, as if by accident, they almost always go for the thighs, I am always startled when they touch me, I no longer know whether it is for real or if I am faking it, it can certainly be dangerous, I don't know the men who lock me up in their cabins and I realise that I cannot easily get off the lorry, that if I scream no-one will hear me, and yet, the more likely the danger the better I feel in those foul-smelling lorry cabins, looking at some football club logo or the photo of an ugly woman, or of some equally ugly children, a framed piece of fabric with an embroidered message, a man has no worry if he has no mother-in-law and no lorry, Ângelo might use this line in one of his performances, it is better than the one about elephants that he likes so much and that no-one else finds funny anymore, in these cabins I have almost always seen the same things over the years, every now and then a surprise, a baby's boot hanging from the rear-view mirror, a human tooth, a dry rose, it is mostly football club logos, a rosary and two or three family photos, the occasional posters of naked women, the truth is it is very difficult to tell these men apart, very few of them kiss me, I don't hold it against them, I don't get upset, I just say this to prove how alike one another they all are, I know that unwanted kisses are bitter, they leave an unpleasant taste in the mouth that even the greediest of tongues can recognise, the men don't kiss me even though they are hungry for my flesh, at that point I become even more coy, I mustn't let my own flesh's hunger scare them away, even if desire is taking my breath away, men are so easily frightened, they have to believe that they persuaded me to allow them into my body, I pretend to be surprised, I resist, I tell them this has never happened to me, I hint that I do not think this is right, but I never go too far in case I come across some benevolent man who will give up, I obey the rules I have set for myself, I have given every man I was ever with the illusion of being unique, I have told them what they wanted to hear, I am the most defenceless prey, the most vulnerable, my blind obedience excites them, they grab me by the head and push me against their cocks, my head bobbing against their thighs, I kiss their sweaty hands, I submit to the craving I awaken in them, my head banging against the hanging rosary, the family photograph, the club logo swinging to our bodies' rhythm, the teenage daughter looking more bored every day, looking dumber than the ugly mother, the cabin feeling smaller, tighter, if I weren't so big I could lie back, I no longer fit in the lorries' sleeper berths,

one size only, I'm sorry

when the weather is fine I lead them, or rather, I pretend they are leading me, to the abandoned lots near the service stations, I let them take me on the weeds that pierce my flesh, after they are sated my excessive flesh becomes intolerable, they say, I've never been with someone like this, I think even they don't know why they need to hurt me, they feel contempt for the desire that led them to wallow in the flesh they now view as misshapen, they despise themselves, they feel ashamed of themselves, I might feel shame for them if I could be bothered, I never was, I stub out the spent cigarette, I run my tongue around my mouth and find a cake crumb, I breathe into my cupped hands to see if the smell of gin has gone, men rarely trust women who smell of alcohol, what I want to happen is about to happen, the tumult of the flesh has never disappointed me, I wait, I look at the map on my lap, I look at the lorries, I read the licence plates, I seek out coincidences in their numbers, their letters, I search for a sign that will let me shoot to kill, I hear

do what I have to

three dry knocks close to my head, I jump in my seat, the shape of a man outside my car window, I cannot see his face clearly, a veil of water running down the glass, the man knocks again with his knuckles, hand shut in a fist, I press the switch and the window rolls down silently, my car window is as efficient as the café's automatic doors, the man comes near, his face now close to mine, I pull back, he is

drenched, water runs down his forehead, onto his nose, his
lips are purple,

the lips of the dying are ugly, don't you think, lady
volunteer

he asks, are you lost, the rain won't let me hear him clearly,
I heard him ask, are you hurt, he asks again, oh, lost, of
course, it could not be hurt, I glance at the map on my lap, I
turn off the cassette player, I begin the role play, a good
hunter is always ready, I look at the man who seems strangely
unbothered by the rain, he is soaked, the sweatshirt, the
jumper, the flesh, the bones, the blood

do you need anything

I will never again need anything

that seems not to course through the hands that are now
pressing on my car, the man notices my apprehension and
takes two steps back, he smiles, now that he is not leaning
against the car I can see he is a tall man, slim, his hair must
be black and straight, he looks at me, does not take cover
from the rain, does not wipe off the water dripping down
his forehead and making him screw up his eyes, he steps
further back, wants to reassure me, steps into a shadow,
a gentle ghost, do you need anything, no, I don't, I answer
still unsure of how to take advantage of the opportunity,
I got caught out by the storm, and I point to his drenched

body to make my point, the wind won't let me hear, he comes close again and he is no longer a ghost, a man now, he puts his hands on the open window again, his pale and thin hands, he smiles, he seems to know I am lying, I notice something bulging suspiciously out of one of his sweatshirt pockets, I am instantly convinced that it is a weapon, I shudder slightly, a weapon, I can't take my eyes away from the bulge, I let him follow my gaze, I am frightened, a pleasant feeling in my stomach, in my legs, in my tongue that seems to twist itself involuntarily, the man slowly takes his hand to his pocket, I swallow hard, a familiar sound, fear growing in my mouth, in my faster-beating heart, my heart beating so conspicuously I don't know how much longer I can take it, the man smiles as he puts his hand in his pocket,

nature in all its fury

he is going to take out the weapon and point it at me, he is a thief, a murderer, how long can I keep up this charade, I look at his hands, he is having fun, he has sniffed out my fear

the sky is running riot

which is not as real as I am making it out to be, if I was really fearful I would shout, I would try to shut the window, I would lock the door, if my fear was real I would turn the key in the ignition and escape, I am not frightened, I was never frightened of any man but I convinced myself I was frightened of all of them, my own private joke, I go along with it, I move

my eyes away from his pocket, I press the switch to shut the
window halfway, the water splashing my face annoys me, I
turn off the cabin light, I start folding the map, the man is
still standing, he put his hand in his pocket, I think, what if
this is it, a knife, a gun, a gleaming knife against my throat,
the blade colder than rain, he says, get out of the car, I stay
still, he shouts, get out of the car you fat whore, how long
will this take, the man pulls a bottle out of his pocket, shows
it to me, I don't recognise the shape at first, fear prevents me
from seeing that it is a bottle, that the man who talks about
the sky running riot is drunk, I sigh, this is the first time I've
come across a drunkard worried about the sky running riot,

do you want a drink to warm you up

I am amused by the drunkard standing in front of me, a drink
would be nice, earlier this evening at the restaurant my child

stop drinking, you're being pathetic

told me off, she is ashamed of me, I smile, how could I have
been scared of a drunkard, this hunt is won, I feel no pity
for the poor prey, I'm not bothered by a drunkard's lack of
judgment, I am not usually considerate and even less so when
I am on the hunt, I have been with men who were so drunk
they forgot me the second it was over, others felt so guilty
they would have run back to their little wives if I had given
them the chance, repentant, I never betrayed my wife before,
I wrapped my legs around their backs, there is always a

first time, you'll see that you like her even more now, I never gave them a second chance and I never regretted it, I need to find an excuse to get out of the car, I never let these men get into my car, it's not a hard rule, just a habit, I follow them wherever they take me but never let them into my car, the disgust a satisfied body can feel is truly unbearable, I can hardly stand their smell on my body, it is so difficult to get rid of the smell of others' bodies, to get rid of others' bodies, I don't want him in my car, I need an excuse to get out, have a coffee, use the toilet, anything, the man smiles

   may I get in

get your hands off, I want to shout, I don't want him in my car, I don't want you in my car, instead I say in my usual voice, perhaps sweeter, I need to have a coffee, a coffee would be nice, the man cannot hear my shouts like he cannot hear my mother

   a coffee, Baltazar, a coffee

   the *chauffage*, Baltazar, the *chauffage*

who is dead, but if she is so long-dead why is she, on these cold nights, still saying to my father,

   the *chauffage*, Baltazar, the *chauffage*

   a coffee, Baltazar, a coffee

I lie to the man, my heating doesn't work, that's bad luck with this weather but bad luck is proof that there can be good luck, I pretend to agree, the man says again, bad luck is proof that there can be good luck,

it's bad luck to take the piss

later I may try to understand how the man is proposing to put his theory to the test, and afterwards he may invite me into his lorry, at the moment he doesn't know what to say to me, I have to wait until the man chooses the words he thinks are best, I cannot jump ahead, the man is still quiet, perhaps he wants to give up, I cannot let that happen, I employ my usual trick, I need to use the toilet, I point to the block of toilets, I press the switch and the window rises silently, I exit, it is raining hard, the man opens the bottle and offers me a drink of his liquor, and what if I had one sip, just one sip of liquor to warm up on this cold night, but I refuse, I cannot risk ruining everything, he drinks, chokes, drinks again, the liquor burns his tongue, his throat, I don't want him to stop, I don't protect him from his thirst for burning, I don't care if the drink sets his body on fire, a flame growing inside his chest, his flesh in flames, the man takes me by the throat, his hand is very cold, I shudder, he pulls me towards him, it is raining so hard, the man whispers, I'm not going to hurt you, I feel defenceless, one of the birds my father chased in their cages,

come here, little bird

one of the birds he caught between his pincer-like fingers, a quiet snap and the bird would have no other sky to fly in apart from the hand in which it lay, come here, little bird, a little feathered body with its eyes wide open, if Ângelo had come with me this would have been a different trip, something else, if, pointless to think, the man strokes my hair made frizzy by the rain, he pulls me, grabs me, his very slim hands, like pincers in the cage, come here, little bird, a quiet snap and a little lifeless feathered body, the eyes wide open, birds are also frightened of dying, my father would put the frightened feathered bodies into a bag,

better to burn them

he was never upset by the eyes now looking at him from some other place, a distant place, eyes can never shut again after they have seen death, endlessly frightened, the man tells me to follow him, I obey, I am so ridiculous under the heavy rain in my high heels and my tight skirt, the man puts his hand on my head to protect me, we make a ridiculous couple, I'm sure that anyone who saw us would laugh out loud, I am tripping over in my pulling shoes, I take them off, I carry them, it feels good to let the feet free in the freezing cold, we run towards the toilet block, once out of the rain I ask, which one is your lorry, I point at the parked lorries, which one's yours, none of them, he says without noticing that in my mind he has no reason to be there, the fear returns, the man pulls me inside the toilet block, I open my hand and drop my shoes, my left shoe falls on its side and the right one lands upright but to the left of the other, that is what shoes look like in films about women who were killed, askew, a misalignment that death does not care about, I look at the shoes, the man bends over to pick them up, what is he doing here tonight, I don't ask, he shakes water off, a dog-like shake, the light is harsh and white, it hurts the eyes, the floor is filthy, the doors to the toilet cubicles are all open, we are alone in the toilet block,

what's your name

what am I doing here in bare feet with a man holding a bottle of liquor in his hand, an assailant only becomes one once there is a victim, this is the proof that the man is proposing, a victim is proof that there has been an assailant, what's your name, perhaps he wants my name so he can write it down in his logbook of victims, a notebook filled with the names of the women who were found dead near the road, or perhaps to have it tattooed over his heart, perhaps he just wants to call me by my name, I make the usual joke,

bêtises, chérie, bêtises

the name of a flower that is also a colour

violet, Violeta

he knows me for sure, if he did not know me he would say Rose like all the others who have tried to guess my name, he knows everything about me, that Ângelo could not accompany me, that Dora is at home, that I will be seeing Denise and Betty, he knows everything about me, he chose me, he brought me out to this toilet block that nobody uses, much less on a night like this one, I fell into a criminal's trap, I am alone with a criminal who picked me out, but why, perhaps he does not like fat women, or fat women in high heels, murderers' motives are always absurd, and how long have these febrile eyes been fixed on me, how long have these deathly hands been chasing me, I ask for a swig of his liquor, it is easier if I am drunk, I won't put up a fight, I ask him to kiss me, my last wish, a long kiss to put me to sleep, a kiss that won't let me feel the hands strangling me, the knife slicing me open, I ask him how it's going to be, how are you going to kill me, he pulls me towards him, looks into my eyes, kisses me, they rarely kiss me, I taste his mouth, I run my tongue against his teeth, one by one until I find a rotten tooth that tastes bad, I linger on the rotten taste, he pushes me up against the wall, I could shout, beg for mercy, I allow him to grab me, birds flapping against the cage bars, clinging to the perch, behind the feeder, and my father's hand every-where, taking them to a sky larger than the birds had ever seen, I am not expecting any mercy, an executioner should not be merciful, he loosens my skirt and it is me that pulls it down and tramples it beneath my feet, I take off my blouse, my back against the cold wall, his hands on my legs, I get rid of the tights, I'm cold, a different kind of cold, the cold of a body that is prepared to lose its life, the man fumbles with the bra hooks, I help him, my breasts fall helplessly over my stomach, two ugly slabs of flesh, I am unashamed, I was never ashamed, the man bends over and takes one of my nipples in his mouth, I fondle his head, a new-born suckling, Dora, my Dora like a blind new-born puppy seeking out the teats, you taste so good, I ask him to say it again, say it again, please, you taste so good, I offer him the other breast, a still blind baby feeding, hungry, I let myself slip down the wall, I am naked, a body awaiting the end, I lie down on the toilet block's dirty floor, I pull him towards me, kill me, kill the lust growing inside me as vigorously, more vigorously than weeds growing in empty lots,

I have heard about love

a body resting on another body, breathing in unison, chest against chest, a hand that falls and another that holds it, the silence that descends on sweat covered bodies, love could be like this, love could be

the boys liked me at the matinees

this peacefulness of satisfied flesh, the man moves carefully, I will pretend to have dozed off for as long as possible but I can't keep still for too long on this cold floor, I have grown used to the smell of piss and no longer think it stinks, but bodies can never get used to the cold, perhaps that is why death can get them so easily, the smell of alcohol coming off him, off me, is not unpleasant, flowers, alcoholic flowers, cut or arranged, with a little added foliage, a cellophane wrapper and a glossy ribbon, flowers must be so miserable wrapped in all that useless cellophane, and the chintzy ribbon must fill them with shame,

bêtises, ma chérie, bêtises

stop drinking, you're being pathetic

you always go too far

I open my eyes slowly, I fix them on the ceiling, a water stain from an ancient leak, the fluorescent lamp flickering, I don't know whether it always does it or whether it is just the storm, the parts of our bodies that I can see in this uncertain light are nice to look at, I close my eyes again, I feel the man's weight upon me, fearful of the words forming within me, how could I think that love might be like this, I stroke his back, I want to say I love you because I have never said it, I want to try out saying it, just try it out, it costs nothing, I keep quiet, cowardly, my throat hurts with the word I am silencing, I have heard about love, and what if this is it, a body resting on another body, the breathing in unison, chest against chest, a hand that falls and another that holds it, the silence dragging me towards a place I've never been,

everyone on this street says that girl does naughty things with the boys whatever is happening must rapidly go back to normality, our lives must carry on without us, the life of the man whose head is on my left shoulder, my life, I am willing to accept that love can last only as long as people are breathing in unison,

bêtises, ma chérie, bêtises

I am cold, the man's body is not enough to cover my own sprawling body, spread out, I see us as if reading a map, from above, a distant gaze, his back thin and hairy, the narrow hips, the long legs, the battered heels, arms outstretched, head on my shoulder, my legs curled around his, our torsos purpled, my toenails pathetically painted in screaming bright pink, my arms, gelatinous appendages encircling his back, my eyes fixed on the ceiling, they see us embracing, they see the flickering light,

when the cinema lights went down the boys would come to be with me

my eyes give up, they shut, if the man said something it would be easier, if he made the same mistake as others before him, for instance, I've never been with a woman as big as you or some other similar nonsense, how merciless satisfied flesh can become, to which I would respond that, unlike him, there was nothing that surprised me, I put all the men who mistreated me right where they belong, a muddle in which I cannot distinguish one from another, nothing distinguishes them from each other, some of them take the humiliation quietly, most of them insult me but I couldn't care less, once my flesh is satisfied who cares what they say to me,

when the film was over the boys pretended not to know me and I didn't care

the man is still silent, I need to get away from what is about to happen, to think about something else, a plan to sell my eco-friendly wax to Denise who is expecting me tomorrow before the salon opens, a glass cubicle in a shopping centre, she will be there with her blue eyelids and her dry lips, her Ukrainian fellow, Serguei, I think he's called Serguei, says with the accent that most language orphans seem to have, Deniz, sleepz bad, iz not very good, he pronounces properly the words bad and good and it means nothing, it is simply curious, I get on well with this Ukrainian like I got on well with the one before him, and with the Moldovan who came before the two of them, there were two other boys, pretty and affable, I can't remember, Denise thinks it's funny to say, I get my supplies of men from Eastern Europe, where else would you find someone like this, and to prove her point she grumpily orders the Ukrainian to go and get coffee, the Ukrainian takes off the apron he wears while sweeping the floor, makes his way to the coffee shop, another glass cubicle in the shopping centre, as he exits the salon I can see he is a large man who moves with difficulty along the narrow corridors, a likeable freak reflected and multiplied in the shops' mirrored windows, once he is gone Denise says, he is so meek it is annoying, not much of a difference between him and a dog, I know that when she starts going on about dogs she is ready to exchange him, the blonde dog comes back with two coffees, I thank him and I have the sense of a tail wagging, the Ukrainian puts his apron on again, satisfied at having succeeded at his task, he starts arranging the hair tints, every now and then he shakes his head and mutters something in his language, Denise is right, I can almost hear him barking, the Ukrainian smiles and Denise makes a fuss, she will find him a new owner, she will cry a little and offer him a few biscuits, Denise is convinced that she is a sensitive person, she often says, there is no-one more sensitive than me, there may be someone as willing to help others as me but I doubt it, she quotes as proof the fact that she keeps buying my wax

it's all a bit tight at the moment, last month I couldn't even pay the rent

despite her business not doing too well, she forgets to mention that she always buys the cheapest ones, I have to push hard to sell her the eco-friendly wax, I won't be buying that wax again, I can't be bothered with such an expensive wax just to be a friend of the environment,

I wouldn't buy it at that price even if I was a friend of the King of China

Denise always has replies like that up her sleeve, and cheques that always bounce at the bank, but she's a challenge, a salesperson can perfect her pitch with a customer like Denise, so hard to persuade, if I want to sell her one of my special waxes, for instance, the one for sensitive skins, she will blow cigarette smoke in my face and

those silly cows with their sensitive skin can go fuck themselves

negotiate hard, she'll ask for more handouts, the stainless steel toothpick stand, or the spoon holder, more samples, she bargains down the prices, and at the end she tells me I need a decent haircut, one good turn deserves another, I make my apologies, I can hardly pay for petrol, and time is short, with so many customers to visit I can't afford to waste time on a haircut, Denise shakes her head and lights another cigarette, when I say goodbye the Ukrainian is gesturing with his head and his hands, he is not like a dog, dogs wouldn't be able to gesticulate like that, when I reach the hallway I hear Denise

you're lucky to have found a fool with a heart as soft as butter

talking about me, she's getting fatter every day, I feel so sorry for her, after all these years I can't just send her away, around here no-one else wants anything to do with her, I feel sorry for her, the way she looks, I would die of shame,

I've been told her parents were important, I think her father had a tough time after the revolution, he was one of those high-ups who were put in prison, but the way she looks, Denise is always telling me she has a heart as soft as butter so it's not surprising that it burns so easily, or that it becomes rancid, it's funny what people say about the heart, Betty for instance is convinced she has a big heart, I'm sure she would be upset to hear that, give or take a few little things, all hearts are the same size, she would also be upset if I told her that the Villa Elizabete she is so proud of is ugly, the iron letters above the veranda, leaning, almost diagonal, *Villa Elizabete*, they're ugly, the tone of green she chose to paint them is ugly, the tiles and plant pots in many sizes and colours are ugly, the poorly laid staircase is ugly, the pruned back rosebushes and bougainvillea are ugly, if I told her that everything beyond the door flanked by two potted rubber trees is ugly, I don't know if Betty's heart would still be quite as big, I can't possibly know, I'm a good salesperson which is why I compliment her on her house, the leaning letters spelling out the name, the tiles, the plant pots, the bougainvillea and the rosebushes, I compliment her on everything, I am a good salesperson, the best, it is so easy to fool Betty, thinking about it, everything about Betty is so small that it is easy for her to think her heart is big, after I leave Denise and her Ukrainian fellow I am going to Villa Elizabete, when I get there I will ring the bell and the dog will start barking from the back garden, a dog with a short light-coloured coat that approaches me baring his teeth, after a few minutes Betty shows up and shouts, Jardel, into your kennel, Jardel, the dog obeys with his tail turned down, ashamed of having been told off, Denise has done well to look east, at least her Ukrainian knows when to bark and when to be quiet, tomorrow Betty will welcome me reeking of lemon from the deodorant she bulk-buys at the hypermarket some twenty kilometres away from her Villa Elizabete, every Saturday Betty goes to the hypermarket with her husband and children, a happy family, Dora and I would often order a Happy Family set menu at the Chinese restaurant, we would laugh at the names of dishes at Chinese restaurants, I should have taken Dora and Ângelo to the Chinese restaurant, we would have ordered a Happy Family set menu, tomorrow Betty will welcome me with her hair tied back with an elastic band, her skin rested from a night's sleep, her eyes looking like mornings agree with them, she asks me in and I am sick with the musty smell of the shuttered rooms, Betty takes me to a little room she calls her parlour and asks me to sit while she goes looking for a notebook in which she writes down what she needs, she is very organised, when she comes back she taps her forehead gently with the tip of the pen, she often has the gestures of someone who is thinking, she always surprises me with some random scientific fact

did you know that our skin is the human body's largest organ, and that it makes up about ten per cent of our body weight that she invariably questions, she heard it on the television only a few days ago but she's not so sure, ten per cent seems too much, five per cent perhaps it is five per cent, in the end the weight of a human's skin seems to be only a matter of opinion for Betty, she talks about the programme, it's very good with that very good woman journalist, she can't remember her name, I try to help her by saying names that she rejects immediately, no, not that one either, I make an effort to change the subject but Betty is determined, how could I forget her name, it'll come back to me in a moment, she's that journalist with the black hair and the very feminine manner, I haven't been watching too much television lately, I apologise, oh but she's been on television for a while, right, sorry, still don't know, the conversation fizzles out, there are so many programmes and so many journalists today that it's easy to get confused, I bet you I'll remember her name the moment I stop thinking about it, it's so frustrating, Betty falls silent in protest at the vagaries of memory and I launch into my refrains,

refrains are so tedious

I talk about the types of wax, the resin base, the honey content to make skin soft but Betty is not listening, she is trying to remember the journalist's name, it's on the tip of my tongue, eco-friendly wax, Betty is paying attention now, we all have a duty to protect our environment, what kind of a world are we leaving for our children, Betty asks, exactly the same one, I think, but don't say it, I wouldn't want to derail her train of thought, Betty returns to what is bothering her, just the other day I was trying to say to a customer, a lovely person, by the way, the name of a soap opera actress I saw at the restaurant, look, it was the day of my birthday, I went for lunch at a restaurant with my husband and children, we entered and there she was, the actress, at the table next to ours, the following day I wanted to tell my customer and I couldn't remember the name, as soon as the customer left it came back to me, I know I'll remember the name of the journalist in a moment, Betty has a boring conversation but pays me quickly and always offers me two or three compliments, how shiny my hair is, how practical my very ordinary handbag seems to be, or when she can't find anything specific, which is unusual, she will make some general observation, you are looking well today, I thank her, besides waxing Betty offers massages and anti-cellulite treatments, her massage table is always ready with a blanket that smells of bleach, I don't like filthiness, with so many diseases out there you can't be too careful, there is a whole world of filth out there that she does not know about, her pale children spend their days behind closed doors at the Villa Elizabete protected from the sun and from the world of filth, Betty always has her blinds drawn because sunlight will ruin everything, if she allowed sunlight in it might ruin her collection of miniature tea sets that she buys from the hypermarket every year around Christmas, my Dora has never seen her there, if she had I bet she would have expressed some surprise, the things people buy, miniature teapots and teacups, the things people think they need,

Dora is content in this job as she was content in her previous jobs, my child has the unique quality of always being contented, of never talking about her heart, even when her current colleagues are complaining, our problem is that we wear our heart on our sleeves, they say, or when the owner of the café where she served coffee and buttered toast put all his heart into the business but still was not able to keep it alive, or when she heard the fine arts students tell tall tales about their broken hearts, or even when she was selling knock-off designer clothes at a ready-to-wear outlet,

the curse of *prêt-à-porter*

in the many jobs she had Dora never talked about matters of the heart and I would not have been surprised to hear her colleagues assert, she doesn't have one, a person with no heart, I would not have been surprised at all, every day Dora works at a different checkout counter, one square metre, today she was at number 37, she adjusted the chair and placed the tiny stuffed bear in the cheque drawer, a little Valentine's Day gift, the artist with the tiny bear in his hands and Dora ever so happy, probably pretending to be happy, maybe even two or three tears, the signs of love are so pathetic, in any case the stuffed toy bear is the only thing that is truly hers in that cage, my Dora shut off in that cage and astonished by what people buy, thinking of people's homes as storerooms for detergents, scented candles, peanuts, set of two oven-and-microwave-safe dishes, my child who learned quickly how to deal with the most common problems to avoid having to speak to her colleagues, her managers, therefore annoying both, arrogant according to managers, ambitious according to colleagues, in any case her self-sufficiency might earn her a promotion, cashier supervisor, if she is patient enough, at the moment the dream is within Dora's reach, cashier supervisor, my Dora who I remember saying something ridiculous as we left the restaurant,

I'm leaving home tomorrow

surely my Dora said, I'll see you at home tomorrow, she did not say, I'm leaving home tomorrow, as always Ângelo must have been telling a joke, so perhaps that's why I misheard, Dora and Ângelo do not like Indian food, I should have chosen another restaurant, when I get out of here I have to buy cigarettes, I must have only one left, two at most, I don't like being without cigarettes, the rain beats down on the tin roof over the toilet block,

I'm leaving home tomorrow

what am I doing here, I think about the house I sold today, about the pack of cigarettes I have to buy, about the women who will wash the floor on which we are now lying, a bucket of water and a mop and we are washed away, scrubbed off, we disappear, the man moves carefully, he sits up, he kneels next to me, almost cutting a nice figure, a life-sized saint, he gets on his feet, I offer my hand, he remains in silence, he stretches out a thin hand that I cling on to with all my strength, I get up, I do not resent my fat body, ugly, slovenly, my badly varnished nails, the man looks lovingly at my breasts as they hang over the folds of my belly, two bags of flesh tipped with too-dark nipples, he bends over to pick the bra off the floor, I am waiting, my legs, two purpled stumps, I know that I look like a cheap whore, it should bother me, I lean on the man to get dressed, we still haven't said a word, the man offers me a drink of his liquor, I accept, I can drink as much as I want, I can run the risk of appearing to be drunk, the feeling of wet clothes on my body is very unpleasant, I cannot avoid the goose-bumps over the fat folds on my belly, rising over my thighs, hardening my nipples, he embraces me to warm me up, he rubs his hands vigorously against my arms, my teeth won't stop chattering, I'm cold, we are holding one another as we lean against the toilet door,

I have heard about love

we are astonished by the storm's strength, a figure is walking around one of the lorries, it looks like a woman, it disappears behind another lorry, we look at each other, I don't know if the man also thinks he saw a woman, I don't want to ask him, the woman reappears, this time we are both sure of what we are seeing, the man squints to see better, he shuffles uncomfortably, the woman comes towards us, she is wearing a plastic bag over her head and a raincoat all the way down to her feet, the coat is too long, someone else's raincoat, someone much taller than her, the man puts the bottle to his lips and drinks, the woman is closer, she is coming towards us, I realise she is looking for us, she was looking for us among the lorries, the woman walks towards us, she seems satisfied to have found us, I look at the man, I am not sure he has realised what I have, perhaps there is a reason, the man lowers his eyes and the woman comes closer, the enormous raincoat, someone else's, and the plastic bag on her head make her look crazy, if she remained where she is she would be nothing more than a crazy woman in the lorry park, but as she comes closer I correct my views about her, she is not a crazy woman, she is an angry woman, a very angry woman, what makes her walk so quickly is not some satisfaction at having found us, it is rage, the woman walks with rage in every footstep, suddenly I understand, the woman is travelling with her husband to protect him and this time she failed, apart from her rage she feels guilt for having fallen asleep, for not having noticed her husband slipping out of the lorry, for having woken up much later, the woman expected to find her husband lying on the floor, she eyes me up incredulously, she asks her husband, with a whore like this, the man waves his hand, tells her to stop, the woman pays no attention, she moves towards us, I feel no pity for this woman, I feel no remorse, the plastic bag on her head protecting her against the rain makes me want to laugh, the woman leans in to spit in my face, I evade her, the woman shouts, you whore, the man pulls her by the arm and tries to shut her up, he must regularly beat her because she recoils and protects her face, I walk away, the woman cries, you whore, she repeats, whore, you'll get what you deserve, the man twists her arm, I walk away towards my car, I leave them, the woman cries, I feel nothing for this woman, perhaps some irritation at her loud crying, the man asks me to stay, don't go, he pulls the woman violently towards the lorry, don't go, the woman tries to break free from the man who is holding her, she shouts, one of these days I'll be done with you and me, one of these days it'll be over between us,

I have heard about love

the man lifts his hand and the woman covers her face again, I leave, I continue my way, I am not angry but I don't feel like staying, I get into the car, I want to warm up, I turn the heating up to maximum,

the *chauffage,* Baltazar, the *chauffage,*

I put the gears into reverse, the man and the woman are further and further in the distance, two dolls gesticulating in the middle of a storm, I speed up, the car zigzags, to take the road I have to drive past the café again, I look around to see if the group of boys is still there, I can't see them, I like the daze that dislocates the café's windows slightly to the left, the neon light shining more brightly, I gaze over the parked cars, I slam on the brakes and stop the car, I am unable to brake gently, I fumble around in my handbag for money to buy cigarettes, I find some of those little papers for notes, the little yellow papers you can stick anywhere, now I have a small block of little yellow note papers in my hand and I'm not sure what to do with them, I start peeling them off and dropping them on the car floor, I am at a service station far from home,

you always go too far

what does bloody Ângelo know about going too far, Ângelo who never did anything exciting in his life, how dare he tell me off over dinner, you always go too far, what does Ângelo know about limits when he knows nothing about my pain, always so close, the desire to forget everything, always so close, I can't go beyond myself even when I'm drunk, I can never go far enough, I'm cold, I'm frightened by the storm, the block of sticky yellow notes makes me so sad, I have no-one to leave a message for, I am still, I should prioritise the things I need to do, buy cigarettes, go to the toilet to rid myself of the man's smell, have a coffee, buy food, sober up, get back on the road, I try to find a pen to write down the order in which I must do these things, I start writing on one of the little yellow pieces of paper, buy cigarettes, then another, go to toilet, and suddenly, don't go, I feel a huge relief as I write, don't go, on every little piece of paper, I write over the grooves left by the pen, my hand pressing down heavily, it takes me a while, I use up every piece of paper in the block, I finish the task, a handful of messages scrawled on little yellow pieces of paper, I open the door and climb out of the car, I still don't know what I will do, I hesitate, one of the employees, not the one who served me earlier, watches me through the café windows, points me out to another one who is nearby, I pull up the wipers of the first car I come across and I stick a message beneath them, I move onto another car, perhaps belonging to the group of boys, there are only a few cars, I plaster another message onto the windscreen and watch it become slick with rain, my handwriting slides slowly across the little pieces of paper, I am holding in my hand a cluster of wet pieces of paper stained in blue, the two café employees watch me intrigued, they are joined by the one who served me cake and coffee, I wave to them, I blow them a kiss, I trip, they all laugh,

   look at that fat bird falling over drunk

I look around for more cars to plaster with my messages but no-one is travelling on this stormy night, it was Ângelo who said it, the outing was cancelled, no-one travels in this kind of weather, it is very dangerous, I make my way back to my car, concentrating hard on not tripping, I have the bits of paper in my hand, I drop them on the floor, I wave at the servers who are now stuck to the window, messages I cannot read, I am drunk,

   if you want to smash yourself to pieces on the road that's up to you

I get on the road, a few hours from now I will be selling Denise and Betty some of the eco-friendly wax I have in the car boot, I am a good salesperson, the best, I offer an infinite illusion, unique access,

gently

I glide along the road that is always the same, leaving it behind even as it renews itself ahead of me, a generous tongue swallowing me, black, infinite, I move on, guided by the cats' eyes at the side of the road, the steel crash-barriers, the wind twisting the leafless trees into sad skeletons, lines sketched in charcoal against the sky, the electricity pylons, like scarecrows holding hands in a line that goes nowhere

laughter is the best thing we can offer others

we sit down, the waiter picks up the rectangular laminated card that says reserved and I ask him to please take away the wilted rose in the glass jar that doubles as a vase, the waiter does as I ask without hiding his bewilderment, on every table in the restaurant there is a rose in a glass jar and nobody ever asks for them to be taken away, I seek Dora's complicity but my child is stroppy, she did not want to come out for dinner and will not forgive me for asking or ordering her to come, I can't remember what made her agree, whether it was my asking or my ordering, I know I forced her, as I always do in fact, because I take it as a given that she belongs to me, a feeling of possession I have never felt for anyone or anything else,

we are a family, shame on us if we stop behaving like a family

Ângelo, oblivious to the wilting roses in the jars, or to Dora's stroppiness, tells another joke, it is his third and we have only just sat down, by the end of the dinner he will have told dozens of jokes at which Dora and I will have laughed the corresponding number of times, it won't matter if we laugh or not, Ângelo will not interpret our lack of laughter as a sign that he is a bad comedian, he'll think we are annoyed, or indisposed, all behaviours have a convenient explanation, there is an explanation for everything, even the end of the Princesa Beauty Salon can be easily explained, this used to be the Princesa Beauty Salon, I say, Dora and Ângelo reply in unison, we know that, they are so predictable, everyone is predictable after a few minutes and even more so after a lifetime,

I have to go out, *ma chérie*

my mother's handwriting on a piece of paper, not one of the yellow ones, not one for leaving notes, the kind of paper that doesn't stick anywhere on the kitchen table, Maria da Guia saying, don't cry, menina, your mother is just getting her hair done, she's making herself even prettier, don't cry, menina, Maria da Guia was an ignorant creature who never saw the inside of the Princesa Beauty Salon, now turned into this Indian restaurant with pictures on the walls of camels and of two ladies dancing for a sultan, impossible for her to understand my mother's need to go to Princesa Beauty Salon every Friday,

stop making a scene, *ma chérie*

the floor is still the same, a giant chessboard, it was here that I sold my first waxes, it was here that, Dora says, this is such a sad restaurant, I reply drily, what you really mean is that the restaurant is not very nice, I am convinced that I always know what Dora really means, there is nothing I don't know about the most perfect part of me, there is nothing I don't know about my child apart from how she exists, what makes her content to spend her whole day sitting at the checkout counter scanning barcodes, semi-skimmed milk with added calcium, vitamins and fibre, 400W food processor with one litre capacity, girl's top 93% polyamide 7% Lycra, whole days spent in that ridiculous uniform, unable to see the blue sky, the starry nights, whole days beneath the plywood ceiling's deathly light, whole days with the sound of beeping machines, not realising that when days are all the same we inevitably grow out of touch with life, if I said it is sad I meant it is sad, that is what she'll reply, she is angry, she hates me even more when I correct her, I cannot ignore any detail about the most perfect part of me, I spend whole afternoons walking the aisles beneath the deathly light to watch my child scan barcodes for 5 kg bags of dry food, 75 W 3-position infrared air bubble foot massager 24-month warranty, individually wrapped Golden Cat apples 70/75, Corn Flakes added vitamins and iron new original formula crunchier 1 kg, plain decorative cushions, 4-piece stainless steel pots and pans set 18/10, my Dora with her name hanging from her chest, every now and then she distracts herself browsing the discount shelves, 100% natural tomato purée ideal for sautés and sauces, double ply paper napkins, I find it hard to believe that my child likes this type of work, that she liked other types of work, when there are no customers Dora amuses herself watching the girls on roller-skates, dancing and gliding along the aisles, we always watched artistic ice-skaters on television, I am sure that is what Dora thinks of when she is watching the girls on roller-skates, that smile, how to explain Dora's smile, it is like Dora's smile when she used to believe she could be an ice-skater, at that point she could still dream of becoming anything she wanted, I did not correct her, it was only later, when I started to feel her slipping away from me, that I began correcting her, I stand in the queue, behind the family putting its shopping on the conveyor belt, veal chops in the three-for-two offer, frozen line-caught white grouper fillets, pack of two ultra-resistant tights, semi-skimmed UHT milk best before 10.07.04, low cholesterol super soft multigrain bread, American-style white sandwich bread thick-sliced perfect for sandwiches sweet or savoury, Dora scans all the products and the woman puts them in plastic bags, the husband takes a car magazine from the checkout display to verify the price of the car he left in the car park, space F 78, second floor, it is the husband's duty to remember where he left the car, the children, a couple of teenagers, one Sónia Rosa and the other Sérgio Ivan, pay no attention, the boy takes a box of chewing gum tablets, strawberry flavour, he opens the box and puts a few in his mouth, the girl tells on him, Sérgio is stealing gum, the mother pretends she did not hear, the boy puts the box back with the others and opens his mouth to show his sister the pink paste, the sister says you idiot and helps her mother put the shopping in bags, she does this when not playing with her hair, tucking it behind her ear, letting it hang down her back, flicking it over the back of her neck, or when calling her brother an idiot, the father scolds her, Sónia Rosa don't call your brother an idiot, the mother remains quiet, machine-like as she fills bags and then fills the shopping trolley with the bags, the sister defends herself, Sérgio Ivan is being gross, the father loses interest in the bickering children, he finds the price for his neighbour's car, he says to his son, Moreira's car is worth less than ours,

we are a family, shame on us if we stop acting as a family

Dora likes watching families who are doing their shopping, she is convinced that a family shopping together can hold no secrets, that she knows all the families she has served, Dora is angry in this seedy restaurant that still has the chequered floor of the Princesa Beauty Salon, if I said it is sad I meant it is sad, at work Dora is never angry, she can't be, she must always smile, when she says goodbye to the family, when she says hello to the next customer, a man asking questions about a video camera, mini DV-LCD 2.5" 123 kPixels 800 kPixels CCD Zoom 10 × 800 photo mode, Dora cannot help him, she picks up the handset and a woman's voice interrupts the romantic ballad being played in every aisle, can someone in electronics come to checkout number 48, can someone in electronics come to check-out number 48, the romantic ballad restarts a few beats later, Dora is helping the customer with the video camera without looking at me, she never looks at me, whether I'm in the queue, or in the aisles with the too-white light, or by the discount shelves, or on the benches near the checkouts, to hurt me Dora avoids looking at me, to hurt me she keeps up her silence,

there is nothing that silence won't kill

Ângelo cannot stand silence, he fights it with unfunny jokes,

what do you get when you cross a centipede and a parrot

he asks the question and we cannot even give him an answer because it is part of our duty to pretend that we don't know it, I disarm Dora with a low blow, you want to hurt me with your silence,

a walkie-talkie

Dora laughs, she always fulfils her duty to laugh, she laughs despite the joke being lame, she says to me, not everything needs to have a purpose, hardly ever does one of us emerge a winner in these clashes, as adversaries we are equally matched, Dora knows how to retaliate against my bitterness, she instigates it, we each know how to inflict the greatest most unbearable pain on the other, we know each other, there cannot be better matched adversaries in the whole world, if only Ângelo could be persuaded that his jokes are out of fashion, if they ever were in fashion,

and what about when you cross a hedgehog and a snake, what do you get when you cross a hedgehog and a snake those elephant jokes Ângelo insists on telling in his performances are a thing of the past and no longer in fashion,

fashion is fickle like that

there was a time when everyone laughed, how does an elephant get through a door, but now nobody laughs, at most a grimace pretending to be a smile, how do you kill a purple elephant, and the day-tripping pensioners all shout back, with a purple shotgun, they show no mercy and ruin Ângelo's punchline, there's nobody as cruel as old folk, on every daytrip there is always one obnoxious pensioner who says, that joke is even older than me, which makes his companions laugh, they all laugh more with each other than they do at the comedian, they tell each other anecdotes about blonde women and about black men, at the end of the performance they complain to the guide,

where did you find such a lousy entertainer

just like the newlyweds or the newlyweds' parents complain after weddings, weddings might be lucrative business for Ângelo if only he could understand that nobody wants to hear

there once was a bride so generous, so generous, that on her wedding night she gave her husband a pair of horns how many teeth should a mother-in-law have, just two, one to give her tooth-pain and another to open bottles with

unpleasant things on such a happy day, the newlyweds or the newlyweds' parents stop him before he starts telling jokes about dirty or hungry wedding guests, they ask him to sing instead, or perform magic tricks, or to leave, they stop him from telling jokes, there's nobody as cruel as newlyweds or newlyweds' parents, he doesn't usually get complaints at children's parties on Saturday afternoons, dressed up as a clown, he is even moderately successful

what's the difference between a potty and a cooking pot

among children who laugh the moment someone mentions potties, the children find him funny until they realise that it would be even funnier to pour orange drink onto the clown's shoes, or to throw cake at the clown, Ângelo carries on in his bad Spanish, so the children can't guess the right answer, at children's parties there is always one obnoxious child who says, let's steal one of the clown's shoes, there's nobody as cruel as children, they attack the clown and it is always the part of the performance children enjoy the most, even then Ângelo continues to tell jokes until the parents send him away, when Ângelo is gone the parents say, this clown was completely useless, next year we'll have to find a better one, maybe even get some references, the truth is that Ângelo cannot amuse anyone, a bad comedian is of no use

Dora is worried that I will want to be honest and tell Ângelo he's no good, he should do something else, my child is so confident that she knows everything yet she knows nothing, I would never hurt Ângelo, and Ângelo would never hurt me, my daughter does not know that this is the one privilege she and I have, I gave birth to her to make sure that there would be someone in the world able to hurt me, that is why she exists, what she exists for,

no-one can hurt us as much as a child

my mother sitting in the living room of the house I sold earlier today wearing the light-yellow pleated dress that suited her so well, or here in the Princesa Beauty Salon, at the back near the hairdryers, legs crossed, thumbing through a fashion magazine, the *dernier cri*,

no-one can hurt us as much as a mother

my mother forever sitting on the sofa of the house I sold earlier today,

Baltazar, you can't allow your daughter to do this to us

my father does not reply, nor does he read the newspaper any more on Sundays, he does not go into work, my father who has fallen into the habit of spending entire days taking care of his birds, even when my mother insists, aren't you saying anything to your daughter, aren't you telling your daughter off, what can a man do who is more trapped in a cage than the hundreds of birds he keeps, what can a man do who finds himself a prisoner in the garden cages and is afraid of the stray cats lurking nearby, my father and the birds made anxious by the cats, not worrying about the trees sagging from lack of irrigation, about the aphid-infested rosebushes, about my mother's irritation, my mother pregnant with me, my father anxious because of the cats, as silent as my own daughter so often is, not to hurt me, not to hurt my mother, putting out bowls with poisoned milk,

the cats always ran away from me instead of running away from my father,

Baltazar, you must stop your daughter from

my child cannot run away from me, my child born despite my mother's shame, despite my father's silence, my mother so angry that she forgot that a lady must at all times

be *chic, très chic*

use words from the only civilised language in the world, remember that as long as Paris exists nothing can be too bad, not me, not my father, not a bastard grandchild, a lady who is *chic, très chic* does not get upset about those barbarians who never learned how to end an argument elegantly, by saying *c'est tout*, that is the best way of ending an argument

you have to get rid of it as soon as possible

I don't know why my mother forgot to say *c'est tout*, perhaps the barbarians' rudeness is contagious, how dare you, how, I am so ashamed to see you like that, when my friends find out, I am so ashamed, my mother forgetting to end our argument with *c'est tout*, forgetting that as long as Paris exists nothing can be too bad,

how can it bother you that your daughter is in that state when you yourself

accusing me, accusing my father, not wanting to know what the appropriate words in the world's most beautiful language might be for that situation, my mother standing by the toilet door, arms crossed, worried,

I'll take you to see someone I know, she is discreet and very good at getting the job done

more worried with the passing of time that made the baby inevitable, wavering between threatening me or

you're coming with me even if I have to drag you there

understanding, insisting on the advice that only a mother can give, on the wisdom of all mothers,

you still have time, your life is already hard enough without it but after

before ending exhausted with a threat, the one she thought to be the most terrifying, my mother with her head on the sofa unable to find a single reason why I would want to keep the baby,

if you decide to go ahead with it forget about counting on me or your father

ignoring the most fundamental one, the privilege of having someone in the world capable of hurting me, that is what children are for, nothing else, and if the child is black, have you thought about that, you were with a black man, weren't you, a black returnee, do you think your father or I deserve, they deserved it, of course they deserved it, they did not deserve the delight Dora gave them, an angel that saved us all,

mon ange, mon petit ange

an angel sitting silent in front of me, convinced that it hates me, angels have the habit of going to extremes, probably from ignoring everything in between good and evil, my angel is waiting for Ângelo to reveal the answer to the question about the crossing of a hedgehog and a snake before she can smile,

angels have heard about us

my angel cannot accept that she incapable of hating me, it is a weakness I passed onto her through the blood running in her veins, I fixed it into the flesh I made her from, Ângelo finally reveals the answer,

barbed wire

and he laughs heartily, Ângelo has a unique ability to laugh at his own jokes, perhaps that is his greatest talent, to laugh so earnestly at the jokes he tells, once he has told a joke it is another Ângelo who is laughing, one who certainly did not know the joke already, who has just heard it for the first time, it may seem absurd but it can happen that there are two of us, or seven, so many, I for instance, sitting at the restaurant, am this person and also another one who once sat at the Princesa Beauty Salon, perhaps that is my greatest talent,

there once was a woman who was so fat, so fat, that she could be in two places at once

to be many people at once, to be in many places at once, in the Indian restaurant with Dora and with Ângelo and in the Princesa Beauty Salon, it would not surprise me to see my mother sitting somewhere behind Ângelo, where that family is having dinner, with her head inside a hair drier with a visor, looking like the astronauts on the television news, my mother reads a magazine, crosses her leg, my mother always

chic, très chic

looking so nice in the light-yellow pleated dress, my mother stretches out her left hand, the stones in her engagement ring click against the glass and glint in the light, one of the attendants comes over and checks how much time is left for the drier, my mother thanks her, a nice smile, I also raise my arm to call the waiter and shake the folds of fat that hang between my shoulder and my hand, a vulgar gesture, an ugly hand, a snake wrapped around my index finger, a cheap ring, a single gesture from me and everyone in the restaurant will know that I am

chic, très chic

one of the most vulgar women, fingernails painted in screaming bright pink, my mother watches me from under the drier with her pearled fingernails, the engagement ring and her marriage band, the light-yellow dress, the tan leather handbag, the tan pointy shoes, a small foot, like Cinderella's,

a boring story that Maria da Guia often told me

I complain about the waiter who is not paying attention to us, Ângelo could launch into one of his endless anecdotes, further back is the place where the salon employees once washed customers' hair, will we be washing your hair today, they ask as they adjust the customers' collars, to keep them dry, they make them wear robes,

one size only

it doesn't matter lady volunteer, it doesn't matter

every now and then the couple, they must be a couple, they are very young, block the view of the salon employees, the waiter approaches, he has very white teeth that seem at odds with his dark and dull skin, with his black and straight hair shiny with grease, the couple raise their glasses, I can see the salon employees again, at the couple's table the girl smiles tenderly at the boy with mousy eyes, if I asked the girl why she looks so lovingly at such an uninteresting boy she would not be able to answer, it looks like all forms of love may need some mystery, they are built one mystery at a time, the waiter keeps smiling, he has not stopped smiling since we arrived, despite my mother

where are all these Asians and blacks coming from

staring at him with repulsion, I am only irritated by his permanent smile, a façade of teeth in a man who appears to have died with a silly grin on his face and not noticed it, my mother smooths out one of the pleats in her light-yellow dress,

they should stay in their own countries, I don't know why
they don't stay in their own countries

how do you kill a ghost, the couple are putting their heads
together and I see the salon attendants washing the heads
of women with stretched out necks, clusters of foam, the
women's stretched out necks, birds ready to be sacrificed,
the attendants make the same gestures they make when
washing clothes in a stream and they laugh like a flock of
chirruping birds, the women with the stretched out necks
are dolls that the attendants are playing with, dolls that
blow soap bubbles out of their heads, they used to say mamã
or papá, or perhaps do some other trick, now dolls do so
many other things, I can picture Dora at the hypermarket
checkout, doll that blows bubbles out of its head comes in
all sizes long or short hair fair or dark straight or curled
rechargeable batteries not included, Dora with her forced
smile scanning the barcodes on the dolls with the stretched
out necks that seem to fully trust the attendants, even though
the attendants might, at any moment, break their necks like
I used to break my own dolls' necks, no, it wasn't like that, I
started by pulling out their eyes, the pieces of coloured
plastic would lie on the floor watching me, I did not want my
dolls to see the lumps aching on my chest, or the enemies
poking through my skin, dark and hard hairs conquering
my body, that is why I pulled the dolls' eyes out, I thought
that would be enough, it never occurred to me that my blind
dolls would keep feeling sorry for me, sitting on my bed, in
an unbearable silence, they pitied me, I realised then that

I had to destroy them, to finish once and for all with those rubber impostors, I dismembered them with my own hands, I took scissors and slashed hair, bellies, legs,

the young menina is very naughty, sometimes it's like the menina has the devil inside

Maria da Guia found them in the bedroom, screamed with fright, and went straight to my mother to complain,

someone in your family, Baltazar

without realising, such an ignorant creature, without realising that by destroying my dolls I was saving them, if I had let them grow old with me they would have experienced the pain that never stopped growing inside my chest, my whole body, nor did my mother appreciate my altruism,

someone in your family, Baltazar

the couple are so engrossed with one another that they don't notice the salon attendants playing secrets and coins with their dolls, a simple game, the dolls put coins into the apron pockets of the attendants who pretend to be distracted and out come the other dolls' secrets, a simple game, practically no rules, a coin goes into the pocket and out comes the secret of the blonde doll who is so good at crying, her husband has a lover who has two of his children, another doll throws in another coin and out comes the secret of the doll with the curly hair who can barely open her eyes, she gets drunk every night, once a secret is out it can no longer be a secret again, the salon attendants know that but to keep getting coins they allow more secrets to escape their pockets through their tongues, or perhaps it is in the nature of secrets to escape, like the secret of the sad doll with the seven-band ring, it took its time but ended up by escaping too, her communist brother was arrested, the secret of the very dark-skinned doll with the shaking hands, her boyfriend is in one of the overseas wars, the secret of the doll with the disjointed arm that changes her hair colour every week, her husband beats her, the dolls are always putting coins and secrets into the salon attendants' pockets, as if the dolls' secrets and coins were endless, when they get tired of playing the salon attendants wrap the dolls' heads in white towels and leave them by the dressing tables, the stylists brush their hair and the dolls cannot stop themselves from doling out secrets and coins, they don't know what else to do, they don't know any other game, Dora turns away when she hears the laughter of a group of girls as they enter, the couple lose sight of each other for a few seconds and look over at the group, so does the family eating in the place where the dryers once were, Ângelo says, it must be a hen do, the girls shake the drops of water off their coats and look around for place to leave their umbrellas, the waiter with the row of bright teeth leads them to a table at the far end with two glass jars with wilting roses and a place card that says reserved, the girls' irritating laughter can be heard all over the restaurant, I regret coming here, the past has no place, the only advantage of the past is that it does not exist anywhere

Dora and Ângelo exchange glances, they are tired of my pilgrimages to places that are no longer what they were, that Chinese place the other day was good, or the Italian,

you cannot use food to make the world smaller

Dora is upset, she did not want to come to this or any other restaurant, she did not want to have dinner with me, my child is so unkind, Ângelo looks at her entranced,

food, my darling, only makes us bigger, the world stays the same as it is, as it always was

we are well matched, we are good adversaries, the best, the world never stays as it is but there seems to be no advantage in that, the Princesa Salon passed on its chequered floor to this seedy restaurant, the Rosa da Manhã and the Estrela da Avenida are now filled with pigeons and posters, the world never stays as it is but then it never changes enough, if it did my mother would no longer be underneath the hairdryer that looks like an astronaut's helmet listening to the gossip escaping the mouths of the attendants, knowing that in her absence, I don't know whether her husband was ever arrested, he was certainly beaten up, they picked him up on the street and told him to stick to bird keeping, they say what comes around goes around, it looks like he was already a bit odd, but they say now he's completely crazy, she never complains, the poor thing, she never has a bad word to say, everything is always alright, the husband, the daughter, everything is always alright, sometimes she talks about her husband's collection of birds, who keeps birds, and that daughter, people who live in glass houses shouldn't throw stones but the poor girl was unlucky, they say she can't regulate her body, she may even have become pregnant by a black man, a black returnee, my mother's secrets escaping into the salon, ricocheting off the dressing table and becoming magnified, they say the poor girl even tried to kill herself once, the secrets of a doll that knows a dozen words in French, which in all circumstances makes her *chic, très chic*, Dora at the checkout counter at the hypermarket scanning the barcode for the last *très chic* doll that says a dozen words in French, the computer telling her it is now out of stock and my Dora becoming small again, a child with eyes puffy from crying, pining for the *très chic* doll that could say a dozen words in French, grandmother died, you have to realise that grandmother will never come back, Dora suddenly growing up and sitting at the hypermarket checkout with that ridiculous uniform, despising me, you know exactly how I feel about you, fascinated by my mother who is complaining at the salon's reception, the place where that young Indian is now sitting,

the girl wasn't even born yet and I was already coming here

grandmother always knew what to do, how to behave, my mother standing at reception, I want to speak to the owner, determination suited her, as did refusing Carminho's intermediation, or the changing times, you should choose your staff better, this girl does not deserve to be here, she asked if I had a booking, made me wait, disagreeing with the changing times suited her, it even suited her to disagree with the new rules that Carminho explained drily, the other customers complained, we have to adapt, my mother always knew what to do, that time she remained quiet, my mother and the times she once belonged to now silent, defeated without a single shout, not a single violent gesture, my mother a pathetic figure

when we are ashamed of the past we become nothing

offering up prophesies, I don't give this salon much longer with those new rules, there are things you cannot change without turning them into other things, but prophets are rarely heard and Carminho did not hear her, she just kept repeating, these are the new rules, my mother defeated in the era she belonged to, becoming an object of ridicule for the others, the new customers,

you've handed the sword to the villain

ill-mannered women who had always been turned away from the salon, we're fully booked, Carminho used to say to them in the same tone in which she spoke to my mother that evening, she never said to them, our other customers don't want you here, they don't mix with the likes of you, just like she never said to my mother, it's not good for my business to have an informer's wife as a customer, someone unable to accept that things had changed, Carminho always knew what to keep to herself, she welcomed those women who wanted to avenge longstanding humiliations, she drove out those like my mother who could not adapt to the new times, Carminho always knew what to do while the salon owner reclined on the chaise longue in her parlour drinking liquor, Carminho had nothing but the salon work, she catered to her newest customers' demands, to the demands of the stylists, she encouraged the departure of the less palatable customers, she tried to protect the furniture from wear and tear, Carminho had a hand in everything, in the end of the salon, the end of its owner, her own end, everything, even the girls on a hen do who have not stopped ordering beers, they were not even born and the Princesa Beauty Salon was already dying, and Augusta, where is Augusta who was always in the cloakroom where the Indian man now takes orders for takeaways, there is a sign on the wall, takeaway orders, in Augusta's time the sign was not there, I never saw the cloakroom without Augusta, by seven-thirty in the morning Augusta was already polishing the counter, by eight she was arranging the numbered tags she handed out in exchange for coats and bags, not that she needed the tags, she knew each customer like she knew the palm of her own hand, she never got their names wrong, or their marital status, or the number of children, their background, their financial situation, their health,

how are you, Madame, how are those migraines

going from bad to worse, Augusta, from bad to worse

and how are your daughter and husband

comme ci, comme ça

Augusta does not need the tags but she agreed to use them when she understood that they gave the salon a more prosperous air, more modern, she did not mind being undermined if it was for the benefit of the salon, I feel sorry for Augusta when she realises that the Indian man took away her cloakroom, she never took a day off, one or two days for sickness or a relative's death, but never any holidays, the Indian man does not know anyone's name, he mixes up the widows and the divorcees, a serious mistake, he does not hang up the coats and the handbags, he does not offer anyone a little cup of coffee, an Indian man very much like the Indian man who is waiting on us, and like the Indian man I saw in the kitchen, teeth so white they must be false, slick black hair, skin like rancid chocolate,

where are all these Asians who all look the same coming from the Indian sitting in Augusta's cloakroom, the cloakroom that once stretched from one wall to the other no longer exists, a few swings of the sledgehammer and Augusta was forever left without somewhere to exist, Ângelo asks,

what do you call a louse on a bald man's head

Dora pretends to be guessing, I reply, a plain-clothes louse, Dora rubs her left wrist with her right hand, a sign that she is fed up, I know her gestures of impatience, she wants the dinner to be over, we haven't even started, Ângelo shakes his head, I did not guess correctly, my answer is not funny, Ângelo replies

homeless

and he lets out a guffaw, his chest going up and down, his breathing interrupted, his face red, homeless, I always felt sorry for him, even before I knew he spent hours standing at the end of our street hating us, I laugh, Dora laughs and picks up the laminated photocopy that passes for a menu, she has made her choice, Ângelo is undecided, he does not like spicy food, he does not like spices, this one, they say this one is good, we lean over to help him choose, Ângelo blows his nose, the smell just kills me, I should not have brought them here, the past does not exist anywhere, the only benefit of the past is that it will never again exist anywhere, I think I'm allergic to these smells, Ângelo complains, and he gets up to use the toilet without noticing the metal trolley with the curlers and the hairbrushes, he might almost trip over the manicurist with her pink overall sitting on a stool with the nail polish basket perched dangerously on her lap, or slip on the hair curler dropped on the floor, Ângelo walks on and reaches the lounge where the salon owner drinks liquor while reclining on her chaise longue, Ângelo will be embarrassed, when he comes back he will tell us that he mistakenly entered a lounge where there was a woman lying down, we will laugh until it hurts, Dora avoids me, she looks at the art on the wall, we are silent, we don't know how to speak without hurting each other, we don't know how to be together without hurting each other, we don't know what to do with our hurt, Ângelo comes back as if he had not walked into the salon owner's lounge, he is more absent-minded every day, he says, I splashed some water in my eyes, I'm better, I ask Ângelo to choose some wine,

are we celebrating anything

the sale of an old house

I could not miss this opportunity to hurt my child, I am only held back from delivering the final blow by the pleasure of holding back,

nobody can hurt a child like its mother can

Dora disguises the blow with a grimace, swallowing hard, she harbours an excessive love for her grandparents, the house where she was so happy and which I sold today, I signed the deed transfer with the silver pen, this time my hand did not betray me as it did when I signed my first ID card, I wrote every letter of my name without trembling, without the smallest hesitation, if I thought it would be easy it turned out to be even easier, I could feel Dora's anger as I signed, the greatest betrayal I was ever capable of, Dora does not know that I made it impossible for her to hate me,

an angel that saved us

that there was no point in pulling away from me to run to her grandparents, I did not want to offer my parents their salvation, a trap, I never intended to save my parents, not even to offer them a reason, Dora went yesterday to tidy the garden, she thinks she can dissuade the buyers from paving over the whole thing, her hands are bruised, she trimmed the rosebushes, she thinned out the row of chrysanthemums, she pruned the night-blooming jasmine, picked the remaining calla lilies, she should not have wasted her time, the buyers will pave over every bit of ground they find,

they don't like plants or animals

our daughter complained, a teenager changing her skin,

no-one like our children to betray us

nor should Dora have wasted her time begging me not to sell the house, we were never talking about the same house, I did not sell the house Dora talks about, I don't even know that house, I was never in the garden where her grandfather taught her the difference between the leaves of the orange tree and the lemon tree, where every year he would pick the season's first fig and offer it to her, the fig tree was the only tree that thrived with neglect, it spread over the entire garden, it did what survivors do, it took everything, at the end of every summer the smell of rotting figs and the fig tree growing even further, the waiter brings us wine, I fill the glasses, I propose a toast,

to the sale of an old house

Dora might note that I am being careful, that I am being merciful, I don't say, for instance, to the sale of the old swing on which my child found her wings, and anyway, the swing is rotting away, Dora's swing no longer exists, two unravelling ropes and a woodwormed plank, the swing that my mother always pushed so carefully

an angel learning to use its wings

rotted away, my mother worried, she did not want the daughter she wished she had had to hurt herself, but Dora insisted, harder, granny,

I want to touch the sky, I want to fly up to the sky

and my mother laughed, she called out to my grandfather, Dorinha wants to touch the sky, and she pushed harder, the idiots would laugh, and then Dora would say, I'm almost touching the sky, Dora with her rosy cheeks, her blonde curls high in the air, I hit a cloud, my idiot father would laugh, I take a sip of my wine, neither of them toasted, I insist, I did not sell the house that Dora remembers, I sold the house that actually exists and the one I remember, the house with the walls that closed in to suffocate me and the ceilings that came down to crush me, no air, even today when I went there, the roof tiles and the windows cracked, the wind whistling on the staircase and the permanent stuffiness, Dora needs to recognise that we were never talking about the same house, I can do nothing against my child's stubbornness, I will never forgive you, my child wants to feel hurt, to hurt me, she has become her worst enemy, my greatest enemy, I look her in the eyes, I raise my glass, I repeat,

to the sale of a house that was falling to pieces, no house, no matter how bad it is, deserves that fate

I will be disloyal like never before, I turn to Ângelo, with the tone of someone sharing some news, Dora did not want me to sell the house, have you ever heard anything so silly, a house falling to pieces, Dora was upset, very upset, the house was not falling to pieces, it was a solid house, it just needed some fixing up, nothing more than that, Ângelo looks at her, moved, Dora continues, it was the place where I was happy with the people I loved the most, the only people I loved, poor child, I laugh, I did not sell any of that, no-one's happiness and no-one's loves, I sold off an old house, you need to believe me that I sold off a house that was falling to pieces, that was all it was, Dora looks at me with such rage that I can feel my face burning,

I know you would have sold it if you could, lucky that your spite can't hurt me

I am proud of having raised such a good adversary, I can do nothing against her memories, against mine, against my parents who never once believed I could touch the clouds, the sky was always off-limits to me, my adversary easily recovers from life's knocks no matter how hard they are, she is well trained, she moves into attack mode, turns to Ângelo, excludes me from the conversation, uses my own dirty trick,

she could never accept that her own parents preferred me, she is so miserable that she would have preferred it if my grandparents lied to her

which interrupts Ângelo as he arranges the paper napkin, he is smoothing out the wrinkles, the same obsessive manner with which he stretches out the bedspread every morning so that the frills hang neatly, Ângelo does not want to, cannot, be involved in our fight, he would lose to both of us, he is far beneath our category, he can only ever play the role he is playing now, we always leave him out, an unspoken agreement, it is my turn to reply, I cannot deny what she said,

Dora was the child my parents wished for, when she was born she lifted the curse of her parentage, she drew my father away from his cages, an angel that saved us, it had never occurred to me that I could offer my parents

you have to get rid of it as soon as possible

some salvation, they could not accuse me of ever being generous to them,

you will get rid of it, you will get rid of it even if it's the last thing I do in this life

if I had done what my mother wanted me to do I would have never heard her say, my granddaughter is so much like me, my granddaughter likes me so much, Dora is waiting for my reply, in our clashes silence always means defeat, even more so in this case, Dora never defeated me, no, she never defeated me yet, she was loved by my parents, she managed to prove that there was something wrong with me, she is threatening to use her trump card, she is about to say,

your parents didn't like you because you didn't deserve it, I don't like you because you don't deserve it

there is something wrong with me and not with my parents, or Dora, or Ângelo, Dora hesitates, she has the trump card to defeat me but foolishly she hesitates, I make the most of my adversary's hesitation, I want to win, I always want to defeat her, I deliver another blow, not the definitive one, strategy is essential in a fight,

the new owners will pave over the front garden and the garden

I know how the front garden's disappearance hurts her, and that of the fig tree in the garden, yesterday she was still trimming the rosebushes, thinning out the row of chrysanthemums, gathering the remaining calla lilies for her grandparents, she is hopeful that the buyers will keep the garden and the fig tree, the garden where as a child she would lie on the grass, her golden locks spread out on the ground, her body warmed by the soft spring sunshine, a child surrounded by new-born kittens

the cats were always running away from me

tickling her, the unsteady kittens climbing over her belly and making her laugh, her back cooled by the humid grass, the kittens getting tangled up in her locks, Dora's laughter, my mother called her, she was always worried that the angel that had saved her would become sick, nobody knows how angels get sick or how they are cured, my father was not yet putting out bowls filled with poisoned milk, he was allowing the kittens to tickle the angel that saved him, no-one dismisses an angel's laughter, Dora with one of the kittens in her hand, can I take it home, and my father not yet putting out bowls with poisoned milk or showing her the stiff carcasses, the stretched out legs, the eyes deader than two pieces of glass, grandpa, can I take this one home, and the grandparents said yes to everything, the goodness of the angel that had saved them was contagious, so too was the gentle laughter of the spring sky, they were happy, the three of them were happy in that house that tried to eject me as soon as I entered its gate, I felt indisposed, I could barely go up the staircase that wanted me to stay downstairs, the steps too narrow, or too slippery, waiting for me to trip, to misstep, the hand on the bannister, they could not keep me downstairs, I would climb the stairs and my heart would beat faster, jumping out of my chest, leaving a gap that frightened me, I would lie on my bed panting, I was cold, I was always cold in that house, despite the sweat that moistened my clothes, I looked up at the ceiling that came down to crush me, a crushed cockroach, the ceiling falling onto me, no, it stood there threatening me, I will crush you, I won't crush you, I turned to one side and then it was the walls closing in to smother me, a fly spinning from the lack of air, so many times I wished for the house to burn, it would have been so easy, I lacked the courage, I was always a coward, I am not ashamed and I am not proud, one trait among many, I would think, I'll spray everything with petrol and light a match, I could see the flames coming out through the windows, spreading over the roof, never again would the orange tree flower in the garden, never again the rotten smell of figs, never again the scent of the night-blooming jasmine, never again that house, fire was the most appropriate punishment, the house turned into a pile of ashes, a pile of ashes that I would spread around with my feet,

and the bird cages are all going, the buyers have no time for plants or animals

Dora does not reply, Ângelo takes this as a cue to lighten the awkwardness, of course they don't have time, almost no-one has time, since he got it into his head to try to understand things there is nothing that Ângelo does not claim to understand, the children pelting him with pieces of cake, the pensioners heckling him, the teenagers filling the stage with cans of beer, nothing, absolutely nothing, escapes Ângelo's understanding, if he were not such a weak adversary I would ask him how he managed to understand that my father, but it's not worth it, I am sure he would tell me some nice lie, I let him rearrange the cutlery, it is the fourth time he moves the knife and fork before putting them back where he thinks they should be,

plants need time

just last week one of my plants died, he confesses sorrowfully, he tries to explain which one, the reddish one in the pot by the balcony, not enough sun, I say without knowing which plant he is referring to, I vaguely remember the mildew, not enough sun, I say again, Ângelo disagrees, I don't think so, it had been there already for a few years, some disease perhaps, plants are like us, they can grow sick

97

without any warning and if we don't pay attention, by the time I realised it was too late, there was nothing I could do, Dora is moved, she promises to buy Ângelo a plant to replace the one that died, she looks over at me, she wants me to know that she is generous to Ângelo, to everyone else, Dora's hand on Ângelo's, they are pitiful,

I'm sure you did everything you could

I let out a guffaw, what a poignant scene, a bit more and you'll have me crying, in fact, we should all cry for the plant, oh, we should put out a notice in the paper, the relatives of the reddish plant, it was the reddish one, wasn't it, friends and relatives of the reddish plant in the pot by the balcony wish to share the sad news of its passing last week and to express their gratitude, one of those notices might be good, for a change, Dora takes her hand off Ângelo's,

stop drinking, you're being pathetic

Dora thinks she is capable of hating me,

and what about your mother, you're not offering your mother a plant

she does not know that I have fixed into her flesh the impossibility of hating me, a trap, you're not offering your mother a plant, I insist,

everything you touch dies

not listening to the silly remark she read in some book, she is always underlining stupid phrases in books and then spewing them out in this tragic tone, poor child, her blow misses its mark, my adversary has missed her chance, I joke,

if only, I'd be much better than laser treatment

if only that were true I would be able to compete with those Spanish laser clinics popping up all over the place promising, say goodbye to superfluous hair, compelling customers, get to the root of the problem, marketing refrains are so tedious, I turn to Ângelo, laser treatment is a dangerous nuisance, skin dies when deprived of its swirls of hair, I reply, the things you read in books are no good for real life, people who write books know nothing about life, that's why they waste time writing, because they don't realise, for instance, that time is precious, Ângelo gestures with impatience, speaking about time, this food is taking some time, and Dora agrees, Ângelo and Dora like one another, they don't need to hurt one another, they exclude me from the little smiles they exchange, I don't care, it's been a while since I stopped caring about the smiles they exchange, about them, it's been a while since I stopped caring about the house I sold earlier today, about the garden, about the calla lilies Dora collected to take to her grandparents, about anything, I am certain that Dora cried yesterday when she cut the remaining calla lilies and placed them by the two stone slabs, here lies, full name, date of birth and death, additional information, eternally missed, a form that the funeral director, I preferred calling them undertakers, filled out after I chose the Napoleon model from a catalogue, I chose the Napoleon model for my mother and later I chose another for my father, I can't remember which model I chose for my father, the funeral director shook my hand and, for the tenth time, offered me his sympathies when

my sympathies

he should have kept them to himself, he might still need them and there was nothing I could do with them, I should have told him to keep his sympathies, we never know when we'll need our sympathies, or that little tin of dried yeast that we've had in our larder for years, the woollen night-gown we've not used for the past five winters, we never know when we'll need things even if we never use them, if it were not for that uncertainty I might put out an ad in the local paper, sympathies for sale, in mint condition, as new, unique opportunity, selling due to change of life, reasonably priced, Ângelo asks,

a parrot crossed with a centipede

Dora and I are not done wrangling, we are at an impasse, Dora should not have squandered her victory by relying on some silliness she read in a book, nothing is as pointless in real life as the nice phrases in books, how gullible are those who take it upon themselves to reinvent life, Dora was embarrassed to have been exposed,

everything you touch dies

Ângelo insists,

a parrot crossed with a centipede

Dora and I revert to our roles, we are the artist's audience, I'm used to it, I go to Ângelo's performances whenever I can, a wretch dressed up in sky-blue trousers and vest, an immaculately white frilled shirt, polished green shoes, a wretch with blue bug eyes, enormous feet, long monkey arms, taking the microphone, it's been a long time since Dora stopped going, she does not like seeing him make a fool of himself, she is hurt by the lack of talent, the failure, I accompany Ângelo whenever I'm able to, I can hear him even before he opens his mouth,

thank you for coming today, I was going to come too but I couldn't

the audience laughs at first but soon they realise that they were misled, that the comedian is crummy, they cough, shift in their seats, the first signs of discontent, if Ângelo had greater awareness, if he were not dumbfounded by being on stage, every audience member regrets paying the price of the ticket, the bolder ones start whistling, the first heckle, piss off, clown, Ângelo unflustered, dumbfounded by being on stage, or by the certainty that laughter is the best thing we can offer others, overlooking the fact that he is not in any position to offer it, I watch another of his failures, I applaud, I pretend to laugh, at the end of the performance Ângelo says

that went well, didn't it

that it was a tough audience, I agree, it went well, I add, people are getting more and more demanding, I offer to buy him a drink, somewhere that we can sit down and have a few beers, and laugh, it's true that the performances always go well, whether it was applause or jeers they last only a few hours, it always goes well, whether people have applauded or jeered it takes the same amount of time to forget, all it takes is for Ângelo to return to his two rooms, the jade elephant, the dancer and the fruit bowl with the swans, a few hours and he's forgotten everything and no-one remembers the clown, perhaps the teenager who threw the beer can onto the stage, like an excited fan who threw some gift at the artist, flowers, they always throw flowers, flowers for artists, beer cans for clowns, flowers are the best thing to give others, even when wrapped in noisy cellophane, tied up in sad ribbons with frayed edges,

a walkie-talkie

Ângelo looks so cute with his sky-blue satin suit and the frilled shirt, at the end some audience members come up to

Ângelo but instead of asking for an autograph they complain and Ângelo understands, he understands everything, even the old folk who get up halfway through his act, not because they are fed up, more probably because they are tired from laughing so much, laughing demands a lot of the human body, it involves a large number of muscles is what Betty heard on the television programme with that journalist, I can't remember her name, the one with the black hair and the very feminine manner, the old people have to get up halfway through his act because they can't take any more, weaker bodies can't take any chances, they stand by the doorway asking one another, laughing with one another when

where did they get this scarecrow

they talk about the scarecrow and that's when I start clapping so hard that my hands hurt, Dora offers me a truce, she is leaving the tie-break for later on, we will have so many opportunities,

so you'll still be travelling tonight

I never reply without knowing exactly where Dora might land her next blow later on,

you shouldn't drink so much

Ângelo can drive

I told you I can't go with you, the outing was cancelled
because of the storm

it was not my intention to force Ângelo to come with me,
I am used to travelling alone, I don't mind, in fact I like it,

that's right, you'd told me, I forgot

Dora looks at me with suspicion, I add some more information to prove to her that I know what I'm talking about, you
called in the morning to let me know but the day was so,
for a few seconds I cannot find the right word, so, busy,
Ângelo helps me out, I am grateful, that's it, so busy, the day
was so busy that I forgot, Dora lowers her head,

if you want to smash yourself to pieces on the road
that's up to you

here we go again, we are so tedious, why can't I end this by
telling her how much I love her, why do I pull further away
from this most perfect part of me, a trap, the waiter brings
our food on small plates, tells us to enjoy our meal, Dora
helps herself with ease, Ângelo eyes with suspicion the food
the waiter brought us, what am I doing in the Princesa Beauty
Salon sitting near a group of girls who won't stop letting
out shrieks, cackles, sighing mawkishly like cheesy love-
birds, why did it ever cross my mind to come for dinner to
the Princesa Beauty Salon when it is a well-known fact that
hairdressers are no good at serving dinners, I chew on the

pieces of lamb, Dora eats slowly, she savours the meal, my child always

chic, très chic

so elegant while I chew loudly and swallow larger pieces of meat, an animal attacking its food, Ângelo tries to guess the spices, what am I doing here, the same absurd impulse that took me to the Rosa da Manhã which has been boarded up for years following a dispute between the heirs, they locked up the blue velvet sofa behind concrete and wooden planks, the blue velvet sofa that so bothered my mother when it started wearing thin, when its springs started loosening, when its back started bending, because it reminded her

have this sofa fixed or throw it out, *je vous en prie*

of her own skin, even more worn out, of her own bones, even more brittle, her own back, even more bent, my mother who knew she would suffer the same fate as the sofa, there is no big difference between ageing things, both of them were growing old but my mother had an angel that saved her and the blue velvet sofa did not, it died boarded up, in a giant pigeons' nest, a hospice for old posters, a dance school to learn the tango, other types of dance were covered up by, God is seeking you, covered up by, voting is your ri—, and by, Grand Circus 3.00 pm on the 17th—, the blue velvet sofa smothered by pigeon shit and by overlaid posters, Ângelo says, lucky that the food does not taste as bad as it smells, Dora arranges the cutlery, from the girls' table a squeal in unison, we look their way, the bride-to-be opens the present her friends gave her, shrieks, you have to put it on, in unison, put it on, put it on, put it on, Dora shakes her head, the girl, at the head of the table, takes something that looks like a veil and places it on her head, instead of a tiara an enormous cock, the bride-to-be laughs with the enormous cock on her head and the white tulle tumbling down to her shoulders, the friends laugh, their laughter bouncing around the room until it dies by the camel drawings, on the black and white tiled floor, the white teeth of the same-looking Indian waiters, Dora says, how pathetic, the bride-to-be touches the fabric cock to respond to one of her friends who keeps asking, come on, tell us if it's bigger or smaller than the groom's, bigger, the others shout, the bride-to-be pretends she is measuring, bigger, this one's bigger, she agrees and pretends to be disappointed, one of the friends gets up to take a photograph, the bride-to-be is so happy, sitting at the head of the table, wearing a veil adorned with a cock, I fill up my glass and raise it,

to the blue velvet sofa

Dora does not raise her glass, she is embarrassed by me, she looks around, since when is she embarrassed by me, I never wanted to know, Ângelo clinks his glass with mine, to the blue velvet sofa, whatever that is, it's a moment in time, nothing more than a moment in time, Ângelo pretends to understand me, he says, a toast to a moment in time, I correct him, no, a toast to the blue velvet sofa, Dora is about to get up, she knows I have had too much to drink, before she gets up I fill my wine glass again and raise it,

to Dora, the most perfect part of me,

I add, loudly, almost as loudly as the friend of the bride-to-be who is shouting, to the bride, the groom and their lovers,

to my daughter and the blue velvet sofa

so loud that Dora rebukes me almost without moving her lips, stop being so pathetic, I am pathetic, me and the bride-to-be and the friends, and the lovey-dovey couple, and the family, Dora sees pathetic people everywhere, why doesn't she see the dolls with their soapy heads in the black basins, the broken manicure chair, the salon attendants with their rustic gestures, the chirruping of a flock of birds, my mother in her light-yellow dress, if Dora could see her grandmother she would run to her like she always did, my mother would caress her hair and then say to Carminho, do something about *mon ange*'s curls, she looks so much like me, don't you think, and Carminho, carbon copy, Dora does not see the salon attendants taking advantage of customers' distraction to steal their secrets,

she doesn't know who the father is

the grandmother was worried that she might be black

it's a miracle she was born normal

if she were like her mother she would have been another tramp

Dora, my child, holding her grandmother's hand in moribund beauty salons, in fading tea rooms with her lips dirty with hot chocolate, my child oblivious to the death all around her, holding hands with her grandmother, an angel protected from the abyss of time, everyone knows that angels are immortal, Ângelo asks for the dessert menu, he is in good spirits, he thinks the veil with the cock is funny, he raises his glass towards the bride-to-be, to the wedding, says my blonde bug-eyed scarecrow, Dora is impatient, she wants to go home, tomorrow she will have to get up early, she has to take three buses to get to work, while she puts on the uniform she will say to one of her colleagues that she had dinner at an Indian restaurant, the colleague says there is a very good Indian over at, one of the managers arrives, the conversation about restaurants goes on, the colleague says she would like to try a Japanese, the manager says her sister-in-law went just the other day to a Thai and African food place, Dora says nothing, my child is in the habit of buying her silence for the rest of the day by saying a phrase like, yesterday I had dinner at an Indian restaurant, my Dora could tell them how embarrassed she was by me, by Ângelo, a bug-eyed scarecrow that she must surely find embarrassing, but she says nothing, the bride-to-be with the cock on her head guffaws, the waiter comes over at Ângelo's request to tell him about a pudding with a strange name, I ask for one, Dora wants nothing, she wants to go home, she needs to be well rested tomorrow so she doesn't mistake organic Spanish turnip greens for organic Spanish spinach, or any other leaf, she has to be in the right mood to pose for the artist who for years has been trying to kill the flesh I made her from, to drain the blood I filled her with, to free her from the inability to hate me, at the artist's house she is another Dora, made of stone, finally free from me,

where do you get the nerve to eat more

this one is easy to answer, very easy, my poor sculpture,

it's about appetite, not about nerve

Ângelo wants to laugh but he doesn't dare, he has to remain impartial in our quarrels, that is the only way we accept him, Ângelo has never admitted it but he likes to see us quarrel, we offer him an excellent spectacle, we hurt each other with every word, daggers thrust mercilessly, with every gesture, carefully dispensed poison, rarely missing an opportunity, Dora gets up, showing no respect, we both know that the quarrel has to go on to the end, we never give up, when she gets up my child knows she is cheating, playing dirty, by handing me victory she is showing that she despises me, I don't care, tomorrow we'll start over, we don't know how else to be with one another, tomorrow we'll start over, Dora heads towards the door, she walks past the table with the hen party, she stops to look at the bride-to-be, what made her stop, she goes up to the head of the table and in a swift motion pulls the veil off the bride-to-be's head, she throws it onto the ground, I don't know what got into her, the bride-to-be's friends do not react, neither does the bride-to-be, my child's anger caught them off guard, the waiter stands still, he is carrying the desserts we ordered, Dora pushes the restaurant door and exits, one of the bride-to-be's friends picks up the veil and places it again on the bride-to-be's head, she looks our way, Ângelo gets up and offers an apology, another girl says, idiot, what a massive idiot, and they all insult my child, the most perfect part of me, the thought of Dora leaving makes Ângelo nervous, of course she hasn't left, she's outside waiting for us, she was always reasonable, she never loses it, she never makes mistakes when scanning barcodes, trolleys and trolleys full of shopping and not a single mistake, any day now she will be promoted to cashier supervisor, Ângelo says,

you always go too far

how dare a disgrace like him scold me, I laugh out loud, I cannot believe that Ângelo wants to tell me off, Ângelo cannot afford to interfere in our quarrels, to take sides,

I never go too far, never, because there is no place that is too far how can Ângelo talk about things he knows nothing about, not even the maps I collect take me far, or far enough, for instance, Wilkes Land, I like Wilkes Land, a place at the end of the world, I like paper places, places I don't associate with anything, places that every now and then can be as far away as I need them to be, everything is so close to me, I am always so close to everything, to the pain of the words I use to hurt Dora, to Ângelo's arm as it holds me, to the house I sold earlier today, to my mother, to my father, to the calla lilies Dora cut to bring to their grave, to the body hair I could never vanquish, to my waxes, I never go too far, I walk over to Augusta's cloakroom to pay, I want to leave,

no-one can escape the past

I trip, I'm not yet drunk but everyone thinks I am, the dolls with the soapy heads, the attendants, Carminho, Augusta, the lovey-dovey couple, the hysterical girls, they all feel sorry for me, there is nothing sadder than an obese woman, some-where between type I and II, stumbling, I smile at the girls, the bride-to-be with the veil and the cock on her head once again, at first it is just my lips moving, then, involuntarily, I am letting out laughs, waves of sound rocking me, my mother smoothing out the pleats on her light-yellow dress, the attendants stealing my secrets that are now burning their tongues, nothing escapes them,

there wasn't a boy in this neighbourhood that she didn't sleep with until she slept with a black returnee and then nobody wanted her if her father hadn't already been batty he would have died of shame

they say every night she's going around falling over drunk

I say to the Indian man, if Augusta finds out you stole her cloakroom she'll slap you, Ângelo pleads, let's go home, he asks quietly, please, I grab the Indian man's arm, Augusta, where is Augusta, Ângelo apologises, he is apologising all the time, my mother shakes her head, at me, at Ângelo who is hanging my handbag on my shoulder, the couple look at us appalled, they are so far from my despair, the girls are quiet, it is the first time they are quiet since they entered, Ângelo drags me out of the Princesa Beauty Salon, the Indian man who usurped Augusta's cloakroom shakes his head, I walk over the giant chessboard, I sold the house I was born in, the blue velvet sofa was boarded into a home for pigeons, the Princesa Beauty Salon is now this restaurant

pourri, completely *pourri*

that my mother refuses to enter, the salon owner died, on the chaise longue she left her broken heart, her wonder-filled eyes, a mysterious smile on her rouged lips

the great mystery of the smiles of the dead

and dozens of empty tablet boxes, the salon owner on the chaise longue, after her heart got tired of taking her to the heaven of other lives, she left nothing else, Carminho shut down the salon, she tidied up the accounts with the heirs and went abroad to wipe the bottoms of old Swiss men, German, English, they are all the same, they all stink, Ângelo is still apologising, he is almost funny in this upset role, if he acted half as well in his performances I am sure his audiences would enjoy themselves, Ângelo pulls me, I am hefty, I resist, my child is out there, she did not escape to the house I sold earlier today, she did not try to save the cages, or the magazine left on the night stand, she cannot save her grandparents from the oblivion I condemned them to, the new owners will get rid of the smell of my father's office, of my bed, of the paper with the roses lining the kitchen drawers, of Dora's bicycle, they will get rid of us, we go out into the street, Dora is waiting for us,

I'm leaving home tomorrow

you talk such nonsense and then you say I'm the one who's drunk

we walk towards the car, Ângelo says he will drive, I do not argue, I am worried about my child's threat, she cannot leave home, I need her, no-one else can hurt me like she does, Dora was born to give me that privilege, she was not born to save my parents even though she did, Ângelo turns on the windscreen wipers, we continue in silence, I look at the blurred city, an ugly painting, I look at the watery road lit by the headlamps, at the softening buildings, the city weakening in my tearful eyes, or in the storm that has finally arrived, the show is about to begin, I ask,

into how many parts can a mother's brain split

neither Ângelo nor Dora reply, they carry on in silence, they are in no mood to pretend they don't know the answer, they are annoyed, they are punishing me,

depends on how hard you hit it

oh, says Ângelo with the annoyance of someone remembering the punchline to a bad joke, Dora remains silent, I tell another joke and then another, neither of them laughs, we don't know what to offer each other

what the sky

the bank clerk asks me to wait until the buyers arrive, the transfer of deeds was scheduled for two o'clock, I say, yes but with this rain it's likely they'll be late, the clerk speaks with excessive politeness, the notary hasn't arrived either, this rain makes everyone late, the bank clerk's words are all said in the same tone, his politeness helps him shut up troublesome people like me, I turn away, the clerk picks up his work where he left it, he is annoyed at having been interrupted, it is the second time I have distracted him from the computer, the first time I was talking about the storm, it's chaos, I like using that word, chaos, it's chaos, I repeated, then I offered details of the chaos, four accidents, serious and less serious flooding, fallen trees, roads cut off, the clerk listened to me in silence, politely killing the conversation, the tragedies I was describing disappeared in the clerk's unflappable face, as soon as he had the opportunity the clerk returned to his luminous screen, he exercises his fingers by stretching and curling them above the keyboard, a pianist doing warm-up exercises, he went back to filling forms, typing in the appropriate blanks, statutory marriage, residents of, landline phone number, mobile phone number, husband's profession, wife's profession, monthly income, surgical interventions, chronic illness, the clerk is not allowed to know any more about people than what the blanks on the form allow, although there is a special section, other observations, for anything important that has not been entered elsewhere, or perhaps to prove that there is not much more to say, that the people who design the forms know what they are doing, the clerk detests having to spend his day gathering this information, a monotonous job, the clerk might even admit to himself that he detests what he does if that did not cause him to loathe it even further, if it were not because he has to pay for the new apartment, his wife's new car, his eldest daughter's computer, the nursery for the youngest, the summer holidays, nobody would force him to wake up early to sit at a desk gathering dreary information about faceless people as dreary as the information they produce, the bank clerk would sleep in every morning or board a cargo ship and sail around the world, he dreamed about that when he was young, the clerk gathers the forms to take them to his boss, one floor above, in his own office, not the open office that the clerk shares with some fifty wretched souls like him, the boss with a larger wood-top desk, a chair with back and neck support, height adjustable, a computer with a larger screen, a speakerphone, a gold-plated pen

make sure all the papers are in order, make sure we don't have any problems

to emphasise his great responsibility, the clerk's boss is bored by the monotonous loan requests from equally monotonous faceless people, were it not for the holiday home, the multi-person vehicle, supporting the son who does sailing, the polyglot daughter who likes travelling, nobody would force him to wake up every morning and come into his office, despite the desk and the adjustable chair, the more powerful computer and the conference speakerphone, the clerk's boss would dedicate his time to organic farming, when he was younger he wanted to be a farmer, and worry about nitrates in vegetables, the clerk's boss signs the loan requests and puts them in folders with transparent covers, after signing in the appropriate space on the forms the clerk's boss collects the folders and takes them to his boss, one floor above, with a view, a larger office, a full wooden desk with lockable drawers, an ergonomic leather chair, a porcelain lamp, a computer with a larger screen, a multi-function conference speakerphone with speed-dial, a gold pen, the clerk's boss knocks on the door and he gives his own boss the folders,

make sure all the papers are in order, make sure we don't have any problems

the clerk's boss' boss is also fed up with the bothersome requests for loans from equally bothersome faceless people, were it not for the little chalet in the snow, the luxury condo, the eldest daughter living in London, the middle son's degree in the United States, the youngest one's delusion of being an artist, everyone's cars, everyone's motorcycles, everyone's cigarettes and drinks, everyone's vanities, and yes, the weekends in New York with his lover, nobody would force him to get up every morning and come into the office with a cramped view, the clerk's boss' boss would go into a silent retreat and would climb mountains as the sun came up, a healthy life, were it not for the life he has he would be a hermit, the clerk continues doing his job

people believe they need so many things

as numbed as my Dora at the hypermarket, people believe they need so many things, the clerk looks out through the sealed glass, the open office has no windows that can be opened because of the central heating or the air cooling system, or some other reason, at first the clerk did not like the sealed glass in place of real windows but he got used to it,

they were worried we might jump out a window

the clerk has the sort of humour that colleagues never appreciate and

if we had even a tiny bit of sense that's what we should do

that makes him even lonelier, the clerk stares at the relentless rain, for a long time now his thoughts have been the only thing he truly possesses, how will I get to the nursery on time, even on a normal day I'd already be late, where will I park to buy some chicken, I should have said to my wife that today was not a good day to buy roast chicken, he would have said it had he not been trying to avoid a conversation, he has learned to spare himself the sound of his wife's voice,

half a spicy chicken and another half with butter for the children, two portions of chips, if they still have some bread, the one baked in the wood-fired oven, bring two and I'll freeze one of them, if we had the bigger freezer I wanted you could bring three or four, so

his wife's voice is so irritating, he couldn't stand that voice even when they were dating, nobody is that self-deluded, besides her voice the wife has the irritating habit of talking non-stop,

make sure you're back in time, I don't want us to be late for the tenants' meeting, I want to see what that annoying building manager has to say about the broken lifts, he lives on the first floor so could do without them altogether, I hope you will help me, just the other day the neighbour in 6B, the one whose roots are always show-ing, she had the nerve to say to me, I mean, she implied that you were scared of the manager

the clerk's wife likes to use the word nerve for anything and everything and this annoys him, the clerk does not remember her saying when they were dating,

I bet you wouldn't have the nerve not to marry me after so many years going out but then again the wife did not speak non-stop as she does now,

> I mean, if there is someone we need in this building it is her ex-husband, she doesn't like anyone to call him ex-husband but if they're divorced I won't call him her husband, whenever her ex-husband opened his cakehole it was to give the manager an earful about everything, that's the only reason I'm sorry they got divorced

the clerk's wife also likes using the word cakehole, which irritates him a lot, the clerk reads what he just wrote and presses delete, he misses typewriters, having to pay attention to what he was doing, he attended the professional development courses the bank sent him on, he added to his CV, good IT and customer management skills, and now he spends his time listening to his wife and pressing delete,

> I am going to complain to the manager about the damp stain on the living room wall, the neighbour in 5F, the one with the dog, she complained and she got her living room painted, I went to see it, you can't imagine the smell of dog, and the sofas covered in dog hair, animals were not made to live in apartments, animals should be banned in the building, the place for animals is on the street

the clerk starts filling out another form, purchase of property, name, address, occupation, monthly income gross and net, marital status, marital asset regime, name of spouse,

spouse's profession, gross and net income, dependants, the clerk verifies the information, compulsory home insurance for a total amount of, life insurance, health, three entries, chronic illness, surgical interventions, hospital admissions, this is the only part that the clerk enjoys a little, he is always surprised by the variety of illnesses, cataplexy, hydrocele, intermittent claudication, he goes home and looks them up in the family medical encyclopaedia bound in leather with gilt edges that he bought some years ago in instalments from a man who knocked at their door, when his wife sees the clerk looking up rare diseases she scolds him

you'll become a hypochondriac like the neighbour in 7H, you've got to stop it with those diseases

but the clerk continues reading the descriptions of diseases, if only his wife's voice would leave him alone on this day with so much rain, they've announced a storm,

make sure you're back in time, you know that our boy starts crying when all the other children have gone home, poor thing, after a whole day at nursery,

the clerk has to arrive before his son's classmates' parents so that his son won't burst into tears and annoy the nursery staff,

we couldn't bear it, not because of us but because of him, just look at the state the child is in the nursery staff's voices are as irritating as his wife's, the clerk has often dreamed about being a serial killer of women's voices, in his dreams after killing all the women's voices the clerk walks around happily in a silent paradise, it's lucky that the clerk does not know how to kill a voice, the silence in his dreams is so inviting, the clerk types into the additional information box on the new form, what the hell have I done with my life, he presses delete and moves on to the next piece of work,

what the hell have I done with my life

the room where I am waiting for the buyers has a nice view across the city, matching black sofas with a modern design, a coffee table with a shiny chrome base and a glass top, I reach for the magazine lying on it, I could look out at the city beneath the rain, I like seeing things from afar, everything seems so perfect when seen from afar, there is no mystery to the love we are given by our creator, it is easy to love us from afar, I look at the city, I leaf through the magazine thinking about what I could be doing instead of leafing through a magazine I have no interest in, right there on the second page

sign up to a pension plan

is a command duly illustrated with the picture of a successful old man who followed it, the old man who signed up to a pension plan in a timely fashion is smiling on a golf course, his teeth so bright, I check whether my stockings have slipped, the packaging for the stockings promised *haute résistance*, they were more expensive, but now the nylon is poised in a threat, as if saying in no time I will be a massive droopy mess, I look impotently at the slipping nylon, the slovenly leg, *haute résistance*, I look at the scuffed shoes and the mud-splattered raincoat, the garish dress beneath the coat, I turn back to the magazine, sign up to a pension plan and become a perfect person, get the old man off the sunlit golf green and leave him standing in the rain waiting for a taxi, expel him from the paradise in the photograph and the old man becomes just another old man like so many others trembling in the cold,

happiness depends on the circumstances

the wind has already broken two of the spokes on the umbrella of the old man waiting for a taxi, he waves his arms, the taxi drives past the old man without slowing down as it crosses a puddle over a blocked manhole, a puddle splattering the old man's body, the old man rages against the storm, the taxi driver, life, he bares his yellowed teeth like an angry dog, the pension plan he had obediently signed up to is worthless, I scan the rooftops, I focus on the street where the old man is looking for a taxi, from here the city looks very pretty, the rooftops are like pieces in a puzzle, the streets are a labyrinth, the treetops are green clouds, the creator chose the best view if we accept that he lives in heaven as some say he does, I carry on leafing through the magazine that smells of ink and has pages that are stuck together and make a funny noise when I unstick them, nobody has leafed through this magazine before,

sign up to a high-interest investment plan

a handsome man driving a convertible illustrates the advantages of the investment plan and the other men pretend they believe they can be like that, something as irrational as faith, I do to the man in the convertible what I did to the man on the golf links, I take him out of the car and the nice road and leave him in the rain waiting for a taxi, because the man in the convertible is young and healthy everything goes well, one quick sprint and a whistle and a taxi stops, I change plans, I place him in a queue for the cinema behind a woman buying tickets for herself and a friend, the woman chooses her seats on the floorplan, the man wants to watch the film beginning in two minutes but never enters the cinema if the film has already started, the man is annoyed, he asks the booth attendant to sell him a ticket while the woman makes up her mind but the attendant says, one at a time, after that the woman takes even longer, she does not know whether her friend might want an aisle seat, aisle seats allow you to stretch your legs, some of these new cinemas are so uncomfortable, the downside is that you watch the film sideways, the man looks at his watch, he's been waiting for over a month to watch the film, it's no use being young, handsome, healthy, having an investment plan, the film he wanted to see is about to start and the one the woman wants to watch with her friend starts in half an hour, the woman checks her change, she hesitates, did you give me the card discount, the lady in the booth explains, I can only offer a discount on one of the tickets, the woman replies, my friend also has the discount card, you need to show it when you buy tickets, she complains, that's not right, I should be able to show it to you later, and the lady in the booth, those are the rules, the man realises he will not see the film today because he never enters the cinema after the film has started, it's a foible, but it's just adverts, his last girlfriend tried saying to him, it doesn't matter, I can't watch the film, the woman puts away her tickets and her change, the man checks the time with the lady in the booth in case his watch just happened to be ahead, or if the film screening just happened to be running late, the woman in the booth says, that one already started but the one on screen three starts in half an hour, and the eight o'clock one starts in ten minutes, the man turns away without saying thank you, the woman in the booth mutters so rude, I observe the man in the convertible after ruining his day by making him meet with the woman in the cinema box-office queue, the little things that make life a living hell, I turn the page in the magazine, I could get off this sofa I am sinking into, leave this waiting room, change my stockings, my raincoat, my garish dress, my body, my face, my frizzy hair,

unhappiness depends on the circumstances

I get back to the magazine, a spread of pages with an interview with the banking group executive, in the corners, at the top or at the bottom, advertisements, an exclusive apartment, two hundred square metre lounge with a view, heated pool, huge car, minuscule mobile phone, I read the pull-out quote, a photo of the executive in a very large office, top floor, splendid view of the city, desk and chair designed by one of the world's top architects chosen from a list of architects that someone drew up, a gold pen, another quote, they took over my family home, the factory, who took over is not spelled out, we had to escape, the years of exile made me love my country even more, we came back because the country needed us, I turn the page, another photograph, a woman sitting on a sofa that the executive rests his hand on, her blonde hair highly coiffed, a dress that fits her so well, her legs elegantly crossed, a pearl necklace, the woman is *chic, très chic,*

how do you kill ghosts

in no time I'll be selling the house, I look out at the city, not the splendid view from the executive's office or the sunny weather that goes with it, a man like him does not have to bother with rainy days, I turn back to the chromed surfaces, the mirrors, my face deformed in the reflection of the table leg, I check whether the stockings have fallen any further, I take off the raincoat, they never have the right temperature in these offices, a dry heat that scratches my throat, we should go away, Baltazar

I should get up and ask the clerk if the buyers have called, or
the notary, interrupt the clerk for a third time having smoked
three cigarettes, time rearranged into forced coincidences, I
should ask if something has happened, I would not be surprised with this weather, I sit up on the sofa, I read the caption
beneath the photograph, joined his wife who welcomed us
at home, my mother alongside my father who chose a garden
filled with bird cages to exile himself, a habit, habits are
hard to break, my father who never understood how much
he loved the country, or how much the country needed him,

listen to me, Baltazar

my mother's pointy heels from one side of the bedroom
to the other, stopping brusquely by the side of the bed, by my
father,

this country does not deserve us

my mother's coiffed hair very close to my father's face, the
pearl necklace almost touching his shoulder, listen to me,
Baltazar, but my father was already far away, he had exiled
himself in his habit of spending hours in the garden looking
at the birds,

your father is not crazy, I don't ever want to hear you
uttering such nonsense

my father did not lose his mind, it was just a habit that took him over, madness is an abyss, not a path that is travelled more or less gingerly, your father is fine, he just needs to be alone, no more than that, I don't want you repeating the stupid things you hear on the street, and so I did not repeat them, and over time I acquired the habit of thinking of all of it as normal, the birds, hundreds of birds, the ever larger cages, against every wall, I got used to the chaos that the garden became, my father never went kooky as Ângelo likes to say, Ângelo is so mean,

nobody goes kooky little by little

madness is an abyss that some wretched souls are condemned to fall into, or into which they condemn themselves, same difference, when my mother used to lie down to sleep with her light on, with her prayer book on her chest, angel of God, we have to go away, Baltazar, my guardian dear, and my father a shadow of what he once was, leave me alone, woman, to whom God's love commits me here, my mother with her light on, be at my side to light and guard to rule and guide, what will become of us, Baltazar, my mother's hands twiddling the rosary beads while my father pretended to be asleep, gradually my mother fell into the habit of always criticising the revolution,

soon, very soon *chacun à sa place*

a habit, habits are so hard to break, at her card games on Wednesdays, she was always asking what the revolutionaries were so proud of, my mother was always saying to her card-playing companions, perhaps they are proud of the colonies now being in the hands of barbarians, or the houses and the land now being occupied by thieves, perhaps that's it, I'd love to know what they are so proud of, my mother insisted while her card-playing companions were still joining in the Wednesday afternoons, they used the disagreement with stupid Clarissa as an excuse to escape the ritual my mother had fallen into, stupid Clarissa who started putting on airs and graces only because her son appeared on television in his camouflage uniform, a dodgy-looking opportunist in my mother's words, a hero of the revolution in Clarissa's words, the truth depends on your point of view, at first the card-playing companions were still trying to get my mother out of her habit

times have changed, Celeste

but with time they realised there was nothing they could do, nothing they could do in the face of the habit that had taken over my mother,

for the love of God be more careful about what you say, Celeste

they are a bunch of opportunists, soon, very soon *chacun à sa place*, it is always the same ones who win, *toujours les mêmes*, the opportunists you'll get into trouble, Celeste

I'm not talking about politics, I'm talking about human nature and there is no revolution that will change it for good or for ill

keep your voice down, Celeste, you'll get into a pickle

if I live another hundred years I will never forgive them for what they did

the card-playing companions gave up on trying to save my mother from the habit of saying inconvenient things and left her to talk on her own, her head on the back of the sofa and saying quietly, a few years, just a few, and nobody will remember any of this, they will all forget, a few years, just a few, everyone will forget so that they don't feel the shame of having failed so much,

the people defeated will never be united

and only a few years, just a few, and now nobody even remembers having failed so much, not the revolutionaries that mobbed us, or, even better, in my mother's words, the gang of thugs that tried to mug us,

the truth is always somewhere between us and others, it does not belong to anyone they will forget that they ever mobbed us, that they considered my father an enemy of the revolution, my mother always spoke of the gang of thugs that tried to mug us, she never spoke of revolutionaries, it was on a beautiful spring afternoon, we had already become used to

revolutions do nothing more than exchange one group of victims for another, your father was unlucky, that's all

receiving the anonymous letters and phone calls, after bemoaning the authors' cowardice my mother would forbid any more talk about the matter, if I asked about the threats my mother

whose side are you on, Violeta, you cannot serve two masters, Violeta

would get angry, she warned that she would not allow me any suspicions about what my father had been, or done, I kept quiet, not out of respect, more out of indifference, I didn't care, I was not interested in the truth, I did not care whether my father was an executioner or a victim, a traitor or a casualty of injustice, I didn't care, in those days which I remember as being all the same I was not interested in the truth, my father would go into the garden to tend to his collection of birds and my mother would shut the living room doors and think of Paris, of the only time she had been to Paris, since my father had found nothing special in Paris and never wanted to go back,

when this is all over we'll go to Paris, how about that,
Baltazar, don't you think it would be good to go to Paris

my mother insisted but my father always said it was a city
like any other, he must have been right, all cities end up looking like one another, that all happened before the days when
cities all looked alike, those days when my mother closed
the doors and thought of Paris my father was already far
away, he was travelling through his birds' hearts, over time
my mother gave up on a return to Paris, with time she gave
up on asking

don't you think we should leave the country, Baltazar

what the neighbours were saying, the butcher, the baker,
at the teahouse, at the Princesa Beauty Salon, over time my
mother lost interest, she became certain that it would all
pass, like the cloud in the theme song of that soap opera,
I am a passing cloud that goes away with time, no-one
remembers a cloud that covered the sun for a few seconds, so
no-one remembers my mother's stubbornness in refusing to
put her mink coat into storage, or to replace her jewels with
fake gold, not even her card-playing companions, who had
for so long advised her to put away anything that might be
considered contrary to the revolution, they remember

if you carry on like that you'll get yourself into trouble,
Celeste

using the disagreement with stupid Clarissa as an excuse to make themselves scarce, they don't remember abandoning my mother, Wednesdays suddenly silent like they never had been and even then mother was pleased to have expelled stupid Clarissa from her home, a creature who thought she could push people around because her son appeared on television with camouflage uniform and long hair, stupid Clarissa who never understood a thing about fashion but who berated my mother and the fashion magazines my mother bought, they are in the attic covered in mildew, when the buyers find them they will leaf through them and laugh at how people once wore their trousers, their shoes, the buyers have no way of knowing about the disagreement with stupid Clarissa, my mother and her card-playing companions sitting at their usual places at the cards table, my mother had rung the little bell, the bell with the silver dinger, and Maria da Guia came over from the kitchen, with her starched uniform, her polished shoes, irreproachable, she never made my mother wait, you could still hear the bell ringing and Maria da Guia would be at the door asking in the tone that distinguishes good housemaids, do you need anything, senhora,

a well-trained maid can appear to be everywhere at once

her card-playing companions envied the way my mother had trained Maria da Guia, my mother asked Maria da Guia to serve tea and stupid Clarissa, without thinking about her words, her tone, continued the conversation that the bell had interrupted,

> as I was saying, I've been trying to tell you for some time, nobody uses fur coats these days, or jewellery, darling, everything is simpler, more popular

in front of Maria da Guia, stupid Clarissa taking the liberty to be inconvenient only because her son had some important post in the revolution, my mother dismissed Maria da Guia, and stupid Clarissa interfered, what I am going to say interests her, stay, she said to Maria da Guia who was distraught at not knowing whether to stay or to go, my mother gave her permission and Maria da Guia stayed, stupid Clarissa said, and this, taking hold of Maria da Guia's apron, one of the pleats on her uniform's skirt, this is no longer the done thing, darling, Maria da Guia blushed and my mother sent her away immediately, there are things that a maid must never hear, stupid Clarissa took out a cigarette, she had stopped using her cigarette case and her silver lighter, I fancy a cigarette before tea, she said, the other card-playing companions were silent, not even their breath could be heard,

> who knows what got into Celeste, always so level-headed, who would have expected Celeste to get into that state

I don't know what went through stupid Clarissa's head to decide to confront my mother in her own house, she defied her in front of Maria da Guia, the other card players started talking about many other things at once to move on from what had just happened, they did not think my mother would reply since everything, especially the son with the post in the revolution, suggested she should remain silent, my mother hesitated, cornered animals always have a moment of hesitation to choose a more dignified death, not to surrender,

what is no longer the done thing is the work and effort I put into buying what I own, work and effort are the only things no longer done, your son and the other opportunists don't even know what they mean

stupid Clarissa put the cigarette down in the plastic ashtray, the card-playing companions gulped, my mother

your son and the rest of that scum may be running the country, and badly, to our disgrace, but in my house and with my maid, and for as long as I can, I'm in charge

expelled stupid Clarissa who tried to defend herself, the expulsion of stupid Clarissa was a warning to the others who remained in silence, rats are the first to run away at a sign of danger, it's true that they make noise, squeaks, my mother's card-playing companions did not make a sound but

no-one who denies the past is welcome in this house

they started getting together in stupid Clarissa's house, mixing biscuits and tea with gossip about the beating my father
took, the anonymous letters and phone calls we were getting,

who knows what got into Celeste, always so level-headed,
who would have expected Celeste to get into that state

every now and then they entertained themselves by taking
pity on my mother, what bad luck with that husband, with
that daughter, my mother who on Wednesdays would still
send Maria da Guia into the kitchen

in this house I'm in charge

and shortly before teatime Maria da Guia had the *petits
fours* ready as usual, a teapot and teacup on a tray, the lace
doily without a single stain, a single crease,

with or without visitors this house deserves the best

nothing had changed for my mother, the same intransigence,
the smallest fault severely reprimanded, on Wednesdays
my mother would sit alone at the card table and enjoy the
petits fours and the tea, and if the *petits fours* were doughy,
or the tea was not hot enough, or the doily was creased,
my mother

where's your head at, Maria da Guia

would berate Maria da Guia, the house always deserved the very best and the fact that half a dozen cowards had run away would not change things, still the teapot was scalded, the flour for the *génoise* sponge was well sifted and the eggs were hand-beaten,

it's not enough that you are better than other maids, you have to be the best, there's a difference, have I made myself clear, Maria da Guia

every Wednesday my mother and Maria da Guia made an effort to keep up what had been so essential in their lives, the same self-delusion that allows me to believe that I am close to correcting my past, to restarting everything, I'll sell the house and life will offer me another opportunity, as if I did not know or had forgotten that life was never generous, life is stingy even in the time it grants us although time is something it has more than enough of, two employees walk down the corridor, I overhear them, they said gale-force winds as fast as, and it had to be today when I had agree to go out with, I get back to the magazine, and this time I do not interfere with the loved-up couple walking hand-in-hand through a field, I no longer want to play at being the creator, I leave the couple in circumstances in which happiness seems possible, I like the flowering almond trees they are walking towards, I am fed up with the buyers' tardiness, in this waiting room I can picture my mother all too easily, for instance endlessly knitting a night-shirt, her hands busy repeating motions

soon, very soon *chacun à sa place*

waiting for the times to go back to what they should be, this morning I picked up the wicker basket where my mother kept her wool skeins, the wicker rotting, the basket filled with skeins of powder instead of the emerald green wool for leaves, blood red for the larger flowers, darker green for the edges of leaves, light pink for the middle of the larger flowers, violet for the smaller flowers, the colours seizing her hands and preventing her from taking the anonymous phone calls,

dirty snitch

from opening the anonymous letters, one or two unsigned sentences in cut-out newspaper type,

you will finally get the punishment you deserve

the stories change depending on who tells them, Maria da Guia had only one story to tell and even then it was different every time she told it, stories are so fickle, and storytellers, and that is why I don't know exactly what happened the afternoon when we were mobbed, the story about that time we were mobbed, we had left the house together, we were going for a stroll,

how about we walk to the square, Baltazar, it's been so long since we went, how about it, Baltazar

I'm sure my mother did not expect my father to agree to the invitation, it's been so long since they had gone out together, that is how I remember the conversation but I cannot be sure that the facts are not different, that my mother

   if I have to spend one more minute locked up in this house I'll go mad

had not been shouting again that afternoon, throwing her knitting needles and her wool onto the floor and pushing my father to leave the house, perhaps to get something he had forgotten to buy for the birds, I cannot be sure that it was not I who insisted on walking to the square with both of them, I don't know how we agreed to go out together that afternoon, even today I don't understand, for a long time we had been ashamed of each other, I don't understand how we ended up going out together that afternoon, my mother came down the stairs with a light-blue skirt and jacket and her blonde hair all brushed, the pearl necklace and earrings, all over the house the perfume that so charmed the bump-kins, my father's parents, that's what my mother called them, country bumpkins, your grandparents are poor country bumpkins, my father was pacing the living room instead of putting on a full suit like my mother asked him to, short steps and hands behind his back, he did not stop walking around in ever smaller circles,

   nobody goes crazy little by little

I put on the wraparound scarf that the seamstress had sent some days before and that my mother complimented, underlining the day's strangeness, it was the first time my mother had ever said some item of clothing suited me, that afternoon I got the only compliment ever from my mother,

look at that, there is nothing as good as classic lines, *ma chérie*

we must have looked like a real family, when we walked past the front garden my mother stopped by the rosebush, I need to get it pruned, she said, it's infested with pests, I looked at the sick rosebush, at the other rosebushes, the ones Dora went to prune today for one last time, it was not worth it, it was not in her hands to save the garden, the buyers were going to pave over everything, I was examining the sick rosebush one more time when my mother said, tomorrow I'll call the gardener and ask him to cut it back, and we left for our walk, in a neighbour's garden children were singing out of tune about the seagull flying, flying, my mother shook her head with annoyance,

the refrains of revolutions are so tedious

they get louder every day, everyone speaks louder, suddenly we are in a country of deaf people, I slam the iron gate shut behind us, it makes an unpleasant noise that gets me told off, you mustn't slam the gate so hard, I saw Maria da Guia looking at us from the window, it did not occur to anyone to invite Maria da Guia to the square, no revolution changes the essence of things, the natural order of things, it was a lovely afternoon, the sky was the colour of the sky, the flowers were the colour of flowers, the mild spring breeze caressed our faces, the three of us walked side by side on that perfect afternoon, we were silent, each of us was thinking about that perfect afternoon, about how such splendid afternoons were still possible, I think we may have even smiled at one another, the clacking of my mother's heels on the pavement bothered me but I tried hard not to let that ruin the perfect afternoon, I did the same with my father's dumb gaze and unsteady steps, the habit of someone who goes for too long without taking a stroll with the family on a perfect afternoon, a habit,

madness is an abyss that some wretched souls are condemned to fall into

I saw the group of men, they were still far away, I saw the flags, I think they were red but I might be mistaken, it seemed to be a group of men, when they were closer I saw that there were some women too but from a distance it seemed to be a group of men with flags, I can't say exactly what happened, I have heard myself telling this story in a number of ways, I heard my mother telling it in many others, my father never told this story, a disability typical of those who are in the habit of speaking to birds, the group came close, it was a perfect afternoon, the sky was the colour of the sky and the flowers were the colour of flowers, the warm air smelled nice, we walked towards the group with nothing to fear, groups of men waving flags and shouting had become a regular thing, normal,

the refrains of revolutionaries are so tedious

we got closer, my mother said, I can't stand seeing or hearing them, they are all so ugly, and their slogans, what ridiculous slogans, my mother talked about the revolution as if it were some sort of underwhelming spectacle, a poorly real- ised stage show, with bad actors, the group started running towards us, I don't know whether my father realised they were coming in our direction,

the struggle continues, fascists out

we crossed the road because of space, we couldn't all fit on the pavement, it was not fear, we heard a shout, I think from the tall bug-eyed man, arms long like a monkey's,

he's running away

at first I didn't understand he was talking about my father, the group crossed the road, ran towards us, that is when I noticed there were also some women in the group, not many, which is why from a distance it seemed to be a group of men and why my mother always said that they were a gang of thugs trying to mug us and swore that it was only men, but there were some women there, it may be irrelevant to the story but I want to make it clear that there were also some women in the group, we stopped, suddenly we found ourselves surrounded, a strange dance, a war cry, the people united will never be defeated, my father saying to one of the men, I think the one that shouted, don't let him get away,

tell them they are making a mistake

the man did not listen to my father's plea, my mother acting as if she were not afraid, her eyes fixed on my father, don't talk to them, but my father insisted,

tell them you know me

my mother tugged at my father, be quiet, Baltazar, my mother looked at the men surrounding us one by one, as if she were incapable of being afraid, someone grabbed and pulled me, instead of being surrounded I was now part of the mob, I was on the outside looking in at my parents who were still surrounded by the shouts, by the raised fists, the threatening phone calls and the insulting letters finally had faces, one man was shouting more than the others, don't let him get away, my father was looking only at him, that man was the first one to talk about beating my father up, he threatened my father, I watched everything from the outside as though I were a revolutionary or a thug since my mother always referred to them as a gang of thugs, or a traitor, or, we can be so many things, my parents were surrounded, the man, the only one my father looked at, gave him the first push, my father stumbled, then it was another man that kicked him, I'm sure it was a kick, my mother was trying to look each of them in the eyes, my father did not take his eyes off the man who incited the others and in my father's eyes instead of anger I saw an unfathomable sadness,

tell them who I am

my mother more disgusted with my father than with the thugs, be quiet, Baltazar, I don't want to hear another word, the man my father was looking at

I don't know who the hell you are

saying to his comrades, these people will make anything up to save their skins, I remained on the outside of the circle, I did not make the smallest effort to move into another position, my mother, at first whispering, leave us alone, leave us alone, then louder every time, leave us alone, then that man, perhaps the leader, we have a matter to sort out with your husband, my father kept quiet, the man spat on the ground, my mother, so do whatever you have to do to us then, here we are, I looked up at the blue sky, not a single cloud, at the flowering jacaranda trees, the purple flowers lying on the ground, a beautiful carpet, it was one of the loveliest afternoons I remember, it was a perfect spring afternoon when I abandoned my parents to the fury of a revolutionary mob, my betrayal framed by a perfect afternoon but only I remember that, each of us remembers different details from events, we had the bad luck to run into a gang of thugs

my mother never talked about my father's slumped arms,
very long, as disproportionate as those of the man who had
a matter to sort out with my father and who my mother
was emboldening, come on, do what you have to do, and
in my mother's eyes a strange rage, an old rage, like a very
deep hurt, my father did not take his eyes off the ground
after the man said,

these people will make anything up to save their skins

I don't know who the hell you are, my mother sized up each
of the thugs, do whatever you have to do, when she looked
at me she said the same thing, I'm certain in my mother's
eyes I could see contempt, no, the right word is disgust, a
gang of thugs and a traitor deserve no more, so in the end
with her voice sounding increasingly confident, do whatever
you have to do, my father with his eyes fixed on the ground,
until the end I remained on the outside of the circle, I did
not say a single word or make a single gesture to defend
my parents,

do whatever you have to do or let us be on our way

my mother took my father's hand and pulled him, I never
saw a man so indifferent to his fate, doll-like, my mother's
determination startled the thugs, the traitor she had put
into the world,

let's go, Baltazar, it looks like these people don't know what they want from us

the man my father had spoken with, his face was not unfamiliar, it was not the first time I'd seen him, my father allowed himself to be dragged away by my mother, I think these people made a mistake, my mother did not take her eyes off the thugs, one by one, they mistook us for someone else, my mother was right, it was easy for my parents to be mistaken for others, they were not different enough to be unmistakeable, normal people, therefore, unlike me, let's go, Baltazar, I'm sure these people will end up finding whoever it is they are looking for, almost free of them my father raised his head to look at the man he had spoken to but the man spat in his face, my mother pretended she had not seen that, it must be a mistake, we never did anyone any harm, my mother pushed a woman away, be careful comrade, the woman growled, my mother walked out of the circle with the elegance of the first person walking onto a dance floor, steady steps, a smile, she walked past me without saying a word, later she would say that she had called out, come on, Violeta, the joke is over, later she also would also say, a daughter that leaves her parents in the hands of a gang of thugs, later my mother would say so many things but what I remember is my mother walking past me without saying a word, memory is so fickle, storytellers are so fickle, the mob dispersed, almost as casually in my memory as it had formed, those days were so full of surprises, the man inciting the others looked at me, I thought I had seen him somewhere before

whole days just standing there at the end of the road hating us

but most people are easily mistaken, when the mob dispersed I no longer knew where I belonged, I could not follow my parents whom I had only recently abandoned, I could not follow a revolution that did not belong to me, I remained standing in the middle of the road, I heard my father plead, let's go home, my mother would not hear of it, a gang of thugs would not stop them from enjoying a bit of sunshine on a perfect afternoon, a gang of thugs could not stop them, my parents walked away, without looking at the mob, at me, my mother said to my father, the afternoon is so lovely, and my father, so old, so hopeless, did not reply, a habit of those who learned the language of birds, my mother looked over at me,

get lost

but what she said to my father was, Violeta doesn't feel like going for a walk anymore,

get lost

it's getting late, I said, I watched my parents walk away, my mother walking assuredly despite the high heels, the tight skirt, my father's steps uncertain, that afternoon my parents sat in a square and ordered black tea and lightly buttered toast, at the end of the afternoon they returned and my mother told the story of what had happened excluding me from all of it, I was not part of the mob nor was I surrounded, I was not there that afternoon, as always Maria da Guia asked if we had enjoyed the walk, well-trained maids are always looking out for their employers even when the employers are out for a walk, my mother told Maria da Guia about being mobbed, or more precisely, about being mugged,

a small mishap with a gang of thugs that was trying to mug us, I can't imagine what will become of this country

and my father went out to the garden, as soon as my mother wasn't holding his hand he would escape to the garden, on the day of the mugging my mother did not yet suspect that Maria da Guia was betraying her, another disagreeable matter that she had to sort out later on her own, after telling the story of the thugs my mother issued instructions for dinner, a pie to use up the leftover stewed meat, she finally sat down on the sofa and picked up the knitting needles and the nightshirt that would not fit anyone, a giant perhaps, that's it, my mother was knitting a nightshirt for a giant, my mother knitted and told herself, it's a matter of time, a few years, not too many, and everything will go back to what it was, time is like a coil in which the future always restores the balance of the past, the only problem was my father's habit, if he had not had that habit the revolution would have been nothing more than an unpleasant episode, a passing inconvenience,

I don't need to know about politics, all I need to know about is human nature

Maria da Guia interrupted her to ask if she should make a salad to go with the pie and my mother shouted, leave me alone, a lady cannot always be *chic, très chic*, Maria da Guia took herself off to the kitchen, a well-trained maid understands her employers' fury, the smell of onions frying in oil brought the house back to normality, to other times, the calmness of smells, of repeated gestures, after that afternoon my parents and I never went for walks together, my father increased his collection of birds, whole days spent in the garden, my mother knitted a flowery nightshirt in an inhuman size, I went with the boys, I did not say no to any one of them, Maria da Guia betrayed us with her communist boyfriend but did not neglect her duties, her uniform and the house always clean, a well-trained maid can go out with a communist and still keep up with her chores, some days, only a few, and the episode of the mugging, the mobbing, was forgotten, the peace of those days would have persisted had a vigilant neighbour not knocked on the door asking for an urgent conversation with my mother, since regrettably my father was, but my mother did not let the neighbour finish his sentence and ushered him in to my father's study,

careful, your maid is hanging out with commies

the neighbour looked around and said, a man's study is a window into his soul and I can see that your husband is a good man, one of the best, the kind that you no longer find, my mother looked around at the study as if she had never seen it and cringed at the sight of the photograph of the bumpkins, of her own photograph, of mine, of the decorative inkpot my father had bought in an antiques shop, of the peacock feathers arranged on the wall in the shape of a fan, of the frosted glass lamp with its golden lampshade, looking around at the study my mother could see that my father, the neighbour interrupted, he apologised again for raising an uncomfortable issue but felt it was his duty, today more than ever we need to know who is living in our homes, we are living in difficult times, troubled times, the neighbour liked to say the word troubled,

but not Maria da Guia, I would put my hands in fire for her

my mother listened to him and assured him that she knew Maria da Guia, really there was not much to know, a creature without secrets, I would put my hands in fire for her, the neighbour replied, then careful not to get burned, you're sure to be burned, and my mother, I know that creature better than anyone else, when she's restless I send her away to distract herself, go to the zoo or to the matinée, I can't be sure she goes on her own but that's not the same as consorting with communists, she never asked for a day off, it is always me saying to her, after you clean the kitchen you can go out a little, or, I'll speak to my husband to see if we can give you a little something, and the creature lowers her eyes gratefully, she never raised her eyes to me, you cannot have seen Maria da Guia, she doesn't have the head to be a communist, it must have been someone who looks like her, if we're honest all maids look alike, they have a common type, you can only tell them apart by their uniforms, if it wasn't for the uniforms nobody could tell them apart, I'm certain you mistook her for some other, my Maria da Guia does not get mixed in those things, I'm grateful for your concern, I'll be careful but I'm certain you've made a mistake, after some time the vigilant neighbour knocked on our door and my mother received him in the study again, there were no conversations about the space even though my mother had rearranged it in between the two visits,

careful, you're harbouring the enemy in your own home

the neighbour got straight to the point, I saw her again, trying to be dutiful I fell into conversation with her, I asked her, does your employer know you are here, and she, arrogant, they are all so arrogant these days, it is not my employer's business what I do outside her home, and she turned her back on me, the neighbour was warning my mother because he was aware that regrettably my father was not in good health,

perhaps you have been lucky so far but your husband might find himself caught up in one of those demonstrations, we all need to know who those people are, we need to know really well who those people are

my mother did not pick up on the question of my father's health, the neighbour apologised again, he did not want to be the bearer of bad news, but he kept repeating as he sat in front of my mother, on the chair in which my father never spoke to anyone because he always refused to discuss work at home,

your maid is getting ideas and you, in your good faith, aren't noticing it, these people are worse than dogs, at least dogs are always loyal to their masters

in truth the study was never of any use, it was a place to display a few framed photographs and where my father would lock himself up to do who knows what, to think about who knows what, at least the neighbour thought the study had some purpose, my mother thanked the neighbour and led him to the door, she sat on the sofa and picked up the woollen garment now too large even for a giant,

that's all I needed now, for the creature to be even more foolish than she seems to be, who knew she would have the head to become a communist, give her a twirl and she can hardly find her way around

and there she remained, with her knitting needles clicking furiously against one another, it got dark and Maria da Guia approached silently to turn on the light, my mother looked at hear, searched her still-lowered eyes, it must be some silly crush, she would allow a man to take her anywhere, even demonstrations, she put down the misshapen knitted flower and went to speak to my father in the garden, what do you make of it, Baltazar, it must be a misunderstanding, don't you think, surely the creature has a good excuse, it has been so hard to train her and she is so well trained, wouldn't you say, Baltazar, and my father agreed with my mother or my mother thought that he agreed since she didn't hear him say a word, my mother came back to the living room and the silence was greater than the absence of words, a silence that destroyed what people were saying about us at the hair salon, at the haberdashery, at the patisserie, at mass, everywhere

because of the husband many people ended up in jail

people saying that my father pretended to be a bit potty to escape, they tried to give him his comeuppance but when they found him so forlorn, who would have the courage to settle accounts with such a pitiful man, they gave him a bit of a thumping and that was that, my mother with the living room doors shut to escape the unpleasant business she had to deal with, my father, me, Maria da Guia,

he pretended to be crazy for so long that he ended up losing his mind, you should not joke about illness

my mother silent because at the hair salon, at the haberdashery, at the patisserie, at mass, everywhere, people were talking about us, the maid wanted to leave but she was threatened, she must suffer in that house, all those birds, the smell and the noise, and that daughter, they always were quite odd, but that daughter, the things you hear about the daughter, there is not a single boy she hasn't been with, my mother sitting on the sofa with the doors shut ignoring Maria da Guia's revolt, nobody ever managed to escape permanently the place they belong, each one of us is fated to be what we are, a maid will never stop being a maid,

> when we are given one life we don't know how to live another

a slut never stops being a slut, how could Maria da Guia live without taking orders, how could I live without whoring around, my mother sitting on the sofa with the doors shut to avoid noticing my father's habits, whole days spent caring for the birds, looking up into their sky,

> nobody goes crazy little by little

a habit, nothing more serious than that, my mother sitting on the sofa with the doors shut to avoid seeing me go off with all the boys, they just asked, wanna do it with me, they did not need to say hello, most of them did not even know my name,

> the name of a flower that is also a colour

wanna do it, and I would go down with them into the base-ment of a house that belonged to someone whose parents were living overseas, I never knew for sure who the owner of the basement was,

my folks had to scram, they'll be back when things get better

I think one day one of them claimed to be the owner but I was not interested, the less they talked the better, my mother sitting on the sofa defeated by my nature, by my father's nature, by Maria da Guia's nature, Maria da Guia who is languishing in a rented room, no more than five square metres, a cage,

come here, little bird

and regrets that my father's merciful hands, one simple twist and Maria da Guia would have no other sky to fly to, don't grab her by the neck too, leave her alone, my father watching the birds all day long, at night he wore a jacket that was too big for him, he was so thin, unshaven, the shoes scuffed, but in his eyes an inexplicable gleam, whenever he went out at night always that inexplicable gleam, the only thing that had not changed, the same gleam from when he was newly married

I'm going to stretch my legs

and walked past my mother, a girl sitting on the sofa pretending she did not know what was happening, a girl grudgingly accepting everything she had been told without asking any questions and trying not to notice the gleam in her husband's eyes, and trying not to notice that the gleam was gone when her husband came back, which happened later every time, while my mother, no, just a girl pretending to be worried, pacing the living room, walking around the sofa set, the little round coffee table in the middle, her heels on the floor, I don't know when she became tired, when she relaxed in the knowledge that no matter where her husband went he always came back, for a long time I suspected nothing, my mother treated the matter like she treated other disagreeable matters,

there is nothing that silence won't kill

my bad reputation, Maria da Guia's infatuation with a communist, stupid Clarissa taking on airs and graces because her son had a job in the revolution, my pregnancy, she treated all disagreeable matters in the same way, silence, nothing survives silence, nothing, I'm going to stretch my legs, I want to say that to the clerk filling out forms, I put the magazine down on the coffee table's glass top and look at the chrome-plated pieces, twisted parts of me, the buyers must be arriving soon, a one hour delay is unacceptable, even on a day like this, I look at the city as it fades in the rain, at the abstract painting on the wall, paintings that hide the shapes of their subjects are so tedious, I kill time, a dog, a woman, a tree, I could ask the clerk what he sees in the painting, or whether he thinks such a long delay is unusual, if the clerk spoke to me he would help me kill some time, I look at the fallen stocking that has not slipped any further but is still threatening to do so, in a moment I will become a gaping hole, huge, shameful, I should have brought the magazine I saw this morning on my mother's bedside table, the cover was ripped, an incomplete headline on which

what the sky

I lingered for a while, I thought up various storylines based on the face of the dark skinned man with slicked back hair, the straight white teeth, even below the, what the sky, that face is what the sky, my mother's body now swallowed by the earth and the magazine still lying on her bedside table as though she had read it last night, I opened the magazine to the marked page and found an unfinished crossword, as though my mother were going to finish it today, for instance, three down, victim of prolonged illness, seven letters, the buyers going up to the bedroom will find the magazine and pick it up with surprise, I don't know this magazine, it must be an old one, the husband says, the wife opens the magazine to the marked page, says, someone liked their crossword puzzles, I am tormented by the irony of those insignificant acts that survive us, a marked page, the top left corner turned down, two or three words left to decipher, what the sky, the woman closes the magazine and keeps it in her hand without knowing what to do with it, where to leave it, the husband says to his wife that not all old things are of value, this house is so full of junk, careful not to start keeping it all

that there is a difference between antiques and old things, the woman is still holding the magazine, what the sky, she asks, do you know who this is, the husband looks carefully at the face of the dark-skinned man with slicked back hair, teeth white and straight,

it looks like that actor who was a poof

he takes the magazine, and now with the magazine in his hand confirms,

it's him, it's that actor who was a poof and died of Aids and everything

the wife makes an effort to remember the actor who was a poof and died of Aids and everything but she cannot, he is from before her time, this actor who disgusted my mother with his fondness for young seamen, the arranged marriage with the secretary, the lawsuit brought by his last boyfriend, the male prostitute who gave him the disease, the wife asks, have we seen any of his films, the husband thinks, I don't know if you saw that one in which he, they still show it on TV every now and then, when my mother saw the sick and ageing actor appear in a TV series she turned the television off in disgust, pathetic, those who are blessed with beauty have the obligation to die beautiful, it is their only obligation

he looks pathetic, he should be ashamed of looking like that, he does not have the right to look like that, when she became ill my mother never left the house again, she never showed herself to others, or even to herself, she covered all the mirrors, and she learned to look away from the tufts of hair growing on her hands, from her scraggy body, she got used to looking far away from herself and, when told she needed to distract herself,

how did I end up in this state, how can a body be so wretched

when Dora or I insisted that she should spruce herself up, maybe wear a scarf or a hat on her head, a long jacket to cover her up,

nobody deserves to see me like this

she thanked us, maybe tomorrow, my mother covered up all the mirrors and locked herself up in the room into which she never allowed any more light, only Maria da Guia would open the shutters, just a little bit of sunlight, senhora, and my mother would become angry, close those shutters immediately, at night when Dora went to give her a kiss, a very weak light from the lamp, a shadow lying on the bed who for a few seconds seemed astonished by the granddaughter you are so pretty, *mon ange*

but soon changed her mind,

take her away, take her away and turn off the light

when my father suggested,

why don't you go out for a bit, Celeste,

have you seen me, Baltazar, do you think anyone deserves to see me in this state

and my father, unusually wise

nobody pays attention to old people, Celeste, nobody pays attention to us

the buyers in my mother's room with the shutters open, the sun glinting on the magazine that the woman holds in her hand, in the end it was the actor who confessed that he had Aids the husband speaks while he measures the walls and writes down the measurements to pass them on to the carpenter, I think he called a press conference or something like that, the woman, I can't remember any of that, the man continues to measure the wall, it was before our time, I think the wardrobe will fit well here, when my mother became ill, three down, victim of a prolonged illness, seven letters, my father wanted to unburden himself of the secret he had always hidden from her, but my mother, who was never able to find anything that would justify the actor's belated act of sincerity,

someone who has kept a secret for a lifetime has the obligation to keep quiet forever, only the weak start talking when the end is near, those who are courageous await the end in silence

was unable to find anything that would justify my father's belated sincerity, much less to forgive him,

I am certain that I know everything about you, Baltazar, the things you make up just to keep me awake at night, *mon pauvre amour,*

she never let my father tell her the truth

how could I not know everything about you after all these years

and if my father insisted, my mother would pick up the little bell, not the bell with the silver dinger that she used in the dining room, but a little copper one in the shape of a doll with a billowing skirt, she would call Maria da Guia and ask her to fill her in on the latest episode of the soap opera, Maria da Guia never understood why my mother, even when she was so ill, still refused to watch the soap opera with her, we must stick to the fundamental principles until the end otherwise it will have all been in vain, a lady must not watch the same programmes as her maids, much less watch them with the maids

the buyer looks at the magazine one final time, the incomplete phrase, what the sky, and says to her husband, you are right, it's in bad shape, the lettering is faded, the cover torn, you are right, and she throws the magazine onto the floor, the things people hold onto, Dora in distress

how can you get rid of everything

when I told her to go and retrieve whatever she wanted from her grandparents' house because I didn't want anything, Dora's voice almost cracking, the buyers are going to throw everything out, and she remembered all the objects at once, the ham slicer on the kitchen's marble counter, the old fado 45 rpm records in the wooden cabinet that was both a radio and a record player, grandmother's dresses, the frame with Dora's photo as a baby, the entire house turned into a single memory, Dora upset,

do their deaths mean nothing to you

her eyes filled with rage, the child's body now grown, the blonde curls in revolt, the most perfect piece of me now cut loose, an absence, and me feeling less complete every day as I try to gather my strength for

go and get whatever you want, I don't want anything from that house yet another fight, my Dora, an angel that saved us, managed to avoid the two tempests that were staring me in the face, she was a child again, a thin child's body, blonde hair tumbling down her back, the hair of an angel,

I feel sorry for you

my Dora who pruned the rosebushes and thinned out the chrysanthemum rows in the garden, my Dora sitting at checkout counter 29 at the hypermarket, every day she moves to a new checkout counter, she calls the manager to get clarification on the tinned pork sausages German style twelve per tin, when scanned it shows one price but the scowling customer thinks it's another, it's always the same problem, posters announce some special offer hoping they might fool people, Dora looks at the stuffed bear that the artist gave her and which she keeps inside the cheque drawer, it is the only personal thing she carries no matter what checkout counter she is sitting at, Dora smiles at the customer as instructed by the human resources manager, until she knows whether the customer is right or not she continues smiling, Dora, wearing a uniform that sits poorly with the obligation to smile, the cashier supervisor opens the cash register with one of the keys in a large cluster and the tinned sausages roll past on the conveyor belt, Dora announces the price that the customer has to pay, the customer hands over her credit card and Dora says, PIN number, green light, it shouldn't mean anything but the customer understands what Dora is saying, another machine bursts into a strange noise, almost satisfied, I don't know how my child bears these noises for so many hours, Dora wishes the tinned sausages a good day, I mean the customer, and she greets the next customer, the human resources manager told her that she must always be friendly, and look tidy, because she is the hypermarket's image, the last thing a customer sees, Dora knows that most customers do not even look at her but she doesn't care, good afternoon, do you have our loyalty card, the customer says no and Dora starts scanning the products, uncovering the customer's secrets, frozen ready-made meals ready in two minutes once unfrozen do not re-freeze, he lives on his own, has problems sleeping, quiet night linden infusion 10 sachets no need for medicine, sanitary towels maximum anatomical comfort high absorption capacity tested in Austrian laboratories self-adhesive wings super effective absorbent system, she was wrong, the man is also shopping for someone else, now Dora doesn't know if it is the customer or the other person who has problems sleeping, she tries to find dark circles under the customer's eyes, find out if the customer is taking the meals on his own, if the man asks for the bill to be split, or if he ties a knot in some of the bags to distinguish them, Dora loses interest, in a moment she will ask the manager for permission to take a five-minute break, one more customer and she'll stop for five minutes, in her breaks she always does the same thing and in the same order, she turns on her mobile and walks towards the bathroom with a honeyed voice speaking into her ear, dial your personal identification number followed by the hash key, you have one new message, to listen to your message dial one

Dora does not mind the permanently honeyed voice nor does she mind doing the same thing every day, Dora knows that the artist will leave her messages in that place that must be full of voices, I can't imagine what the place is like where all the voices go, almost nobody leaves messages on the sticky yellow pieces of paper that I still leave everywhere, on the shelf, on the bathroom mirror, the kitchen counter, the phone, the artist's voice in a new voice message,

I miss you

and Dora smiles, she presses the keys again, the voice always honeyed, you have two old messages, the miracle of being able to hear again what we want to hear, I love you, see you tonight at home at the same time, Dora smiles again, she leaves the bathroom, walks towards the busy staffroom, the butcher and the fishmonger are discussing a television programme, an assistant baker is moderating the discussion, the girl in the roller-skates, a university student, looks around at everything with a bored look on her face, Dora walks up to the vending machine and drops some coins in to get a coffee, she places the plastic cup in the designated place, she walks to the other machine and drops some coins in to get a sandwich, she presses the right button and a clingfilm-wrapped piece of bread drops out, she eats under the watchful eye of the supervisor who is always saying,

come on then, let's serve some customers

my Dora does not smoke but most of her colleagues have cigarettes in their hands, it becomes impossible to be in the staffroom, not a single window or vent, the smoke up against the walls, curling around the ceiling, and those women won't stop lighting cigarettes, yet my Dora never has an unkind word to say about her colleagues, she does not argue with her supervisors or with the floor managers, she does not try to dupe them by locking herself up in the bathroom to kill time, an angel that sticks to her schedule and does not mind having two triangular slices of stale bread with a greenish slice of ham and a coffee for lunch, the fishmonger leaves,

I've got to go, looks like everybody remembered to buy some fish today

without the smell of fish in the staffroom the butcher seems to have grown in size, her blood-stained apron taking up the whole room, Dora's five minutes are up, Dora heads for the bathroom again without stopping in the corridor where two colleagues are chatting, she overhears, this rain is killing me, she looks into the mirror, arranges her hair, rubs a little bit of hand cream on her hands, makes sure that the uniform is straight and returns to the checkout, she turns off the mobile, once again starts scanning products, she thinks all lives should have a barcode, if there is a mistake you should be able to call the cashier supervisor who would sort it out with his cluster of keys, for instance, if the artist's voice were saying, I don't love you anymore, the cashier supervisor might show up with the cluster of keys, my Dora has so much future ahead of her that she can waste it thinking up silly ideas at the hypermarket checkout, when her shift is over she returns home in a packed bus, people press further into each other and she climbs on, managing with some difficulty to make her way to the back,

in case of emergency break glass

then she has to take the metro, she likes to stand by the door,

in case of fire activate this alarm

she reads the instructions and is never afraid of anything, unless it is the artist telling her one day, I am no longer waiting for you, she is convinced that is the only thing she is afraid of, if only I told her that she should be afraid of everything, that only those who find a suitable adversary can succeed in life, she would give me one of her mean looks, you should worry more about your own life, my angel knows that I don't have much of a future, I am one of those obese people somewhere between types I and II whose life is shortened by all statistical calculations, I keep quiet but even then Dora, cruel, as only angels can be, pleads, leave me in peace, the peace she talks about is my silence, my absence, Dora who is afraid of nothing save the artist's voice mistakenly telling her, I don't love you anymore, if that happened my Dora, the most perfect part of me, would call the cashier supervisor who would come to her aid with a cluster of keys, the artist's voice now corrected, I love you, my Dora would look at home in this waiting room where everything fits together with the precision of a technical drawing, she would not sink into the sofa, her stocking would not slip, my Dora so much more like Ângelo than I ever thought she could be, the most perfect part of me getting on famously with Ângelo who also spouts pure nonsense about the sale of the house, different from the nonsense he spouts during his performances, but in any case it is nonsense that I try not to take seriously

nobody can correct the past, full stop

to avoid getting upset with him,

you do everything to hurt Dora, full stop

when he is angry Ângelo says full stop, if he wants to make the argument even bigger he adds, end of paragraph, Dora is right to be angry with you, full stop end of paragraph, if I try to tell a joke,

remember what happened to the thief who stole the full stops silence, he got a long sentence, I say, it was you who taught me that one, remember, he reproaches me, I thought you wanted my opinion, of course I did not want his opinion, I told him about the sale of the house like I talk to him about permanent hair removal,

it gets to the root of the problem

or about the storm, except storms don't happen every day, I want to know what Ângelo thinks about the sale of the house, about the pain I cause Dora, he becomes such a bore

you can't rid yourself of the past, nobody can change what has already happened, not even what is going to happen

I prefer Ângelo in his sky-blue satin suit, or as the scarecrow who does not want to lose the calm in his life and so every night folds back the bedspread along the seams, who makes sure the jade elephant's trunk is facing towards the door, as if bad luck could not come from any other direction, who admires the two porcelain dolls standing immobile on top of the cabinet as if they were real dancers, the fruit bowl in the shape of swans swimming in malodorous water, he is satisfied with his two minuscule rooms, he does not let the thought cross his mind that he could still improve his situation, the two miserable rooms he lives in, the unsuccessful performances, if he only once thought he might still be able to improve his situation he would never again have a moment's rest, so it's better if he doesn't think that, a wise attitude, I reply to the scarecrow with the becalmed life

but it makes us feel better to believe that we can, don't you think

who is so scared of losing his calm, Ângelo who cannot bring himself to think that he might be able to change everything, even the revenge he was so keen to carry out, if I did not feel so much pity for Ângelo I would tell him that he still has time to let go of the hate that keeps him attached to life, of the two rooms crammed with junk, of the absurd notion that he can offer people the laughter he cannot give himself, he amuses nobody, I cannot do Ângelo any harm, I always protected him, from me, from others, from the boy who stood at the end of our road, even though he always took care to stay far from our house, hours and hours standing at the end of our road hating us, when he grew, of all the revenges he could have chosen, Ângelo went for the cruellest

I never disliked you, I never wished you any harm

after planning hundreds of revenges he chose the cruellest

he was a good man

by choosing to understand us, forgive us, there is no revenge more terrible than a victim's forgiveness, my mother would see the boy standing at the end of the street and would lock arms with my father, a happy couple, my father, knowing he was there,

he did not see me, I am sure he never saw me

would come into the house with my mother without hesitation, without looking back, he would shut the door and turn on the light, the boy remained outside, maybe even in the cold, the rain, the sun, no matter the weather he was there hating us, nurturing his hatred for us, my mother would instruct Maria da Guia to serve us lunch and the boy was out there, we ate, we slept and we woke up and the boy was out there, my mother walked my father to the gate, I left for school and the boy was out there, how much time did Ângelo spend at the end of our street, sufficiently far away from our house, maybe not as much as I thought, perhaps only enough to confirm that my father

I'm going to stretch my legs

did not know him outside the two miserable rooms my father paid for him and his mother,

that man does not know you, never forget that that man does not know you

Ângelo learned to like the lowly life that we forced him to live, the two minuscule rooms where not even the light could squeeze in, not a house full of light like the one I am going to sell, from today everything will be different, tonight I will take Dora and Ângelo out for dinner, I want to propose

to the future each of us will have

a truce, from today everything will be different, I still don't know how, the future is hard to imagine, this waiting room is nothing like the one I had imagined for this day, it does not have the decorated ceilings, the dark wooden furniture, the green glass lamps, a pencil pusher and some blotting pads, yellowing papers, moustachioed men wreathed in cigarette smoke and bent over from coughing, I allowed the past to hoodwink me, the future needs only our imagination, it does not need the memories that we foist on ourselves, I never imagined this building, the room in which I am waiting, the room in which the clerk and his colleagues are at work, the partitions concealing half of the employees' bodies, the plastic desktops, the computer screens, I never imagined a room filled with half-employees who all look the same, if I took my time to examine each of them I might discover something that makes them unique but if I just glance at them nothing distinguishes them from one another,

without their uniforms all maids are indistinguishable, a very common type, olive skin with an oily sheen, a smell of soap and bleach, their arms slumped as if in a silent protest that will never leave their lips, unless it is the places in which they sit, I have never sold a house but it seems easy, one more signature and I will never again be owned by it,

your daughter cannot even sign her own name, Baltazar, are you sure there isn't someone in your family who

how do you kill ghosts

the buyers must be arriving shortly, and what if I can't sign my name, what if the letters start slipping away from me like that afternoon when I went to get my ID card, none of that will happen, if Ângelo or Dora had come with me I would not be having these crazy thoughts, the attendant at the Identification Bureau asking me to sign my name and the letters began running away,

she can't even sign her own name

my mother dragged me over to a wooden bench and ordered me to sit down, I lowered my head, look at me, Violeta, look at me, I knew that if I looked at her I would start crying and irritate my mother even more, don't cry when I'm talking to you, look at me, Violeta, my mother gave up, to this day I don't know what she wanted to tell me, that night she waited until my father was in bed

we have to talk about the girl, Baltazar

I always liked listening to my parents talking, they thought I was asleep but I was behind their bedroom door, I did not care too much about the subject of their conversation, I just liked listening to them, that night, we have to talk about the girl, Baltazar, and that was enough for my father to shut his book, turn his light off and roll over, you worry too much about nothing, and my mother, with her night lamp still on, her eyes fixed on the ceiling and her hands on her chest, exhausted, have you paid close attention to your daughter, my father quiet, like Ângelo remains quiet when it is convenient, cowards, have you paid close attention to your daughter, are you sure that in your family, my father tugged hard at the bedsheet, infuriated once again as he was every time my mother made the accusation,

enough with that, Celeste, I told you there is nobody like that in my family

leave me alone, Celeste, neither of them felt responsible for what I was, for me being born this way, my mother replied, and there isn't anyone like that in my family, either, could she not simply be the first one, my father asked, have you thought of that, my mother was quiet, she turned off her bedside lamp and made the sliver of light at my feet disappear, the things I remember, it was so many years ago,

how do you kill fear

today I won't tremble, I brought the pen that my mother bought my father for their silver wedding anniversary, engraved with their initials as if they had been happy together, today my hand will not betray me, I am very close to correcting the past, somebody in your family, I said no, nobody in my family ever got rid of a house, nobody ever was so disrespectful of the dead, could she not simply be the first one, I am the first and the only one since Dora, an angel that saved us from the curse, is so perfect, so pretty, the first and only one, years later my mother experienced the loneliness of being the only one when the doctors said,

someone in your family

no, not that I know of, without adding, I am the first, I hear steps, I cross my legs, I check the stocking, an unknown woman enters the waiting room with a fake leather folder, she must be the notary, I say good afternoon, I introduce myself, I am the seller, the buyers are late, I've been waiting for over an hour, I don't tell her I am fed up of being here, they must be on their way, says the woman who neither sits nor puts down her folder, there was an accident nearby, traffic is hellish, they must be caught in the traffic jam, I only just managed to get in, the clerk I interrupted twice approaches us, he corrects me, she is the second assistant notary because the notary and the first assistant notary were busy, I don't care, I had never before noticed the surplus of information about things I have no interest in, unless it has become necessary to think of everything as important, the clerk asks us to come with him to another room, the second assistant follows him and I follow the two of them, the clerk lets me walk ahead of him, probably as instructed by some human resources manager, or a workshop leader in the latest training session,

> the rules of politeness and courtesy must be observed whenever possible

the clerk directs the short parade along the carpeted corridors, I am sorry we don't need to take the lift, I like riding lifts and rarely have the chance to do it, we reach the room, this is it, says the clerk, as soon as the buyers arrive, the clerk leaves us without finishing his sentence, the meeting room we are in has no view and no sofas, only one large polished wooden table with six chairs around it, the second assistant and I sit face to face, I see myself reflected on the table's polished surface, the second assistant pulls a bundle of documents out of the fake leather folder and places them carefully on the table, every now and then the second assistant's wedding ring taps the wooden tabletop and makes an unpleasant sound, I am sure that every time the ring taps the table it leaves a mark but I can't see them from where I am sitting, with the documents arranged, the leather folder at her feet and the silver rimmed glasses on her head, the second assistant is now able to turn her attention to me, she places her hands on the polished tabletop, considers my cheap whore appearance, tries to establish whether I really am one, or whether I am only a ridiculous woman who has no notion of her appearance, the second assistant is seeking out the evidence, my body says a lot, all bodies say a lot, they refuse to keep quiet when they should, for instance in a room like this one where deeds and other serious things are signed, a solemn room,

when we are given one life we have to take it everywhere with us

the second assistant observes me while I try to confirm whether her ring is leaving marks on the table, not that I'm interested, but I have nothing else to do, I lean forward, I watch closely, if my stockings were not slipping I would make up some excuse and get up, but instead I have to remain seated and I can't be sure that the ring has left any marks on the table, the second assistant is finding it difficult to reach a conclusion, I'm glad she can't see the stockings slipping, unless she went on all fours under the table and looked at my legs, which is unlikely, the second assistant is obviously struck by the dark circles under my eyes, a clear sign of lack of sleep, but she is unsure about their origin, in any judgment deciphering evidence is essential, the second assistant does not know if she is in the presence of a chronic insomniac, she thinks, if I looked like that I too would be sleepless, she considers respiratory difficulties, everyone knows that fat people have problems breathing, the second assistant is inclined to blame the dark circles under my eyes on a health problem, I am absolved,

when we try to run away from the life we are given we always lose our way

I am a ridiculous woman who has no notion of her appearance, it's not surprising with a body like this, the second assistant smiles, she cannot waste an opportunity to feel pity for anyone who needs it, all the world's unfortunates are entitled to the pitying smile that the second assistant offers me and which I make an effort to return, it is not really a smile, more of a simulation, cheeks pulled back and a line of teeth on display, but the second assistant has already decided that she will take pity on me and my forced smile will not deter her, she is fond of a proper tragedy and will not allow a forced smile to stop her from helping, the cripples, the freaks, the obese, for the second assistant they are all a consolation, she and her children have been spared those fates, the second assistant relishing the beneficent relief of not being like me, she did not expect such a pleasant surprise on a day that started so badly, in fact for a long time the second assistant's days have started and ended badly, she was safe as long as she was inured to it by the repetition, today started as all her days tend to start lately, her husband shouted

turn off that bloody alarm

but the second assistant no longer hears him, she only felt his unpleasant breath, got up, went to the bathroom, the basin blocked, so much money spent on the plumber, not to mention the mess he makes every time he goes, and still the puddled remains of soap and toothpaste, hair, the second assistant picked up the rubber plunger and placed it over the plughole, first round, second assistant nil basin one, second round, second assistant nil basin two, the second assistant does not take her eyes off the duck hanging from the wall with a clock in its belly, if only there were a sporting contest, or a television competition, how many clumps of hair can you pull out in thirty seconds, the second assistant could compete seeing as she trains every morning and thinks herself superbly fit for that sport, third round, second assistant one basin two, the second assistant triumphantly pulls out a clump of hair, she was getting ready for the fourth round when from the bedroom her husband

stop it with that bloody noise

shouted at her, the second assistant abandoned the contest because orders from higher up have prevented her from continuing, the second assistant does not like to think that she has given up on anything, almost two years ago she bought a book that instructs her to Invest In You, its second chapter, Never Give Up, made her think about life differently, the second assistant put on the clothes that she had taken the care to bring into the bathroom to avoid inconveniencing her husband, the beige skirt, a little tight, the white blouse, the v-neck pullover, she put on her makeup, a dark line on each of her upper eyelids, a little bit of colour on her cheeks, on her lips, she picked up the deodorant and sprayed, pffffffffft, powder of roses on her neck and wrists, her husband in bed, don't you know I'm allergic to those bloody deodorants

the second assistant does not want to interrupt her husband's sleep, she left the bathroom in the dark and walked to the living room, where the eldest son was asleep, tiptoed past the daughter's bedroom door, she went to the kitchen to find the bag with the apple and the sandwich she made for her lunch, she brushed past a fork that was hanging off the draining board, it clanked noisily into the stainless steel sink, the son from the sofa bed in the living room,

I'm sick of all this bloody bullshit

the second assistant picked up her bag, tiptoed past the daughter's bedroom door, the house in darkness, she knows the layout by heart, she tripped over something out of place, a shoe, a dossier, she almost fell over, the daughter in her bedroom,

can nobody be quiet in this bloody house

the second assistant had almost reached the front door, she only needed to walk past the bar she has been paying for over two years, thirty-six payments, a moment of madness in one of the many weekends spent at the shopping centre with her husband, they walk back and forth without looking at the shop windows and without speaking a word, at the right time they go to the food court, one hamburger for each, they continue in silence, sometimes one of them says the fries are cold, or the beer is flat, you should have brought more napkins, they get back to the corridors, the light always so bright, the music always so loud, a few more steps, the legs so tired, earlier one of them had suggested, how about catching a film, and the other, what are we going to watch, the films all end up being shown on television, they remain silent, one more lap to make sure they are truly exhausted, they go home and sit in front of the television, after a while they nod off, they wake up with kinked necks, they get into bed, rest, the day is finally over, one of those weekend after-noons the husband stopped in front of a shop window and

since this fella has to work so hard he could at least have a little bar and a few of these stools

a fortnight later a van brought the bar and the two high stools that filled up the only available space in the living room and made her husband happy because now when her brother-in-law came to visit her husband could go to the bar, which he barely fits behind, and serve a whisky in the manner of a real bartender, then pour himself one, come out from behind and sit on the other stool, alongside the brother-in-law, they both spend the whole afternoon sitting on the high stools drinking, meanwhile in the kitchen the second assistant and the sister-in-law are exaggerating the benefits of hydrotherapy to persuade themselves that something is going right in their lives, they are dividing their damned bodies into ever smaller parts to emphasise the benefits, my knees, one says, my core, the other responds, they divide their damned bodies which as a whole only give them pain,

the forms should have blank spaces for supplementary lives

at seven in the morning on the day of the storm the second assistant walked past the two high stools and the bar deluding herself with the possibility of coming back to a different house, as she leaves she thinks that later the husband and the children will be kinder to her and that they will resemble a happy family, she picked up her raincoat and her umbrella and closed the door quietly behind her, turning the key twice because of the robberies, pressed the broken button to call the lift, she is scared of getting an electric shock, just the other day there was news of someone who got one, the lift's light came up from the floor, she opened the door and checked her makeup in the mirror, she saw that the line on the right eyelid was not straight and was too far from the eyelash, she knows she should not be looking in the mirror because she cannot do anything about her makeup now but she cannot resist and so she goes out into the street knowing that one of her eyes looks bigger than the other, the second assistant opened the umbrella, her legs felt weak after she ran to the bus stop, she arrived at work with her boots and her raincoat soaking wet, she hung up the raincoat with a label that said 100% waterproof in large letters, she greeted her colleagues and told them about her day so far, about the son who was already defrosting the bread in the microwave oven when she woke up, he was going to another job interview, the daughter wanted to lend her a thicker coat because of the storm, then her husband had driven her to the bus stop because of the storm,

what the hell am I doing with my life

with the day restarted and now going much better the second assistant turned on the small radio she has on her desk and listened to the hourly news throughout the morning, the announcement of the storm that evening, gale-force winds as fast as, rain levels above, a meeting of those with political responsibility for, a demonstration against, the last hope in the struggle to eradicate, the number of casualties on the roads, some pop star's ramblings, the second assistant listened to the hourly news which was always the same and very much like the news she had heard the day before, and the days before that, the news consisted of a pop star's ramblings and the storm, even though it had already been raining for more than a week and a pop star was born every second, that morning the second assistant could not imagine that she would be made to feel so happy by the simple fact of my existence, that she would choose to absolve me of everything especially my looking like a cheap whore, the second assistant looks me over one more time to make sure she hasn't missed anything, she looks out for a wedding ring around my left ring finger and becomes even sweeter when she can't see one, who would marry a thing like that, the absence of my wedding ring makes her feel satisfied about her own ring which every now and then still taps the polished tabletop, an unpleasant noise, it is some time since the second assistant has felt so intimately satisfied, the boundless pity she feels for me causes her a pleasant excitement, the second assistant should stop while she feels so uplifted but she cannot resist looking for another thing about me that will enhance that pleasant feeling, she is so satisfied to have found me, she can picture me at the doctor, the second assistant hates going to the doctor, the last one, who accidentally discovered she had an ovarian cyst, scolded her, told her she should have regular examinations, and if doctors are so judgmental with her, a woman who by all accounts seems normal, then with me they are bound to be absolutely censorious, have some shame, that is no way to look, come back when you look half decent, she pictures me sitting in front of the television every evening eating four times as many biscuits, as many chocolates, as many crisps as she does and feeling four times as guilty, she pictures me on weekends at the shopping centre sitting down because I find it difficult to walk around, the second assistant has not decided whether she pictures me sitting in one of the corridors and watching normal people walk past or in the food court with a tray stacked with food, she can't make up her mind, she pictures me in those shopping centre toilet booths that even she finds too tight, the lack of air she feels as she closes the door behind her, or when she gets onto a bus or even into a car, she finds it all so challenging, the more she thinks about me the more satisfied she feels about her own body, about her own job, about her own husband, about her own children, about her weekends, about her life, the second assistant should stop observing me before it's too late but she is feeling so good that, greedily, she persists, now she is openly eyeing me and no longer hides the satisfaction that I am causing her, she is watching me intently, confident that she will find in me something even worse that will make her feel even better, her eyes stop at the splodge on my neck, the first thing that crosses her mind is the most vulgar, a love bite, she cannot believe it, it isn't possible, nobody would want to touch a freak like that, she recovers from her shock, it must be a scratch, some animal, these sorts of people always have animals, it must have been the dog, and again she pictures me at home, in front of the television, with a tray stacked with food and with a mongrel dog at my feet, or a cat, one of those grey ones, completely unremarkable, it must have been a cat with its claws, or a nip from the dog, these sorts of people are always playing with animals, poor thing, the second assistant has recovered from her mild shock, a dog or a cat, she is once again satisfied, she stops looking, it is becoming too risky, what if she discovers soon that she was wrong, the second assistant was never too ambitious and so she stops looking me over, she gets back to the documents that she had spread out on the table, and it is now with her eyes on the documents that she feels something is wrong, something she can't explain that runs contrary to what she has been thinking about me, the second assistant raises her eyes again, not as unashamedly as she did a moment ago, a cautious gaze, there must be a mistake, I seem arrogant, but on the other hand the smile, she thinks my smile is ironic, she thinks I am making fun of her, the second assistant is beginning to feel annoyed, a creature such as this would not dare make fun of me, the second assistant stops, she does not want to give up the pleasure that my existence has given her so far, the second chapter in that book, Never Give Up, she is certain that no dog or cat could have given me that blotch, that I am being arrogant, that I am scoffing, the last thing she needed, she comes up with an answer, shame, yes, it is shame that makes me act in this strange way, the second assistant would like to believe that I feel a deep shame but there is something about me that prevents her, she decides to risk it and looks up at me, challenging me, confident that I will lower my eyes and confirm that I ashamed to live like this, but I appear even more disdainful, it is not only disdain, something else, it is so difficult to know what one feels, the second assistant is annoyed, the feeling is more and more unpleasant, the second assistant refuses to accept that I seem to pity her, how can a freak like this consider me to be unhappy, how can she pity me, the second assistant refuses to accept that I pity her for the life she has, if she accepts that a freak can take pity on her everything is lost, the second assistant's bitterness does not stop growing, it is almost a form of pain, if even a freak like that can take pity on me, the pain makes the second assistant furious, the pleasant feeling my existence gave her is suddenly gone, this is something the second assistant cannot forgive, what the hell is wrong with my life if even this freak takes pity on me

I spread my fingers on the table knowing that my fingernails' screaming bright pink is entirely out of place in this meeting room and on this table, the second assistant is riled, I lean back in the chair and look at her without the conciliatory smile that circumstances demand, the second assistant takes this as a provocation and reaches the conclusion that I have gone too far, I have crossed a line, not even the slightest trace remains of the pleasant feeling she had only a moment ago, now it's a deep irritation, a crossness that makes her teeth grind, her stomach tighten, the second assistant tries to calm the fury that has taken over her, don't let a freak like this one ruin your day, Invest in You, she tries to remember the book's fundamental principles but it doesn't work, she is more and more irritated, and why did I have to come across this today when I was in such a good mood, the second assistant won't even admit to herself what it is that hurts her the most, if even a freak like this pities me, if I cannot even feel pity for an aberration like this, the second assistant gets up and leaves the room, a few steps and she is out of my reach, beyond my wickedness,

the menina is a naughty girl, the menina is a very naughty girl

she turns to the clerk, I won't wait for another minute, everyone knew what time we had to be here, we are all grown-ups, the clerk makes an effort to dissuade her, the rain, the traffic, but the second assistant continues arranging the documents she had laid out on the table, the clerk is startled, he has known the second assistant for years and it had never occurred to him that the meek little wallflower could get angry, so many signings of deeds delayed, or even cancelled, and the little wallflower had never raised her voice, with every delay the wallflower would pipe up in her little voice, I'm here to solve problems and not to cause them, with every delay the same refrain and the forced grin that exposes her crowded teeth, what shall we do now, and she waits for someone to suggest a date that she will confirm in the diary, and while she looks through the diary, it's like I always say, what I want is to solve people's problems, not to cause them, the little wallflower never gets irritated, she is always available to sort out any unexpected issues, the clerk did not believe that the little wallflower could get angry, I won't wait for another minute, they are messing with me, I remain seated, I am responsible for the second assistant's fury and for the clerk's surprise, the second assistant's top shirt button has become unfastened and the clerk admires her milky skin, the second assistant is collecting the documents she had arranged on the table, the tight skirt shows off her rounded hips, her bottom, the clerk touches her arm, which startles the second assistant, she stops for a moment, on rainy days it's always pandemonium, and announcing that there will be a big storm makes everything worse, everything goes crazy, they must be held up in a traffic jam, the second assistant looks at the clerk's hand that touched her arm, a strong hand, attractive, the second assistant wonders if the clerk also shouts every morning, turn off that bloody alarm, no, such an educated man surely does not shout, the clerk wonders if the second assistant also makes her husband quarrel with the building manager in the tenants' meetings, no, she always seems such an understanding woman, of course she wouldn't, the second assistant and the clerk smile at one another for the first time ever despite having been acquainted for a long time, they discover with some satisfaction that tomorrow they are due to meet again for the signing of another set of deeds, the second assistant had never realised that the clerk's eyes are dark, or that his hair is slightly wavy, with his right hand the clerk twists the shiny wedding ring on his left ring finger, the second assistant copies him, they are thinking, I have as much to lose as you do, as much to gain, the clerk's wife knows that her husband will forget to bring home everything she ordered from the butcher, that he hardly ever fulfils his errands, she does not know that she will be sharing him with the second assistant, what we know about others does not help us understand what really matters, the clerk's wife can foresee some of the things he will be distracted by but does not foresee that a few weeks from now the clerk will be missing his gym sessions to cheat on her, she cannot foresee that her husband will be lying on a bed in a hotel room paid by the hour saying to his lover, I'm not lying completely, this is a workout too, and that they will both laugh, the lovers soon learn to disdain those they are cheating on, those who allow themselves to be cheated on, the second assistant's husband cannot foresee that his wife will be lying on a bed in a hotel room paid by the hour saying to her lover, he sneezes so much because of the perfume that his nose looks like a clown's, and that they will both laugh, the lovers soon learn to amuse themselves at the expense of those they are cheating on, those who allow themselves to be cheated on, the clerk's wife notices her husband's unusual lateness but says nothing because tonight, at the tenants' meeting, the clerk will ask the tenants to sack the building manager without knowing exactly why he is doing it, when he lies down later the clerk thinks about his meeting with the second assistant and does not hear his wife muttering, I bet the next-door neighbour will have something to say tomorrow about that jerk of a manager, he is thinking about the second assistant's unfastened shirt button, about her surprisingly milky skin, at the end of her day the second assistant goes back home as always and for the first time since she bought it she does not regret the thirty-six monthly payments of the bar and the two tall bar stools, she is not annoyed by the still-open sofa bed where her son sleeps, the empty yoghurt pots strewn around the living room, when her husband asks, so are we having dinner today or not, the second assistant responds politely, I bought the meat pasties you like and I'll just make some rice, while she chops the onions she thinks about the clerk's dark eyes and cries, the husband says, with that bloody storm everything's gone crazy, and the second assistant says affectionately, I spent two hours waiting for some poor souls who got stuck in traffic, and she feels the clerk's hand touching her arm, the second assistant starts setting the table and for the first time ever she is not shouting at the children, she is laying out plates, glasses, cutlery with a mysterious smile on her lips, the son stops watching the television for a moment, and says, your face looks strange, the second assistant serves the meat pasties on a platter with the same smile on her face, and the daughter, is someone coming for dinner, why do you ask, because we never take the pasties out of the box, and the second assistant, they taste better on a platter, tonight the second assistant will be amiable over dinner, her husband will warn her, you're not fooling me with that face, I know that you're preparing some bloody surprise for my birthday but you know that I don't like surprises, the second assistant does not say, I had completely forgotten about your birthday but, how about we invite your sister, her husband and the children for dinner, and she thinks instead about the clerk's star sign, he must be a fire sign, the clerk and the second assistant realise they are not alone in the meeting room and are startled, they wonder whether I have noted what is happening between them, they share the notion that ugliness might be compensated for with special powers, they have images of fat fortune-tellers and wizards with hunchbacks, to break the awkward silence the second assistant says, horrible weather, and I nod in a gesture that might mean that I agree or simply that I heard what she said, the latter is actually true but the second assistant chooses to understand the former so that she can keep talking about the storm,

the more we want to escape the life we have the more it clings to us

I pay her the same attention that I give to the waiter at the café, to the woman who cleans in my building, to the taxi driver who brought me here, in other words, hardly any, her monologue goes so smoothly that soon she is talking about the outstanding fees, she says how much the buyers will pay for the deeds transfer, and how much they would have paid had there not been any changes, the clerk is listening attentively, the power of a patch of skin is truly remarkable, the second assistant no longer wants to go away, the clerk does not want to go back to his computer, when the buyers enter the meeting room I am the only one who is fed up by the delay, the buyers blame their tardiness on the damn rain and a traffic accident that held them up, they talk about firemen, flooding, fallen trees, the buyers take off their raincoats and leave them dripping on the backs of chairs, in only a few seconds a large damp patch starts to grow, they sit down, they won't shut up, we left the car three blocks away, we walked over here, it was the best thing to do, it's chaos, today the man is speaking more than the woman but it is usually the other way around, OK, says the buyer, let's get on with it, and I who have spent my whole life trying to be free of that house start trembling, the excitement of being a step closer to correcting the past,

nobody can correct the past, full stop

the buyer starts again, by noon the traffic brigade had already registered forty-five accidents, two dead and twelve seriously wounded, I think it's twelve, it might be seven, seven seriously wounded, the woman disagrees, I think it's twelve, the clerk is waiting for a pause in the conversation to inter-rupt, I think it's twelve, the buyers disagree on the number of seriously wounded but agree about the dead, they never mention the slightly wounded, on the front page of the newspaper the husband put on the polished tabletop is a headline for a story that continues on page 19, Deadly Rain, half a dozen lines about deaths on the roads,

if you want to smash yourself to pieces on the road that's up to you

the second assistant takes the documents she brought in the fake leather folder and slams them onto the tabletop, the buyer stops talking, the clerk says, can we start, and asks for our documents, I rub my sweaty hands on my garish dress, what if I can't sign, what if the letters run away from me like they did when I was going to get my ID card, I pick up the pen that my mother gave my father for their silver wedding anniversary as if they had been happy, happiness is so easy to imitate, the second assistant notary reads out, on the twelfth day of the month of

shards of glass everywhere

because it is the last time I open this iron gate, the gesture, so insignificant, becomes important,

because it is the last time I hear the gate creak I find myself moved by its groan and the yellowish rust it leaves on my hands,

it is the last time I enter this house, the walls that closed in to suffocate me, the ceilings that came down to crush me can never again do me any harm, very shortly, at two o'clock to be precise, I am signing the deeds and then I am free, I will never again belong to this house, I wipe the yellowish rust on my coat, I go to the garden, the skeletons of rosebushes, the chrysanthemums no longer flowering, the night-blooming jasmine, a scrawny bush whose name I never knew, the calla lilies Dora cut yesterday to take to her grandparents, two rectangular slabs of stone in a cemetery, the garden is waving at me, it is saying goodbye to me,

bêtises, ma chérie, bêtises

the lavender has withered, I never liked this patch of earth even though every spring my mother

of all the mysteries I choose that of flowers that are reborn
every year

would call me to see the flowers, nonsense, what mystery
could there be in a patch of earth and half a dozen flowers
that came to life every spring, a bigger mystery was why my
mother would be so dazzled by a patch of earth and half
a dozen flowers that would be dead in a few days, I won't
deny I felt some satisfaction about Dora's failure, no matter
how hard she tried she could not save this patch of earth,
the house showed her how ungrateful it could be, I warned
her but Dora would not believe me, she was happy despite
the scratched hands, the chipped and grimy fingernails, the
dirt-covered clothes, she was convinced she could cheat
death, as long as the plants in the garden kept flowering, her
grandparents

they're dead, Dora, your grandparents died and there is
no spring that will make them be reborn

would still be alive, they died, Dora, your grandparents have
disappeared from this world and neither I nor you believe
in an afterlife, your grandparents no longer exist, every
week Dora would come to clean the house, pull out the
harmful weeds, pick the rotting figs off the ground, entwine
the branches of the creeping vine, houses demand such care,
every week Dora would come home exhausted from her
efforts to keep her grandparents in this life, they died, Dora,
hardly anyone remembers them, perhaps a dozen old people

who have outlived them, Maria da Guia, me, Ângelo, you, whenever I tried to set her straight Dora looked at me as if from far away, from very far away as only angels can look at us, and she came back to this house, she did not allow her grandparents to die, she did not mind the bruised hands, the blisters, the scraped knees, as long as the house continued as it had always been her grandparents would still be alive, I on the other hand never made a single gesture to keep my parents in this life any longer, I don't like this house, never did,

it is the most beautiful house I know

every time she came back from this house Dora would have slipped further away from me, closer to the love she gave her grandparents and which I understood without understanding, it is the most beautiful of all houses, the place where I was happiest, I could see her, a child lying on the garden's lawn, her blonde hair spilling, arms and legs spread out, an angel

I want to look at the sun

lying on the ground but longing for the place it came from, since angels are born in the sun, my Dora, an angel that saved us, wanted to go back to the sun, to see all the light in the world, the stray kittens walking over her fragile body, licking her angel wings, her hair, tickling her, my father abandoning for a moment his habit of being crazy, an angel that saved us, your father was never ill, you make up such silly things, *ma chérie*

he spent entire days looking after Dora but nobody, at the café, at the bakery, at the barber, nobody said, he spends entire days looking after his granddaughter, nobody said, he's crazy, even Ângelo, instead of saying he was completely kooky, started saying, what most shocked me was his strength, it's amazing how he went back to his old self from one day to the next,

madness is an abyss from which you cannot return

a miracle and nobody thanked me, not my mother, not Ângelo's mother, not my father, not the bastard son, it's true that when I had Dora I never imagined for a second that I would be offering salvation to anyone, to my mother's husband, to Ângelo's mother's lover, to the bastard's father, an angel that saved us and that until the very end tended to the garden in the hope that the buyers

we don't have time for plants or for animals

would not destroy it, so that whenever she walked past she would see her grandparents in the things they planted in this life, the irony of those insignificant things that outlive us, sick roses, barren chrysanthemums, a night-blooming jasmine with no scent, the buyers will pave over the garden and throw out the birdcages, whenever she walks past the house Dora will have nothing in which to recognise her grandparents, her grandparents who she will finally realise are dead, the buyers, somewhat uneasily, told me about their plans for the house, another house, this one will no longer exist, the buyers thought I might be upset,

do whatever you have to do

they were wrong, they could not have been more wrong about me, pave over the garden, throw out the birdcages, demolish the house, the buyers saying awkwardly, we even thought about getting a guard dog but in the end we decided to get an alarm because it's less of an effort and more effective, after we pave over the garden we'll put in a fountain, and they pointed at the centre of the patch of earth, near the rosebushes, a little water feature, we want things that will make the house look pretty but won't give us too much work, Dora should not have made so much of an effort, in a week's time a builder will come in and tear it all up, we still don't know whether to pave over with concrete or paving stones, what we don't want is a patch of earth, the wife says, when it rains it becomes a muddy mess, and in the summer, in the summer it must raise so much dust, unbeknown to them the buyers became accomplices in my revenge, I could not have chosen better, if only we had more time, the buyers had said, confident that the girl,

they don't like plants or animals

a teenager who was in the process of changing skins, would not mind too much, they don't know that there is nobody like a child to betray us, the daughter repeating, they don't like plants or animals, they want to build a garage to park their cars, the little snake accused them, I look over at the flower bed from which Dora picked the last few calla lilies to take to her grandparents, two rectangular slabs of stone decorated with calla lilies, it is the last time I enter this house, my revenge is complete, I have now killed us all definitively, my mother, my father, the plants, the birds, the house, Maria da Guia, Ângelo, Dora, me, we are dead, from today everything will be different, I put the key in the lock, it is the last time I turn the key, my hands tremble with excitement, I repeat, a few hours from now I will stop belonging to this house, a few hours from now, I stop, and what if I can't live without belonging to this house, what if the same thing happens to me as happened to Maria da Guia

when we are given one life we don't know how to live another, menina

who never learned to live without having to follow instructions, and now the door opens as if the house was keen to welcome me, this house was always deceitful, so deceitful that it set Dora up against me, the most perfect part of me,

you are so ridiculous, houses do not like or dislike people, it is people who like or dislike houses there is no more painful struggle than the one our own flesh wages against us, there is no way I can win, I am doomed to lose, this house took everything from me, Dora's understanding,

I don't understand how you can sell the house, I don't understand how you can do it

don't you see that the house is bad for me

stop it with your stories, your clowning around has not worked on me for a long time

if Dora had at least once seen the house with the walls closing in to smother me, she never saw it, instead the deceitful house remained still for Dora, as if unable to move at all, but I brought its feigning to an end, I put the umbrella down by the main entrance, the hall's tiled floor is wet with windswept rain,

where's your head at, Violeta

I turn on the light, such a gloomy day, I push the living room doors and slam them against the wall, the glass panes tremble,

you cannot possibly defeat me, *ma pauvre chérie*

I cross the living room to open the blinds, the latches are stuck, the glass panes, the few that remain unbroken, are dirty, dirtier than the pieces of sky they reveal, the light, if that is what you can call the brighter patches on the worn sofas, in any case the light moves across the living room, the rickety wooden dinner table, the chairs' torn upholstery, the card table's dull green baize, I sit on one of the sofas, waiting for Maria da Guia to turn up in her uniform,

without their uniforms all maids are indistinguishable

a very common type, olive skin, their eyes lowered as if in a silent protest that will never leave their lips, the wide hips, the strong arms, I sit on one of the sofas and wait for the clean and starched uniform to come along and ask, in that specific tone that only well-trained maids have,

does the menina need anything else

a special tone that my mother recognised immediately, when her card-playing companions needed to hire a maid, my mother would say, the tone they use with us, by their tone you can immediately tell the quality of service, all I need is to hear them say a word, it was her tone that gave Maria da Guia away when she fell in love with the communist, my mother only discovered that the maid's affair with the communist

she is acting different, she's not talking to me in her usual tone

was more serious than her previous flings when the maid stopped using her specific tone, it takes so much effort to train them up that we can't just let them leave, that's all I needed, my reckless maid in love with a communist, filling her head with crazy ideas, just imagine her saying, I have a right to live my life, you do not own me, senhora, imagine reckless Maria da Guia behaving so outrageously, it was an unpleasant matter that my mother solved the way she solved all unpleasant matters, she expelled the communist, she expelled stupid Clarissa who had a revolutionary son who spoke on television in camouflage uniform,

there is no place in this house for someone ashamed of the past

if I ever see that hoodlum loitering around here you'll end up on the street

I remain seated on the sofa and there is no sign of the uniform with a broom in hand to scare away the mice squeaking in the upholstery, the uniform now languishing in a rented room, no more than five square metres, whenever I go there, which I rarely do, only when I have nothing else to do and I feel like talking to a frayed piece of fabric, a buttonless jacket, two sleeves moving with some difficulty

I'm sorry this is not very fancy, menina

as they boil water for tea, I'm sorry about this cheap teapot, menina, and they offer me biscuits out of a package, I'm sorry about the biscuits, menina, every now and then she smiles, which seems impossible because uniforms don't smile, which is perhaps why she says, I'm sorry, menina, but I am so happy to see you, maybe even cry two emotion-filled tears, which seems impossible because uniforms don't cry, I'm sorry, menina, Maria da Guia keeps apologising in that very specific tone even though she is languishing in a mildewed room, a constant wheeze, I'm sorry but my asthma is getting worse, menina, Maria da Guia who had the bad luck of outliving her employers, a sick bird in a cage, waiting for my father's pincered fingers

come here, little bird

to free her from her troubles, a quiet crack, the eyes wide open, a little useless body,

where do birds fall when they die

I get off the sofa, I shake off the dust, I go to my father's office, I enter without knocking on the door and strangely my father does not ask me to get out, Violeta, how many times have I told you to knock, now go out and knock so you won't ever forget, my mother looks up from her fashion magazines,

this girl does everything she can to upset us

my father's desk is empty, I go out of the office, I knock on the door and ask for permission to enter just to please him, from her place of non-existence my mother

this girl does everything she mustn't do

eyes me wearily, I knock on the door with my knuckles, may I come in, and from the other side of the sliding door, silence, my father's voice muffled by the door which I pull to one side, I like this door because it does not swing wide open like the others, my knuckles on the door, may I come in, father,

this girl won't let anyone get on with anything, not even death

but it is mother who makes father uncomfortable, it is always mother

sorry father, just stay dead and I promise I won't inconvenience you anymore, but don't get angry as you did when mother told you that Alice's husband was taking a job in one of the colonies, don't get angry, my mother saying, Alice called a moment ago to tell me the news, she isn't very happy about it but they'll make a tidy sum, the children are staying with the grandparents, everyone knows you just can't trust those schools, she's sorry not to be going to Guidinha's wedding, she's Margarida's daughter, remember her, you don't remember, my father remains silent, and my mother raising her voice a little because of the television, Alice was not expecting her husband to take up the commission, what is a commission, I ask, this girl is impossible, can't you see that your father is busy, poor Alice, only yesterday we went to see two seamstresses because of Margarida's daughter's wedding and today she gets this news, of course she's upset, and they'll have to spend Christmas there, where is there, I ask, in Luanda, and do they have Christmas there too, this girl asks such silly questions, there is Christmas everywhere, can't you see that your father is busy, I'm sitting at the desk, my father, his long face, the coughing fits turning his face red, his trembling fingers,

come here, little bird

this girl says such silly things, how about a change of air, Baltazar, a tour of Africa might be pleasant, we could get out of here, where are we going, mother, nobody can talk with this girl around, go to your room, she's impossible, wouldn't it be good, Baltazar, and my father, worn down, maybe, Celeste, maybe, my mother with her light-yellow dress that suits her so well, legs crossed, pearl necklace, I can almost picture her in the bank magazine, the blonde brushed hair, legs crossed,

chic, trés chic,

we could go away, Baltazar, a trip to Africa, where to, mother, where to, I told you to go to your room, Alice is worried about the weather not agreeing with her, or the people, such nonsense, two years go by quickly wherever you are, she was always a worrier, it's true that she'll miss us, we are used to one another, but she will get to know new things, she wanted to come back for Christmas but her husband didn't agree, if he allowed it she would always be back here, they would never leave, I never met such a weak woman,

be quiet, Celeste, be quiet

unhappy women fall into the habit of performing monologues, a few weeks from now the clerk will no longer be able to stand listening to the second assistant's complaints, hotel rooms are too expensive to waste on conversations about the incompetence that the first assistant shows in everything she does, and the clerk will say, speaking of doing things, but the second assistant is already complaining about her family, about her husband's bad disposition, the son who can't get a job, the daughter who is good for nothing, while the second assistant speaks the clerk regrets having spent so much money on a hotel room and thinks about ending it all, unhappy women fall into the habit of performing monologues, not long after that my mother, stranded in that silence in which my father always left her, received an envelope made of very thin paper, air mail, *par avion*,

dear friend, I must tell you that this country seems to be cursed, so many diseases, you would not believe it, if I told you that every day I dream of leaving dear friend, your main duty, as is mine and that of all married women, is to be with your husband wherever he goes and to do it without complaining because he already has enough difficulties outside the house

Alice wrote letters but my mother and her other card-playing companions heard nothing she said, nobody hears someone screaming from the other side of the world,

dear friend, I don't know what I'm doing here

dear friend, I saw your children yesterday, they have become such handsome boys

dear friend,

nobody heard Alice screaming from the other side of the world,

dear friend, my husband is bringing the children over for Christmas so once again we will spend it here, I have so many dreams about the motherland that I feel like I have a double life, by day in this godforsaken place and by night in our beloved motherland

and meanwhile the letters went back and forth, air mail, *par avion,*

dear friend, I cannot spend another day in this place where the earth is so red it can only have come from hell

over time Alice's letters stopped being newsworthy, my mother and her card-playing companions hardly spoke about Alice, every now and then a few quick mentions, she is always complaining, I never met anyone who complained so much, it's true that those people must be different from us, it's not just the blacks, even the whites who live there are different from us, but why so much complaining, and they were quickly back to the card game, or the *petits fours* and the tea that Maria de Guia served with lowered eyes, after the tea her card-playing companions congratulated my mother on the *petits fours* and on the iron hand with which she managed the maid because

dear friend, yesterday we got together as always and we all remembered you most fondly

a good maid is such a difficult thing to hold on to, my mother knew how to hold on to everything, the maid who left the communist she was in love with, my father who left Ângelo's mother and the bastard child they had, Dora who left me, the letters to Alice, feeble words that lost their power long before reaching the sky under which Alice lived,

dear friend, if I told you that the sky here is grey like I never thought a sky could be, and the sun is so fierce it hurts

here in the desk's left drawer are the letters, the bundle of letters from Alice, years of words sent by air mail, *par avion,* that the buyers pick up and read, the husband says, holding up Alice's handwriting,

it's amazing to think that we once had an empire

and the woman is examining the inside of the envelope with the black diagonal line across the top left corner, the woman had never seen an envelope like that, my mother was apprehensive when she received it, she did not recognise the handwriting, it is not Alice's handwriting, and yet the address is the same, my mother and her card-playing companions with the piece of news in their hands,

it is my sad duty to communicate the death of my beloved wife

it had been so many years since they last saw Alice that they did not know what to do with the news of her death, I mean, it had been so many years since they had left her for dead that the letter only seemed to remind them of some unpleasant business, one of the card-playing companions was anxious, do you think they'll send the body over, and then another, I hope not,

an empire, can you imagine having an empire

the woman says, I didn't know they had special envelopes to announce someone's death, maybe a lot more people died back then than they do now, maybe that would justify the special envelopes, the woman puts down the envelope with the black diagonal line and says wistfully, it's funny how people had time for everything back then, even to worry about envelopes, we should also think about those things, the husband closes the letter drawer, he agrees, they had enough time for all these things, my mother and her card-playing companions knew those envelopes well and wasted no time, despite having too much of it, after Alice's death they ordered a mass and prayed for her soul, it was only later, when they heard the details, which Alice's husband did not consider it his sad duty to communicate, that they became more interested, it is undoubtedly the details that keep us attached to stories, when they found out the details, Alice's death became, over the next three or four games, the main topic of conversation

she threw herself out of a window

after one of the card-playing companions found out that it was not tropical fevers that killed Alice, her husband had shacked up with a mixed-race woman and poor Alice couldn't stand it, finally one good reason for my mother and her companions to care about Alice's death, had it been a disease, and a tropical one, there would not have been much more to say, but there is a lot more to say about a woman who threw herself off a fifth floor, for instance, that she fell awkwardly onto the pavement, a victory for the enemy, no man deserves dying for, Alice died at two-fifteen on a Thursday smashed to pieces on the pavement when it was thirty-five degrees centigrade, without ever having written,

> dear friend, I can finally rest because the sun won't hurt me even as I lie on the pavement at two-fifteen when it's thirty-five degrees centigrade

in fact Alice never wrote again despite having more things to say, dear friend, my husband is going back to the motherland on the airlift and is taking the mixed-race woman and the little mixed-race children they had, my children, such handsome boys, are walking hand in hand with the little mixed-race children, and you and all the companions who play that idiotic game will say to one another, we saw Alice's boys wiping the snot off the little mixed-race children's noses, Alice's boys took the little mixed-race children to the patisserie, it inconceivable that Alice's boys, Alice finally with so many things to say and she never again wrote a single line, the dead are difficult to understand, capricious, after three or four meetings my mother ordered everyone not to talk again about such an unpleasant business, stupid Clarissa agreed immediately, she was one of the more docile ones until her son was employed by the revolution, the others kept quiet,

> it would have been better not to know the truth, don't you think, Celeste

my mother told Maria da Guia to close the shutters because the sunlight was very strong, the living room fell into darkness, my mother and her card-playing companions went back to their game and the afternoon

we can always avoid knowing the truth, Clarissa, we can always avoid knowing what we don't want to

was the same as any other, Alice's death did not change anything about the afternoons, about the card players, about my mother, it changed nothing, if the husband had not fulfilled his sad duty of communicating, my mother and her card-playing companions would not have twigged despite the lack of letters, who is going to write about me on half a dozen pieces of card, it is my sad duty to share the news that my dear, my dear what, is no longer among us, the news of my death in the letter drawer, one card among many, the season's greetings cards, the birthday cards, the postcards, my father said nothing when he heard about Alice's death, he might have used the juncture, nobody says juncture anymore, it's funny how words fall into disuse, he might have used the juncture to say, I also have a lover who gave me a little bastard, I set them up in a basement nearby to make it easier to visit them, it's only two miserable rooms but you have no idea how much I like being there, how much they hate living there, you have no idea, I shut the letter drawer, the buyers will burn Alice's letters, my school note-books, my father's course books, my mother's short novels, Maria da Guia's washcloths, the buyers will leave us burning in a bonfire they'll stoke on an empty lot, hell is to be forgotten

they found the most efficient way to get rid of us, Maria da Guia should have shown up, perhaps she is scared of my mother,

someone saw you this afternoon, if you can't explain yourself we'll have a serious problem

this afternoon I'm at the bank, mother, I came to sell the house, the second assistant acted as notary and carried the paperwork in a folder that looked like leather but wasn't, today mother can be proud of me, I don't know what happened the day I went to get my ID, today I wrote my name out very neatly, all the letters came nicely out of my hand, I did everything the second assistant asked me to, my name here, then again over there, and at the end my signature, I wish mother had heard the second assistant say how pretty my signature was, that place was a bank, and I know it doesn't look like much, I didn't know what it would look like, but if I had to respond, someone saw me at that place this afternoon because I was selling the house, I was selling us, I have no excuse, good or bad, it was me at that place and I don't have a good excuse, so we have a serious problem,

this girl is impossible, I'm not talking to you, I'm in the kitchen talking to Maria da Guia

Maria da Guia leans discreetly against a cupboard to steady herself, my mother waits for Maria da Guia to say what she needs to, a minute or so later Maria da Guia says what my mother wants to hear,

> when we are given one life we don't know how to respond to another

someone saw you this afternoon, I am near the kitchen, my mother might need me, for once she could pretend she needs me,

> it would help enormously if you remained quiet and still, quiet and still

> head lowered, finally quiet and still

or for once she could pretend she needed my father who developed the habit of keeping birds,

> you have to speak to Maria da Guia, Baltazar, the neighbour was telling me

> he pretended to be crazy for so long that he ended up losing his mind, you pay for what you do

> would my mother please need me at least once

> it would help enormously if you remained quiet and still

my body hanging by the seatbelt, my eyes fixed on a drop of water,

father is crazy, Ângelo calls him kooky but it all means the same

please, Violeta, can't you see I have to deal with an unpleasant matter

my mother stepped away from Maria da Guia, she looked out the window at the garden, called my father,

Baltazar, help me so that your daughter can see how wrong she was about you, as always she was wrong about everything, even after that incident she still thinks that

my husband is coming now, he's also curious, you must have had a strong reason to go to the place where you were seen, Maria da Guia, a creature who always lowered her eyes, dared to look up at my mother, my father remained in the garden and said nothing, so I don't know whether I'm wrong,

come here, little bird

my mother was in a hurry to sort out the business with the silly maid who fell in love with a communist but the creature was not lowering her eyes and would not say what my mother deserved to hear, I am very sorry, senhora, but I met a boy

who, or, it was the maid next door who suggested it, the mat-
inee had already started and animals at the zoo are always
the same, or, I swear to God I was caught up in the crowd,
the creature challenged my mother, her eyes raised, hands
down instead of clutching her apron, as they did when she
broke something or burned the food, while she waited for
Maria da Guia to say what she had to, my mother looked
at my father through the kitchen window

someone saw you this afternoon

and saw him opening the door to one of the cages, my
father's small and fearful hand was suddenly unrecognisable, his fingers like a pincer, the cruel hand

you can't fight your fate, little bird, it's not worth it

picked up a bird, in a matter of seconds the bird had no
other sky to fly to other than the heartless hand it was lying
in, my mother still sure that it would not be long before
Maria da Guia said what she had to say, like it would not
be long before my father stopped killing the sick birds, the
defective ones, the ones born too small, the ones born too
large, the ones with ugly colouring, the ones that, soon,
very soon *chacun à sa place*, no life can be told only in its
details, all events have their *fait divers*,

a bird is worth nothing compared to the cage

thank you for your concern, I will speak to my maid but I'm sure it's all a misunderstanding, my Maria da Guia would never dare, I know her, I know her very well, I created her, she is my creation

be careful, one bad apple spoils the barrel

my mother looked at my father's hands filled with the feathered bodies with wide open eyes, death is always a surprise, for the birds too, I bet,

so this is it, this is what everyone talks about

my mother looking at Maria da Guia who is leaning against a cupboard, her hand next to the ham slicer before it became covered in rust,

someone saw you and if you don't have a good excuse

mother wants an apology but I am going to tell her the truth, I sold the house to get rid of her and father once and for all, what else could you expect from a freak, don't pretend you don't understand, don't pretend you don't know that's what the children call me,

you were at a communist rally, what do you have to say for yourself, Maria da Guia if it were up to her Dora would keep the house and would never let you die in peace, I could not let my angel mingle with ghosts, angels cannot mingle with ghosts

I'm leaving home tomorrow, not one day more

and angels cannot get upset, I don't know why I was so rattled by Dora's threat

do whatever you have to do

when it had been so easy to defeat her, we need one another to hurt each other but we don't have to be together to do that, even from far away we are able to hurt each other, if distance made any difference I would no longer feel any anger, my parents are far away forever, if distance made any difference my heart would not be filled with anger, it had been easy to defeat Dora,

if you want to leave the door is open

I missed an opportunity, Dora thinks she defeated me, that I was scared like Maria da Guia when she cannot stop clutching at her apron,

a sick bird is a risk to others in the cage

the birds should be scared of my father's hands, Maria da Guia in love with a communist, could there be a more serious sickness than that, my mother was still waiting for Maria da Guia to offer an apology,

a sick bird is a risk to others in the cage

my father could have used his acquired skill to twist my neck, a quiet, very quiet crack and we would no longer need any final reckoning,

mother is waiting for father to twist my neck

this girl says such silly things

my mother could not expect anything great from my father, or from me, or from Maria da Guia, who is about to lie to her, to tell her what she wants to hear, these people are worse than dogs, who will at least fight for a piece of meat to the bitter end, they are worse than the people Alice complained about in her letters, the envelopes with the very thin paper, air mail, *par avion*, Alice in front of an open window wondering what to do with the truth, a beautiful view of the bay, palm trees and the sea extending as far as the eye could see and Alice choosing to embrace despair, she was always so weak, that woman never had a knack for being alive, it's a question of temperament,

dear friend, after all these years in this hellish place I was convinced I was immortal, if it weren't for my husband's happiness, the unbearable whiff that clings to his body, here they call it catinga, they have such funny words

Alice with the window she jumped out of wide open, Maria da Guia caught between a cupboard and the kitchen table, her back to the window, the people defeated will never be united, refrains are so tedious, my mother lost her patience, raised her hand

that's all I needed, a communist maid

instead of grabbing her knitting needles and the wicker basket to get busy knitting the dust that has taken over the house, had she gone looking for the knitting needles and the wicker basket with the spools of wool my mother would have lost sight of my father chasing after his birds and would not have forgotten that a lady must, under all circumstances, be *chic, trés chic*, or about dreaming of Paris, which only ever existed in her head, had my mother gone to find her knitting needles I might accept that the unpleasantness of my accident could not be solved, though different in nature from the unpleasantness of the foolish maid in love with a communist solved with a slap to Maria da Guia's face, these people are worse than dogs, dogs get kicked and they still remain loyal to their masters, and Maria da Guia

does the menina need anything else from this communist maid

follows me, with those silent steps that only the best trained maids have, it won't be long before she leaves me here on my own, I walk past the side table with the telephone, I say, if the phone rings I'm not home, I don't want to speak to anyone,

it's been ages since that phone rang, menina

much less with Dora who continues to threaten me, if you sell the house you'll never see me again, if you sell the house you can forget about your daughter, she even gave me a suggestion, a single suggestion, if I really needed the money I should think of, but I said, I don't need the money, the wax business isn't doing brilliantly but I have enough money,

you are selling the house out of spite

so it is out of spite, then, let's agree that it is, my parents should not have trusted me, you cannot trust a freak, especially one that forced her own birth, sooner or later freaks carry out their obligation of taking revenge on their creators, let's say it is also out of spite that I want to take revenge on Ângelo, if that liar calls on the phone tell him I that I know who he is, did you hear me, Maria da Guia, if that liar calls on the phone tell him that despite what he thinks I am not mistaken, I remember him very well, I am alone, Maria da Guia languishes in a rented cage, a sick bird hoping that my father's hand, I go over to the phone, pick up the black Bakelite receiver and listen to the dialling tone, always the same, eeeeeeeeeee, I let it linger in my ear, eeeeeeeee, the dial is covered in numbers, if I dial them in a certain sequence I will hear, hello, how can I help, I'd like to speak to Ângelo, I'm his sister

there must be a mistake, Ângelo doesn't have a sister

if I dial them in a certain sequence I can hear the voice of Ângelo's mother who I never met, I always saw her from far away, besides the colour of their skin, an ugly dark tone, maids have the same oily sheen, a smell of soap, the wide hips, the rough hands, they are all so alike, Ângelo's mother did not have that specific tone of voice that distinguishes the best help, many times I dialled the numbers and always the same arrogant voice, incompatible with the one a domestic should have, I've already said that you are mistaken, Ângelo does not have a sister, I insisted, dialled the numbers, I wanted to speak to Ângelo, I'm his sister, and Ângelo's mother, a poorly trained maid, insolent, stopped taking the trouble of replying, she just hung up but I carried on speaking, I thought I was leaving a message like the ones the artist leaves for Dora, Ângelo's mother never heard me,

to take revenge his son went to bed with his freak of a sister

she left me forever in that place where unheard voices go, a place that can hold all the voices in the world, a place larger than the world itself, when Ângelo showed up at the hospital

I pretended and let him pretend that it was the first time we'd ever seen each other, instead of

I know who you are, I know what you did to me

telling him the truth, it was easy to pretend because Ângelo was very different from the boy I had met, when Ângelo showed up at the hospital he was already a scarecrow stuttering the words he had rehearsed,

this may not be the best moment but

a poor performance like all of Ângelo's performances, which I interrupted with

we never really know anything about other people, I never imagined my father knew so many people, it's been a merry-go-round of visitors

a lie, I wasn't going to tell Ângelo that nobody had visited, that it had been a long time since his friends, neighbours, colleagues had left my father for dead, that this death was only a formality, Ângelo became nervous and stuttered through the lines he had prepared, I am, I am, I finished his sentence, a friend, I'm sure you are a friend, my father always liked having friends, he was a very cheerful man apart from the habit of keeping birds and spending too much time with them, the habit of having two families, the habit of denouncing people

no, that was a habit my father did not have, I knew all of my father's habits, it was Ângelo who made that up to get his revenge, I'm glad I did not let him

I am also his son, it's a long story, I don't know if this is the best moment

say the truth, I had a good reason, with my father dying everything else was irrelevant, or perhaps my pain would not allow me, I had good reasons but I interrupted him because I was just not interested, I did not want to know anything about a life that was coming to an end, it seemed inconvenient to know the truth about a man who for all practical purposes had ceased to exist, and though I was not very interested in what Ângelo had to tell me, I was more worried about what might happen if I let him talk, the performance of a family being reunited, the hugs and the tears, the awkward silences, I interrupted Ângelo because I wanted to be in peace as I waited for the doctor to carry out his duty and tell me that my father was dead, a duty like so many others he has, greeting the neighbours, voting, finding gifts for birthdays, engagements, christenings, replying to season's greetings cards, separating the rubbish, a duty carried out with no further need to talk about it, not a single word out of place, the softly monotonous voice, the calm hands, the untroubled eyes, a brief conversation, no more than five minutes because time continues to run out for the

living, even in the face of that seemingly eternal thing ⟨
is death, that afternoon at the hospital Ângelo wanted ⟨
trick me and even today he is convinced he managed it, he
thinks I don't remember him or the pain he wanted to cause
me, now when he calls I answer and ask him again

> when you slept with me did you know that I was your
> sister

what I already know the answer to, Ângelo will lie to me, he
will swear that he had never seen me before that afternoon
at the hospital,

> I swear by whatever you want me to that I had never seen
> you, I saw you for the first time that day at the hospital

and I will reply, annoyed, you spent hours standing at the
end of the street watching us, it's funny that you had never
seen me, normally Ângelo gets irritated, you are always so
disagreeable, I had seen you from far away but the first time
I spoke to you was at the hospital when he, Ângelo never
says my father or our father, he says he, or your father,

> that man does not know you, never forget that that man
> does not know you

Ângelo continues lying to me to avoid having to confess
one of the many revenges he plotted, I could say are you
sure that the afternoon when we were mobbed, or, are

you sure that me and you, are you sure we didn't, the phone rings,

where's your head at, Maria da Guia

perhaps it is the seamstress calling to say that the dress I ordered for the signing of the deeds is ready, pick up the phone, Maria da Guia, before my mother's hand comes flying down again, the pearl bracelet slipping down her forearm, almost reaching her elbow, another slap on the other cheek without Maria da Guia offering it, no communist follows the Christian commandments, Maria da Guia's face burning, because of the tears, these creatures' tears are excessively salty,

maids, when healthy, have that ruddy skin tone

Maria da Guia must have been used to that heat on her face, it must not have been too different from what she felt when she was kneading the *petits fours* or hand washing clothes in the basin, the heat of rage must not be too different,

phone call for you, senhorita

who is it, I ask, I never took the trouble to look at the creature, it's the seamstress, menina, Maria da Guia always called me menina, the menina behaves like a tramp, the menina does dirty things with the boys, my mother with her hand raised, taken over by a desperate longing to slap the communist maid, Maria da Guia's hand hesitating between protecting her face or protecting her employer from that desperate impulse, maids, when well educated, always think about their employers first,

senhora must never hit me again, senhora must never hit me again

Maria da Guia chose to protect my mother, my mother caught by the benevolence of the hand that held her back, the phone does not stop ringing, it must be the seamstress calling to say she did not finish the dress because she has to sell encyclopaedias door to door,

the curse of *prêt-à-porter*, the damned curse of *prêt-à-porter*

I could also complain, you can always find reasons to moan when you want to,

the curse of laser clinics, the damn curse of Spanish laser clinics

the deeds transfer is happening shortly, I should go and get ready, yesterday evening I painted my fingernails, this morning I straightened my hair, I like to feel the hairdryer's hot air on my neck so I took a long time straightening my hair, the rain didn't help, a car splashed my raincoat with mud and my hair became wavy again, the shoes got splattered and looked terrible, before I arrived the street looked pretty, and my mother

that dress does not suit you

did not compliment me like on that perfect spring afternoon, the dress did not suit me and the seamstress in the room, the sewing room,

I'm a dressmaker, not a miracle-maker, if I were I'd be on an altar

shrugged her shoulders, if my mother insisted on any repairs the seamstress responded tetchily, that is what scared her customers away, not the curse of prêt-à-porter, nobody can stand a rude seamstress, my mother did not hear the seamstress' remarks,

I'm sorry, you are absolutely right, what a silly idea of mine

so worried was she, apologising for the freak she had given birth to, the seamstress' hands were all over my body, like a piece of meat, look, if I tighten this here it will pull in over there, and here in front, look, see how it looks if I tighten this frill, my mother embarrassed, you are right, you are absolutely right, look at this, on any other body I would not have this problem, on any other body this dress would fit like a glove, the fabric and the design are first class, and later that night my mother lying next to my father, with the lace quilt rolled up at their feet, the prayer book or the rosary beads in her hands, like some martyr,

Baltazar, are you sure that nobody in your family

my father furious, leave me alone, Celeste, leave me alone, Maria da Guia stepped away from my mother, she unfastened her apron, took off her uniform, trampled with her feet the thing that distinguished her from other maids, at the hypermarket my child is not even distinguishable through her uniform, at the hypermarket my child looks the same as all the other girls in uniform, Maria da Guia turned her back,

enough, senhora, enough

at the hypermarket Dora never turns her back, she can hardly move behind the cash register, if an ill-humoured customer

look here, you're bruising the onions

gets angry, Dora smiles and handles more carefully the bag of locally grown onions 2 kg, the digital mini weather station LCD screen memory for maximum and minimum temperatures and humidity date and alarm, garden polytunnel

14 hoops 7 clips 2 pegs 2 cords, the bag of Carolino rice extralong grain carefully selected, the multipurpose baskets with swivel wheels resistant material easy to assemble, my Dora is fascinated by the number of things that people think they need, by the number of people that own useless things, Dora spends her whole day at the hypermarket checkout

I'm not here for you to steal from me, you scanned that toilet paper twice

smiling, nobody ever complained about her, Dora knows she is part of the hypermarket's image, according to what the human resources manager told her she is the last thing customers see at the hypermarket, that is why the smile is so important, Dora is a good employee, the best, even on her breaks, toilet, staffroom, the vending machine for coffee and sandwiches wrapped in clingfilm, breaks can be for five or for ten minutes, she is a good employee, the best, my Dora is in the toilet, she does not hear me shout,

pick up the phone, Dora, pick up the phone

my child takes in the news

there was an accident on the road

without saying a word, angels have difficulty speaking, she could say she is my daughter, that we were in the habit of hurting one another, that our damaged love is the only thing we have, angels have difficulties with words, if she could Dora would say she forgives me for everything, the sale of the house that I couldn't stand, my need to brood over the past, but as Dora says nothing to the men who found me

reeking of alcohol

they cling to irrelevant details, for instance, my state of inebriation, the trickle of semen dribbling down my legs,

she was partying

they do not mean ill, it is the details that keep us attached to stories, my angel might reclaim the story these men are telling about me, she might give them other details, perhaps more important, pick up the phone Dora because Maria da Guia won't be there on time, the rented room where she languishes is far away and her rheumatism slows her down, pick up the phone because

I'm leaving home tomorrow, not one day more

angels never get angry, it's impossible, but stranger things have happened, I didn't think angels might wear uniforms at the hypermarket checkout, it's a question of space, the birds' wings cannot fit in such small cages, I mean the angels' wings, on second thoughts perhaps Dora is not an angel, perhaps I have to resign myself to the idea of her being made of flesh, perhaps, pick up the phone Dora because the man wants to fulfil his duty to inform you

reeking of alcohol

about the accident that left me caught in this position, about the things strewn all over the ground, because it is beyond his sad duty to inform, the man will not go into some of the details,

she was partying

the blood running from my mouth, the sound of the crickets ringing in my ears, if Dora were an angel she could save me, if I had let her be an angel, if I had not sentenced her to death the moment I gave birth to her, I made her in my own image and likeness, I myself sentenced her to life and to death, she cannot be an angel, pick up the phone, Dora, the man fulfils his duty to inform and Dora takes her revenge by not sharing with the man any details that might redeem my story, details like the fact that I think of her as an angel, pick up the phone,

I'm leaving home tomorrow

and where exactly are you going if the only thing you have in this world is your own shadow and even then you need some sunlight, and your eight hours a day at the hypermarket, vest 100% combed cotton dryer safe no visible seams, digital thermometer LCD display easy to read 60 seconds for oral rectal or axillary use accurate up to ± 0.1°, habits are so hard to break, my father keeping birds, silent Wednesday afternoons after the altercation with stupid Clarissa, Ângelo standing at the end of our street hating us, habits are so hard to break,

when we are given one life we don't know how to live another, menina

Maria da Guia ignored the sunlight dappling the kitchen tiles, she picked up the apron and the uniform she had trampled underfoot and walked towards the stove, a habit, Ângelo grew up strong like all bastards do, stronger than harmful weeds, a habit,

a man like him could not marry someone like my mother

once he grew up he developed the habit of plotting his various revenges, another and another until he settled on the cruellest, of all the possible revenges he chose the simplest and the cruellest, he can understand that his father would have chosen my mother to marry, he can even understand that my father suggested to his mother that they move into the two hidden basement rooms where he still lives today, he understand everything, he must have learned from his mother

I understand that you don't want to ruin your life to marry me

nobody can correct the past, full stop

who never took pity on my father, a cowardly man, crying, Ângelo's mother would get annoyed,

I'm marrying her but I only love you

a serious man does not cry, a serious man does not fall into the habit of keeping birds,

and what if I just don't show up at church tomorrow, what if I don't marry her

when have you seen a groom with his eyes swollen from crying, have you lost your mind

and my father begging her for a kiss, my father was always so pathetic, my father begging her for a kiss,

I love you, I only love you

not suspecting that the following day Ângelo's mother would go to the church holding hands with her boy to witness the wedding, nobody noticed the woman who entered the church holding hands with a boy, they were all looking at the bride's tiara, they were admiring the groom's black and shiny tailcoat, nobody noticed, the morning was too hot for the month of May, Ângelo asked his mother to take off his woollen jumper, Ângelo's mother squeezed the groom's little bastard's hand, we'll go in a moment, the boy asked,

who is that woman dressed in white next to daddy

and the woman scolded him,

that man is not your father

Ângelo never again said my father, he never says my father or our father, he always says he, or your father, at the end of the ceremony the boy wanted to go and talk to his father and the pretty lady dressed in white,

why is that man not my daddy anymore

the woman crouched down so she was level with the boy's eyes

that man is not your father, your father died

the mother's hand took the child by the arm and pulled him away from the pretty lady dressed in white that my father was embracing, that photograph in the living room, and far away from the guests crowding around them, my parents embraced and the photographer rearranged the three-metre veil on the grass, he asked for a smile that my parents framed and put on the dining room sideboard, whenever she looked at the photograph my mother said, your father is not photogenic at all, the guests crowded around the newlyweds, they were all in the album that Dora used to look at when she was a child and that went into the bag of souvenirs she rescued from her grandparents' house, Dora liked it when her grandmother shared details of the wedding,

such a lovely day, *mon ange*, when the time comes you too will have a lovely day like I had

Dora never heard the details that mother remembered, the tiara always slipping out of place because her hair was too thin, the veil catching everywhere, the Cinderella shoes crushing her feet, the shiny tailcoat suffocating my father, my mother's parents unsure they had made the right decision,

after all we don't know anything about him

Dora heard the details that my mother made up for her, the absence of my grandparents, the country bumpkins,

people like us make a posh wedding ugly

was covered up by another couple standing in for them, these were your great-grandparents, your grandfather's parents, and the groom's guests, four colleagues from the seminary and two colleagues from work, how ashamed I was when I saw your father's guests

mingled with the rest of the wedding party, the seminarians wore cheap suits and the two work colleagues were a bit better but their wives, only your father would have invited those wretches to our wedding, how ashamed I was when I saw your father's guests, my mother would tell Dora, your grandfather and I had a very big wedding, one hundred and fifty guests, I don't know whether Ângelo and his mother were counted among that number, my mother never said anything about that badly dressed woman crouching in front of the boy,

I don't ever want to see you cry again, never again

the photographer asked the newlyweds to climb into a black car, the photographer plumped up the veil, straightened the groom's crooked necktie, then asked, can the groom please smile a little, my mother never said that she saw the woman get up holding the boy's hand, mother and son watched the newlyweds leave, a guest said to her husband, she's probably a maid who worked at Maria Celeste's house, these people when treated well become very close, probably a maid who came to offer congratulations, the mother took a few steps with the boy,

tell me what happened to your father

and the boy, without hesitation,

he died, my father died

the mother hugged the boy, that's it, she wiped his tears, mother and son disappeared behind the church's shrubbery, about the wedding day my mother never said to anyone, not to me, not to Dora, anyone, that if they looked carefully at the edge of the photographs they might see the groom's son and lover, an oafish woman holding hands with a snotty child, only an idiot would allow the lover to show up with his bastard son at his wedding, only an idiot, the story of the wedding always had

a lovely day, *mon ange*

additional details, shared with Dora, with me, the details never included how shortly after the honeymoon my father asked his lover to run away with him

I can't live another day without you, another day with her

and because his lover did not agree he sat down in a chair and cried,

where is this all coming from, where do I get the certainty that that's how it happened

he put his head on the tabletop and sobbed for over two hours, the lover did not come close and did not let the son come close, my father was always so pathetic, the lover said something to the son, the boy came close, would you like something to drink, senhor, my father took the boy in his hands, not the ones that would later handle sick or defective birds so mercilessly, other hands still new, hopeful, my father pulled the bastard in to kiss him, the boy wiped my father's tears off his cheeks,

would you like anything, senhor

come to your father

the boy ran away to the other side of the table, the table now holding the shrivelled apples in the fruit bowl with the swans, the apples withered under the cross-eyed gaze of the swans,

how do you come up with those ideas, Violeta

my father died, I told you my father died

don't turn our son against me, I beg you

act like a man

my father, a scarecrow very much like his bastard son, with as little grace as his bastard son, put his hands in his head and implored, don't do this to me, I ask you for the sake of our son that you don't do this to me,

I know without knowing how I know

the boy, concerned, says to his mother, the man hasn't stopped crying, and the lover says, he doesn't know how to act like a man, he never knew how, when you are older always behave like a man, my father hid his face, ashamed, he never knew how to act like a man, the lover carried out with every moment the cruel revenge she had planned,

you weren't going to ruin your life to marry me, I understand that, how could I not understand

and she taught that to her bastard son, my father, a hopeless wretch, could not stop pleading, come here, I'm your father, I'm not dead, look at me, tell the boy I'm his father,

say that one more time and I'll kick you out onto the street

my father became the gentleman who visited them every day, the landlord says he won't pay for the plumbing for the toilet, and the gentleman would take out his wallet, the boy needs some shoes, the boy saw a bicycle that caught his eye, if perhaps you, and could it not wait until next month,

I told you this was not a way to live

the lover spoke louder and more angrily and then my father, don't worry, my love, I'll find a way, even if later at night, my mother, money seems to just disappear from our hands, and my father, if what I earn isn't enough for your luxuries then you'll have to be patient, and my mother, I just don't understand how we spend so much money, that's all, and my father getting more upset, I can't believe you can't talk about anything else, Celeste, and then at dinner my mother, and if we took the girl to the doctor, perhaps there is a new treatment, my father arranged the cutlery, if something can't be sorted then it's sorted, I think my mother pitied me, the freak daughter that my father's heart had created caused her grief, whenever my mother spoke my father put on his jacket and

I'm going to stretch my legs

left the house, whenever I spoke my father put on his jacket and left the house, whenever my mother kept quiet my father put on his jacket and left the house, whenever I kept quiet my father put on his jacket and left the house, nothing my mother or I did or stopped doing ever kept my father from leaving the house, long before he went kooky my father was already going out every night to stretch his legs, when Ângelo talks about my father's life he says before he went kooky, after he went kooky, at first my mother and I pretended it wasn't happening but soon we stopped doing it, throughout his life my father had a lover who gave him a bastard son and he never heard a single complaint from my mother, from me, while the lover was teaching her son to be vengeful, cruel, as soon as you understand things no executioner has power over you, my mother and I experienced the terrible power of understanding,

he has a duty towards them

a man like your father would not ruin his life by marrying a woman like my mother

even today Ângelo understands everything, I am sure that when my father went kooky mother and son celebrated their victory in their two miserable basement rooms, they had destroyed my father's life, my mother's, mine, a few years ago after some beers, many beers,

I always felt he was more ashamed of you than of me even though I was

Ângelo, such a weak adversary, confessed that my father was more ashamed of me than of a bastard son, Ângelo never managed to say the word bastard, say the word, Ângelo, because words stop hurting us if we say them repeatedly, pain itself stops the longer it is within us, the longer it lingers within us, why don't you also admit that

my father was ashamed of the freak instead of being ashamed of the bastard son

you were happy about punishing my parents, your mother told you, he married a woman who was going to make him rise in life

a lady must be *chic, trés chic*, under all circumstances

and all she gave him was a freak, to his understanding Ângelo added the further refinement of forgiveness and so he is forever

I forgave him everything

trapped in the revenge that holds him back, even today Ângelo bores me with his stories of cowards, my father, his mother and mine, of impossible loves, of bad luck, the same cast, in those stories Ângelo and I are secondary characters, I never knew what to do with this story, I never wanted to understand my father or forgive him, I never wanted to understand my mother, the lover, the bastard son,

he liked all of us in his own way

I want my father and his own way to go fuck themselves

after a few beers I don't know what I'm saying, I never again talked to Ângelo about us, I will sell this house, the habit of lingering in the past is dangerous, if I get distracted I might never leave here, from today everything will be different, I am free, today I'll settle my accounts with life and the past will never again do me any harm, the past is a hungry leech, I don't want to be trapped in the past, neither by revenge like Ângelo, nor by love like Dora, the past will use anything to keep us trapped, memory is the worst form of torture, memory won't let me rest even when I can no longer feel my body, hanging by the seatbelt, that night I got drunk in

Ângelo's two miserable basement rooms, or perhaps it was another night when I went to visit him, I frequently got drunk when I visited him, perhaps to be able to laugh sincerely at his lame jokes, when I was drunk I saw my father in that house with his lover and their bastard, fulfilled like I never saw him in this house, maybe this house also hurt him, the walls also closed in to suffocate him, the ceilings came down to crush him, this house also hurt my father, I used to get drunk and instead of laughing at the jokes I would start shouting at Ângelo,

> stop pretending, you don't forgive him one day, not a single day that you had to live in this dump, even less the life he forced you to have

I know Ângelo, he offered me drinks so he could hear me shouting, we may not be made of exactly the same flesh, the same blood, but I know Ângelo's hatred as if it were my own, that night or some other night, Ângelo slapped me,

> you don't know what you're talking about, you're drunk

I remember picking up the jade elephant and threatening to break it, to liberate him from the bad luck of being trapped in that revenge, I wanted to liberate him from his bad luck but Ângelo implored me, put the elephant down, please, he was scared like I never saw him before, I put the elephant down with its trunk towards the door, I looked at the paralytic dancers on top of the cabinet and the fruit bowl with the swans, Ângelo only exists in those two miserable basement rooms, people exist intermittently, I for instance never existed when the boys were going out with my friends, my friends never existed when the boys were fondling me in the matinees, the few times I protested they'd say, I'm doing you a favour, nobody wanted to be seen with a dumpy monstrosity like me, and if you tell anyone I'll say you're lying, the past is a dangerous swamp, darker than the cinemas, my mother got all excited when she heard I was going to the cinema with a boy, the enthusiasm was not much use,

make the most of it, you probably don't get too many of these invitations, Maria da Guia can act as a chaperone

no boy ever went to pick me up at home and Maria da Guia never acted as a chaperone, in the beginning I asked, what time are you coming to find me, are you mad, look at yourself in the mirror, so I went alone to be with the boys

we didn't know you liked the cinema so much, Violeta

who laughed at me, sometime later mother managed this matter like she managed all unpleasant matters she had to deal with,

there is nothing that silence won't kill

so unlike the other girls, the decent ones, I arrived alone at the cinema, other girls came holding a boy by the arm, they always came with a cousin, a younger sister, an aunt, and they would not greet me, the boys would openly ask for the hidden seats, the other girls would say to the boys they were holding by the arm, she's got a reputation, the other girls' mothers, I don't want people talking about you like they do about that poor thing, even though I arrived alone I was in high demand, there was always a boy on each side, as soon as the lights went down I felt their hands on my legs, going under my arms to reach my breasts, they pulled my hands towards their groins, nobody ever saw anything, the ushers, the sweet vendors, they never saw anything, the boys chose the right seats to do it, they always talked about doing it, during the intervals they gave their places to others who sat alongside me so we could do it again, the lights went down and the new boys would pull my hands towards their groins, when the film was over and the other girls left arm in arm with the boys who took them home and I would leave alone, the boys would shout, did you like it, Violeta, there's more of that next week, and they would laugh, the following week one of them would call on the telephone and say the name of the film, I once had a whole row of boys waiting to change seats at every interval, before the documentary reel, the cartoon films, the credits, and the oafs changed places to grope me, to make me grope them, to do it, the other girls in decent seats, centrally located, and me in the upper circle fumbling with stiffened cocks, during the long interval the boys would go and talk to the other girls, I walked around the cinema on my own, I'd buy a lollipop or a chocolate bar, during the interval none of the boys knew me and as soon as the interval was over they would run to me, argue over the seats, they wanted my hands rubbing their cocks only recently initiated in these pleasures, in the intermittent way in which we all exist those pimply boys fondling me during matinees never existed for the decent girls they went on to marry and have children with, my mother never existed for Dora, Dora's grandmother never existed for me, Ângelo's father never existed for me, my father never existed for Ângelo, Maria da Guia does not exist outside of this house, she could not run away with her communist boyfriend and cease to exist, on the kitchen floor Maria da Guia's tears fell into the puddles of light dappling the tiles,

I'm sorry, senhora

louder, I'm sorry, senhora, and my mother pleased, keeping away from the sun-dappled tiles because a lady must not bronze her skin, it's not your fault, it's the fault of those who are out and about shouting nonsense, let's just forget this unpleasant business,

the people defeated will never be united

Maria da Guia remained in this house until my mother's end, until my father's end, it was I who kicked her out, in the cage where she languishes Maria da Guia never forgets to ask,

the people defeated will never be united

does senhora need anything, does senhor need anything, in that particular tone that only the best maids have, does the menina need anything, a cage, no more than five square metres, which she keeps clean, she scrubs and polishes the floor, hand washes the curtains, habits are hard to break, Maria da Guia all covered in wrinkles, maids get covered in wrinkles very swiftly, they have a soft skin that shrivels, they all look alike, they all smell alike, soap,

does the menina need anything

I am waiting for someone to come and save me, an angel, Ângelo, the lorry driver, the lorry driver's wife, Denise, the Ukrainian, Betty, Betty's pale children, the buyers, the second assistant, the clerk, the old man on the golf links, the man in his convertible, the Indians in the restaurant, the bride-to-be with a veil and a cock, the bride-to-be's friends, Carminho, the blue velvet sofa, the server at the café, the boy with the T-shirt that says *smile*, someone who has read the messages I left in the service station, something will save me, I cannot remain stuck

c'est fini, c'est fini, ma chérie

in this suffocating house, I am allergic to the dusting of salt everywhere, when tears dry they leave salty dust that corrodes everything, the desk in the office is all stained, my parents' framed smile is no longer on the shelf, Dora took it in the bag of souvenirs

who would have said that your grandparents fit in a bag,
that what is left of them fits in a bag

that she brought home yesterday, I know how to hurt my
daughter, we are good adversaries, Dora knows how to hurt
me, for you not even a bag, nothing, I want nothing from
you, so we are even, my Dora never tried to escape her
origins, she has complied with her duty of smiling as the
human resources manager taught her,

nobody can hurt us as much as a child

she follows the manager's orders to smile, in the staffroom,
the supervisor, your turn to work, and Dora immediately on
her feet even when her colleagues mutter, what a pushover,
Dora, the most perfect part of me, leaves the staffroom,
does not reply, an angel, a telephone ringing will not scare
the angels asleep in heaven, trumpets, heavenly trumpets,
the men who pulled me out of the wreckage tell Dora who
hears the news in silence, the men cling on to irrelevant
details, they step away from my story, the one I am telling,
I shut the office, it is the last time I slide the door shut, my
father will remain inside while his son, the bastard, Ângelo
likes to say kooky and does not like to say bastard, stands at
the end of the street hating us, a regular boy with the habit
of spending hours standing at the end of the street hating
us, of living to avenge that hatred,

I understand why he did not give me his family name

a regular boy while I, in a few hours I will be selling this
house, the buyers will turn the office into a little television
room, they will have walls knocked down, will raise others,
move doors around, the house the buyers are going to live
in does not exist for me, this house does not exist for the
buyers, the house where Dora was happy with my parents
does not exist for me, the house where I was unhappy with
my parents does not exist for Dora, this intermittent way of
existing, the buyers' daughter, a teenage girl changing her
skin, in my room, without knowing any of my gestures, my
fears, my desires, a stranger sleeping in my bedroom and
the sun shining on the same places, offering her the same
sunlight it gave me, the buyers' daughter sleeping in my bedroom and the rain making the same noise I heard, the rotten
figs at the end of the summer with their same smell, the same
patch of ground with the markings beneath the swing on
which Dora flew up to the sky, the buyers' daughter cannot
see my parents drunk with love for the angel that saved them,
perhaps if the kitchen was not so dark, perhaps she would
see the rusted ham slicer over the counter, the soot-covered
stove, the worn out stone of the kitchen sink, if it were a nice
day the sun would shoot through the blinds and draw little
bright ovals on that piece of floor and the buyers' daughter
could see the same things I see, if there were sunshine the
kitchen would be filled with light in the same places, in
the early afternoon the sun starting to shine into the maid's
room, it was not Maria da Guia's room because the only
thing this house ever gave her was work, we always called it
the maid's room and in the end it was always Maria da Guia's,

it takes so much effort to train the help and this one is
so well trained

near midday my mother would say, we have to get the
maid's room painted, she was an abstract creature, not the
creature who was crushed by this house and yet outlived
her employers,

these people are worse than dogs, at least dogs die missing their masters

a small room destined for a very specific type of creature,
a common tone of voice, the olive-tinged and oily skin, they
are all so alike, a smell of soap, you can only tell them apart
by their uniform, I climb the stairs, upstairs are the bed-
rooms, my parents', mine, the one for the guests we hardly
ever had, which later became Dora's, an angel that was not
born black,

you were with a black man, a black returnee,

what luck, a black angel could not have saved my parents,
even if they needed salvation my parents were picky, a black
angel could not save them,

who is the father

it could not be the black returnee because their granddaughter was so blonde and had such fair skin

she doesn't even know who the father is, she was never well in her head

who is the father, my mother wanted to know remembering the scruffy foreigner she once saw with me, I climb the staircase for the last time, the too narrow steps, slippery, waiting for someone to trip, to misstep, the wooden staircase covered in the same salty dust that is corroding the house, birds crying in the cages, the importance an act assumes because it is the last time, it is the last time I climb these stairs, the last day of this life, I no longer exist as I knew myself, on the first day of my life I still did not exist as I knew myself, it is ironic how the first and the last days of our lives escape us, I climb the stairs, the rain drips through the cracked roof tiles and glimmers on the dark wood, with rain like this how could Ângelo stand at the end of our street hating us, he could have travelled with me, the old folks cancelled their outing so Ângelo could have come with me instead of fixating on revenge, I enter my bedroom, turn on the light, open the shutters, I took to the road on my own, Denise and Betty were waiting for me, with any luck I'd sell them some of my eco-friendly wax, the special one for varicose veins, I'm a good salesperson, the best, I always respected my enemies, I fought them openly, the Spanish laser treatment centres have an unfair advantage, I would not be surprised if one of these days the customers from all those Spanish laser clinics found millions of ghosts thirsty for revenge growing back all over their skin, those allegedly permanent solutions are no match for the staying power

of my enemies, Denise likes to hear me rant about laser
treatment and the Spanish clinics,

I don't ask her to leave because I find it amusing to listen
to her nonsense

the Ukrainian fellow does not amuse Denise and she is going
to break things off with him, she has enough sadness in her
own life, Betty does not need anyone to amuse her, she needs
only her Villa Elizabete, I always had customers waiting
for me, not only them, not only at the usual destinations,
others, at other destinations, I never knew how to travel
without someone waiting for me, unless it was on my maps,
the paper worlds I collected, this chest of drawers is full
of paper worlds, places I don't associate with anything, a
landscape, an animal, a flower, places that exist only for me
to fill them however I want, the buyers will find my maps,
the woman will say to the man, I have never seen a map
collection before, the husband will take one map and then
another, they are all out of date, these countries no longer
have those borders, they are no good, the man drops my
maps on the floor disappointed, this house is full of rubbish,
I open my bedroom window and I can see Ângelo, instead
of thinking about the jokes he'll be telling at his next performance he is standing at the end of the street hating us,
Ângelo who dies a little every time he tells one of his elephant
jokes, nobody laughs at elephant jokes any more, if he were
not dumbfounded by being on stage

perhaps he would never again show up to entertain the old-timers in his sky-blue satin suit, old people are always so ungrateful, a horde of toothless people complaining, the food's decent but the funny man doesn't have a funny bone in his body, the old men laugh at their own wit, Ângelo blind and deaf on stage convinced that laughter is the best thing we can offer others,

I don't ever want to see you cry again, I don't ever want to see you cry again

where did Ângelo get such a ridiculous notion, I sit on the mouse-nibbled mattress, this house is a huge mouse nest and even then I don't feel avenged, I look at my dressing table's broken leg, the cracked mirror that triples me and makes me incomplete at the same time, my clothes in the wardrobe, the seamstress' rough hands

I'm a dressmaker, not a miracle-maker, if I were I'd be on some altar

on my body, if I tighten this here it will pull in over there, look at this tummy, no matter how much I try to hide it, my mother apologising, you're right, you've done your best, I got dressed up for the deeds transfer, my garish dress that suits me so well, I painted my fingernails in screaming bright pink, straightened my hair, washed the raincoat, it was not my fault if the rain, if the car that splattered me, if one of the stockings, it was not my fault, before leaving the house I looked pretty,

ordinaire, très ordinaire

my mother thumbing through the fashion magazines, catalogues of deceit now mildewed in the basement,

perhaps this one might not sit so badly on her

the seamstress biting her lip, I'm not sure, and this one, how about this one, the same sneer on the seamstress' face, if she weren't so fat, my mother putting the magazines down, in that case let's do what we always do, a cache-cœur and a straight skirt in a dark colour, not black, girls shouldn't wear black, navy blue, or anthracite grey, dark burgundy, I chose a garish dress and painted my fingernails in screaming bright pink,

the menina will be late for the deeds transfer

I will sell you and your communist boyfriend

the menina is a bad girl, the menina is a very bad girl

the cache-cœurs and the straight skirts in dark colours are in the wardrobe, I catch sight of myself in one of the unbroken pieces of the dressing table mirror, curly hair and rounder face, a ball, a bit of eyeshadow because eyes look dead in the middle of all that flesh, eyelids coloured in blue and green, black eyeliner, fake eyelashes, rouge, a little pink piglet, blood-red lipstick, lips like raw flesh, the buyers asking themselves ironically, I wonder if she has a mirror at home, if she saw herself in a mirror before she left the house, I caught sight of myself in this broken mirror with the three incomplete faces, in the one at my house, the one in a shop, even a bank with a mirrored entrance, I caught sight of myself, but if I hadn't I wouldn't have minded, I've seen myself for as long as I can remember, I know what I look like, the second assistant saying to the clerk, how about the seller, I wouldn't be surprised if she'd been turning tricks, she looked like a cheap whore, I object, that is something I must object to, an expensive whore as all whores should be, it's the virtuous women that let the side down, a little golden hoop around the left-hand ring-finger, two or three children, a restaurant meal on their birthday, a little set of pyjamas from the mother-in-law for Christmas, it's the virtuous women that are cheap, whores are duty-bound to be expensive, my mother badgering my father,

you need to speak to your daughter, Baltazar

somebody in your family must have behaved like that, somebody must have looked like that, I would say, I'm going out, I'll be late, since when is that the right way to behave, who are you going out with, I'm going out, why would you care what I say if I could be lying, somebody in your family, Baltazar

I leave my room, enter the one that belonged to Dora, the most perfect part of me, an angel who was not born black and could therefore save my parents, my mother saying, we've arranged the room for the girl, we like having our granddaughter with us so much, and my father, always so weak, we like having her here a lot, my mother, it's not right for a child to be stuck in the car just coming and going, Baltazar, tell your daughter that such a small child shouldn't be stuck in a car just coming and going, it's better if you leave her here with us, I agreed, when I had to travel I left Dora with them, my mother would sit on the edge of this white lacquered bed and look at her granddaughter, an angel that saved their descendancy from being cursed, when I arrived to pick up my daughter I would find her wearing a pink dress with little white spots, white shoes, a ribbon in her hair, I open the wardrobe, Dora took all her clothes, I leave Dora's room, in the corridor a water stain in the place where I used to sit and listen to my parents, their bedroom door open and the bed without the lace quilt, I lie down without worrying about getting it dirty, on my mother's bedside table there is a magazine, what the sky, the sky did not fit into Dora's bag of souvenirs, the sky does not fit anywhere in this life, I open one of the drawers on my mother's nightstand, out of date medicine, a lower denture with two teeth, various loyalty cards, member of, membership number, user number, so many loyalty cards, a certificate, twenty-five years a member of, I had never seen the drawer in such disarray, sitting on my parents' bed the walls close in to suffocate me, the ceiling comes down slowly, I feel ill, I close my eyes, bright spots of light, the room turning, the vengeful house confronting me

traitor, now you'll pay for everything

but I know that I won, this house cannot do me any harm ever again, in a moment the room will stop turning and the objects in it will be still, in a moment I will stop feeling dizzy, I will not feel thirsty, my tongue will stop feeling heavy and will unstick from the roof of my mouth, in a moment I will be able to shout out for help, I am cold, in a moment my body will obey me, a piece of flesh I no longer feel, I open my eyes, I can see the house from a place I had never been in before, I finally learned to fly

I want to touch the sky

like Dora in the swing, I am far away, very far away, in the sky that did not fit into Dora's bag of souvenirs, I hear a siren, I'm sure it's a siren, it must be the ambulance I called for my father, a hand on his chest, something to do with his heart, not pain, or tightness, something less defined, the trembling hands on the black Bakelite stethoscope, I think my father is dying, a siren, my father was dying fast, it's funny how things go, my mother died slowly, from a long disease after the doctor asked, anyone else in your family, not that I know of, my mother felt the loneliness of being the only one, sooner or later she would have to taste the medicine she had given me,

what came over Celeste, she was always so reasonable, what came over Celeste that she just let herself die so young

sooner or later she would be the subject of conversation between the card-playing companions, like Alice had once been, like me, my mother's death discussed over tea and *petits fours*, for a while, not very long,

all I need is to know about human nature

everything is forgotten fast, especially the old who pretend to have a bad memory, a siren, the position I'm in, this noise that isn't the rain, in this house the rain does not make that noise, chirp chirp, crickets, they can't be crickets, there were never any crickets here, I want to buy a cricket, here it is, senhora, but this cricket is missing a leg, and does senhora want the cricket to sing or to dance, not funny, Ângelo, I can see why you get heckled at the social clubs, Dora is asleep, tomorrow she'll tell her artist that she argued with me, that she only has him,

I love you

the most perfect part of me

I have heard about love

the siren won't stop, they have come to the wrong place, my father is, say the word, say the words because the more you repeat them the less they hurt, isn't that what you are always saying to Ângelo, say it, my father is dead, I was not the one who called the ambulance, I let my father die without talking to him about Ângelo, about Ângelo's mother, about the shame he felt about me, the siren, lights, lights sweeping me up in a strange rush, men talking,

now you'll pay for everything, you dirty snitch

I recognised Ângelo in the group of people mobbing us, I recognised Ângelo's voice in the anonymous phone calls,

tell them they are mistaken, that you know me, I'm your sister, your little freak sister

we need to call for help

two men with hi-vis safety vests, a siren, lights, blue, yellow, the drop of water my eyes are fixed on, a drop of water clinging to a shard, a vertical piece of glass, how long can my life await me, seconds, hours, from today everything will be different, my future in the drop of water shining like crystal a dark mantle covering me

when the two men finally manage to reach me one of them whistles and says, nobody survived, and the other nods his head, agreeing, look at the state of the car, I've seen some beaten up frames in my time but this, the men reached me with difficulty, they were slipping in the mud and the torches in their hands drew faltering circles of light, near me the men complained, hell of a night for someone to go and smash themselves to pieces here, by here they mean the inaccessible stretch of ground I landed on, a steep descent covered in brambles that scratch the men's hands, when the men saw my car from close up

we need to ask for help

they realised the two of them alone could do nothing, one of them rubs his hands together to warm them, he takes out his phone and dials a number, she must have hit that central divider, it's completely bent out of shape, she must have been driving very fast, she still zigzagged for a few more metres, those skid-marks we saw on the pavement, then further ahead she crashed again, went through the barrier and landed upside down right here, these guys got lucky with the headlamps, if the headlamps had not remained on nobody would have found the car, we can't get a signal, the man puts the phone in his pocket, they say it's for emergencies but when you need it either there's no signal or the battery is dead, they should give thanks for the headlamps, I mean, if they could still give thanks, I don't understand why they are talking as if there were other people here, I don't know if that's how the accident happened, when I woke up I was already in this strange position, I don't know what happened before, these men are in charge of supervising the road, there are some strange jobs, days and nights driving from one side to the other, the two men were passing when one of them, the co-pilot, saw my car's lit-up headlamps, unless I'm mistaken a car ended up down there, the other took a look but wasn't sure, a car would not have ended up that far,

I want to fly up to the sky, touch the sky

the colleague insisted, those are a car's headlamps, the driver turned on the siren, he stopped by the metal barrier, they looked out to the empty field where I landed, we'll have to get down there, I don't know which of the two turned off the lights and locked the car, both cursed the rain coming down on them, bloody weather, so far this evening the two men had not yet had a rest, there were calls for assistance all over the place, accidents, breakdowns, things blocking the road, one of the men, I don't know which one of them was driving, said, what a storm, looks like the devil is on the loose, the men jumped over the barrier, they slipped in the mud, they wanted to walk fast but could not, the men's torches lit my travel bag tangled in a bush, the waxing products, the free samples, the account book, as they came close one of the men whistled,

nobody survived, it's impossible that anyone survived,

and wiped the water dripping off his hood and onto his forehead, it's raining like I've never seen, a wall of water, get me out of here, Denise and Betty are waiting for me, I've never missed an appointment with a customer, I'm a good salesperson, the best, the most punctual, the one with the best sales pitch, the one who never gives up, get me out of here, one of the men walks around the car, it looks like there's only one person,

get me out of here

why can't they hear me, I shout louder but strangely I cannot hear my own voice as I used to, it must be because of the noise of the rain, one of the men, the eldest even though there is no great age difference, with a crash like this I wouldn't be surprised if other passengers were thrown out, I wouldn't be surprised at all,

don't waste your time, there's nobody else, Ângelo called this morning to say that the old folks' outing had been cancelled, without the old folks there is no performance,

I was travelling on my own, I was listening to nice music, don't waste your time looking for Ângelo who folds the frilly bedspread back along the seams and is sleeping in the bed where my father and his mother would lie down together, bastards are capable of anything, imperfect beings, incomplete beings like bastards, are capable of anything,

the younger man said, I'm going to look around, the older one walked around the car, let's see what we find here, he peers in, shines the torch on me, the drop of water fills with light, it looks so pretty, I had never seen a drop of light, there's a woman, he shouts out to the younger one who had walked away, there's a woman, the other one from further away, if it's a woman she must have been accompanied, no woman travels alone on a night like this one, let me see if I can find someone over here,

don't waste your time, why can't they hear me, it must be because of the vaguely pleasant drowsiness, the slight jolt, like when we put our weight on an arm and it falls asleep, before long I will start feeling the pins and needles that jab the flesh, before my eyes are free of the water-drop, it won't be long before the men can hear my shouts

inside the waterdrop I can see the younger man looking for someone accompanying me, the torch drawing circles, I never thought light would look so pretty inside water, the older man is still near me and complaining about the rain, about the wind, about my car, a pile of twisted metal and broken glass, perhaps he'll be able to open the door, he tries to get his hand through the broken glass, the glass is shattered into pieces that glisten everywhere, a piece of starry sky on the ground, the man gives up, he walks around the car not knowing how to get me out, the man realises that the other door is no longer there, just a piece of plate metal, he tries to pull open what was once a door but he can't, tries again, nothing, we'll need a chainsaw, he concludes, yes we'll need the chainsaw, the younger man says, perhaps coming in through the boot, I don't think that would work, anyway we wouldn't be able to get her out, the younger man approaches, I don't see anyone else, I think she was on her own, all these things must be hers, the crickets are once again chirping in my ears and won't let me hear anything, the men peer at me, I cannot hear them describe me, my body, my face, they have reached a conclusion about the state I'm in, the crickets become quiet, and one of the men, I can't tell which one, they are so similar,

there's nothing we can do

he sits on a piece of plate metal, puts his hands on his face, I wish you hadn't seen the headlamps, we'll be here all night, this is crazy, my customers are expecting me first thing tomorrow, Denise always wakes up in a bad mood and if I am late she'll be worse, not even the coffee that her Ukrainian fellow gets her in the shopping centre bakery will make her feel any better, I have to be on time so Denise won't get angry with me, Denise does not forgive an obliging dog, nor does she forgive a delayed freak, and Betty cannot stand tardiness either, nothing was ever late at Villa Elizabete, the children grew up fast and already have the pale sadness of grown-ups, I never saw anything be late at Villa Elizabete, one of the men says he is going back up to call for a tow-truck,

there's nothing we can do

Dora is sleeping on a wrought iron bed with birds and flowers on the headboard, a curled up child's body, convinced that tomorrow she is leaving our house, the body of a child with its knees pulled up into its chest, arms crossed, the stray cats walking all over my child who lay down on the grass blinded by the sun, how can the men say there is nothing they can do when in a short while Dora will be sitting at the hypermarket checkout scanning barcodes for apples, royal gala, granny smith, red delicious, golden, russet, pink lady, fuji, golden delicious, so many different apples and the days are all the same, there is never a special offer that says, with the purchase of one full week get 25% off a day, or pay for two happy days and get three, there is never a freebie for regular customers, have three hours that feel like spring, or a special clearance shelf for defective days, the wasted minutes or the hours overslept, discounts, cheaper days, if days were not monotonously alike one another they might be on sale in the fresh produce section, happy days, melancholy days, terrible days, run-of-the-mill days, calm days, wilting days, 100% organic days, packaged or loose, so many different apples and the days are all the same, this day, which might well be the day of my, and even so this day is still the same as others, before going to bed Ângelo emptied the ashtrays, hung the tea towels up to dry on the oven door, closed the toilet lid, just another day in Ângelo's life, this cannot be the day of my, if it were the dancers would be dancing on top of the cabinet, the jade elephant would turn his back to the door and ignore bad luck, the swans in the fruit bowl would drown in the cedar oil used to polish the table, if it were, the lorry driver from the service station would rip apart his wife instead of falling asleep in her arms as he has for the past thirty years, if there were anything different, some detail, something insignificant but I'm certain that even if I were not here things could not be the same, if I no longer existed the day would not start as usual

bêtises, ma chérie, bêtises

nor would the rain fall as precipitously as it has done ever since the dawn of the world, if this were the day then Dora would wake with a start, Ângelo with a fright that left him out of breath, Denise would forget about getting rid of her Ukrainian while Betty would get rid of her collection of miniature teapots and teacups, I am certain that something different, even if it were insignificant like most things are, one of the men says it might be better to wait in the car to avoid getting too cold, there's nothing we can do

the other says they might try to get to me through the boot, it's not safe, and anyway you wouldn't reach her, I am finally unreachable, I always wanted to escape from the hands touching me all over, the words targeting me, poisoned arrows, and now that I am strangely unreachable life seems to have a sense of humour similar to Ângelo's,

you always go too far

a sort of performance that everyone boos at the end, some of the more impatient ones cannot wait until the end, a small disagreement like the one happening between the two men now, one of them thinks they should pick up the objects strewn all over the ground but the other says it is best to do that when help arrives, both men continue to walk in the rain, one of them, how can I tell these men apart, so many apples and these men are the same, only a moment ago one of them seemed older but now not even that, one of the men picks my diary off the floor, he wants to put it in his pocket, under the rain the blue handwriting starts to run, very soon it will all be a blue stain,

do not go away

the man stares at the names and the numbers as they disappear, the one walking ahead calls him, the man throws the diary away, he cannot read a blue stain, a message on a little yellow paper, the men who are going to pull me out of the car are on their way,

where do I get the certainty

the men walk away with their torches, the circles of light look pretty in the rain, the raincoats, the men walking, the men moving away, they look pretty walking in the rain, they are leaving me alone, I don't mind waiting alone, I was always able to entertain myself with anything, like the idea of being dead or any such silliness, the men only say silly things anyway, how can they say that there is nothing to be done if from today everything will be different, they cannot reach me but

this girl is impossible, nobody can talk with her around

they should pick up my things that are strewn all over the ground and that I will need, Denise will want the free hand-outs and Betty will want the samples, not to mention, these insignificant things cannot outlive me, a page in a magazine with the upper left corner folded down, the wrapper of a wax for women with varicose veins, unfinished crosswords, an accounts book, the men have climbed the slope, they jump over the barrier, reach the car, get in, one of them sits behind the steering wheel, he turns the key in the ignition and puts on the heating, he is cold, very cold, I am not cold even with all the car windows smashed, the *chauffage*, Baltazar, the *chauffage*

I was never cold on those journeys to my grandparents' house, at my mother's request my father would press a button on the dashboard without taking his eyes off the road, a quick gesture, my mother would stretch her hands out to warm them over the hot air that made my stomach churn, Maria da Guia with her head back and eyes closed to hold back the car-sickness gathering in her mouth, I'm sorry, senhora, Maria da Guia standing on the roadside vomiting, none of us held her head, or brought her any water, we looked away to avoid feeling sick ourselves, Maria da Guia all alone on the roadside wiping her mouth with a hand-kerchief, the biggest problem with car journeys is the creature who always gets car-sick, I think she's still afraid of being in a car, twice a year we visited the country bump-kins who were always very grateful, old ignoramuses who did not know what that *joie de vivre* was that their daughter-in-law talked about, the saint who saved their son,

a splendid journey, wasn't it, Baltazar

long journeys that did not leave a crease on that light-yellow dress that suited my mother so well, on the little jacket she slung over her shoulders, nothing ruined my mother's perfection, not even the husband who kept birds, or the freakish daughter, or the communist maid, the husband's lover and their bastard child, stupid Clarissa who gave herself airs, Alice's husband holding his two mixed-race children by the hand, the one and only thing that ruined my mother's perfect life, victim of prolonged illness, the one and only thing that took away her *joie de vivre*

somebody in your family

life is a devious thing

the men putting their hands out towards the hot air,

there's nothing we can do

the bumpkins would put their labour-worn hands out to greet us, my mother would wriggle free to go to the bedroom where she composed herself after the journey, it was the only part of the house that, at her request, had any form of comfort, she would sit in the *boudoir*, not even at the bumpkins' house did she lose the habit of using her half dozen words in the world's most beautiful language, she called out to Maria da Guia,

see if you can put on a better face because the one you have is frightful

sorry, senhora, sorry, I'll be fine in no time, maids when well chosen never get ill and never have a long face, Maria da Guia helped my mother hang her pearl necklace from one of the ornamental details framing the mirror, fix her hair here and there, refresh herself with eau de cologne, remove the clothes from the suitcase, empty the *nécessaire*, arrange the face creams and makeup, and only then did she go to help the mother bumpkin, my mother would linger in the bedroom, she did not want to sit at the kitchen table, eat whatever the bumpkins had prepared, she took her time, my father called her, an impatient call, we are all waiting for you, Celeste, and my mother would come out of the room with a smile that seemed authentic, Maria da Guia already wearing her uniform and standing by the table, my mother trying not to look at the bucket of pigswill hanging from a hook over the fireplace, the bumpkins' metal pots, the clay bowls, she turned her head without breaking her smile,

life is a devious thing

she apologised for her lack of appetite, said something about the toast she had eaten not long ago, the coffee that had disagreed with her, the tea that was too strong, she never sat at the table because the bumpkins made her so sick with the smell of the pigswill as it cooked in the bucket, my father and I ate in silence, Maria da Guia had to wait until we all finished to eat what remained of the potatoes and cabbages, she liked the taste, the taste of my childhood, she used to say, while we were seated at the table my mother walked from one side to the other clickety-clacking on the wooden floor with her high-heel shoes, she produced a silk scarf she had bought for my grandmother to go to church, some woollen long johns for my grandfather, wrapped in colourful paper and a bow, so you're warmer in the winter, she walked from one side to the other and the bumpkins thanked her for the presents, my mother said, just a little keepsake so you know you are always in our hearts, the bumpkins wanted to believe this, the truth is that the car had not even warmed up on the way back and already we had forgotten them, when she was back at her Wednesday card games my mother

we had some lovely days

never complained about the bumpkins, about me, about my father, she would say, a few days in the country always do us good, Baltazar can get some proper rest, the girl likes animals, I always have something to do, when she talked about lovely days my mother was referring to my father sitting on the veranda for hours at a time, to me chasing the chickens and the rabbits that the bumpkins raised and then fed us in a display of abundance, to her sitting alongside my father copying the recipes from last year's recipe book into the new year's recipe book, while I chased the chickens in the garden I could hear my father, the girl is spooking the animals, but my mother

this child is impossible, nobody can ever have a moment's peace when she's around

pretended she couldn't hear him, in her careful handwriting she copied out the recipes for Teresinha's galantine, Milu's pasties, someone else's sponge cake, remembering the flavours distracted her from the bumpkins' presence, the girl is either going to hurt herself or one of the animals, my father insisted, and my mother would get up irritated and from under the awning would shout, come inside, come inside now, Violeta, and get back to the recipes that Maria da Guia would later prepare, the recipe books remained in one of the kitchen cupboards, I doubt that the new buyer will one day be able to knead the puff pastry just so, or that the daughter, a snake in the process of changing her skin, would eat the *petits fours*, my mother hand copied recipes instead of eating the freshly cut fruit that the bumpkins offered her, or thanking them for the embers they stoked in the fireplace at night, how could my mother talk to people who did not even know about the world's most beautiful language, when the time came to leave

Baltazar, is there anyone in your family that doesn't have that miserable air

my mother would say goodbye with a kiss and from the car would wave delicately at the bumpkins who were not in the wedding album, in our house there was only ever a small photograph in which you can hardly see them and even so it was hidden away in the office,

people like them make a house ugly

my mother's parents are in the wedding album, and framed in the dining room and in the living room, ever-present, and for the bumpkins there is the little photograph, as soon as we started the journey back the bumpkins ceased to exist, everyone exists intermittently,

we had some lovely lives

I for instance may have stopped existing every now and then, I am not cold, frightened or in pain, I am not surprised that I can't feel anything, one of the men throws his hi-vis safety vest onto the back seat and says to the other, don't forget to play the lotto, I've bought my ticket, the other man leaves his vest on, I don't usually play, so here is one way to tell them apart, the one who plays lotto and the one who doesn't, people always have a way of arranging themselves so that they can be distinguished from one another, a desire to be unique that only disadvantages them, this week there's a jackpot, says the one who plays, the one who doesn't play looks at the rain, have you thought about how everything can end at any moment, we are all calves on the way to the slaughterhouse, the player does not respond, the non-player continues, have you imagined that it could have been your wife, or one of your children, the player brusquely, it wasn't, I don't have to imagine anything, if I was imagining things I would have stopped working on the road some time ago,

why do they talk about me like that

when I win the lotto, we have to think positive to help lighten the twisted mood, he likes to say twisted mood, when I win the lotto I'll buy a grove and plant olive trees, a simple life, the non-player, I can't stop thinking about where that woman was going, whether she realised that, the player, stop it with your useless thoughts, play the lotto because we don't have too many chances to get rich, the non-player, my biggest fear is one day coming across one of my own in that state, just driving along the road from one place to the next and then one day, the player, what would you do if you won the lotto, the non-player, a guy needs to work, I actually like what I do, but I keep thinking about one of my own all smashed up on an empty patch of ground, the player, you're getting on my nerves with this talk, I always play the same numbers, one of these days I'll get lucky, one of these days, then I'll buy the farm and wake up with the roosters singing, do you still remember waking up with the roosters, the non-player, I don't think I ever woke up with the roosters singing, the player, c'mon think about what you'd do if you won the lotto, the non-player, I really don't know, maybe I'd buy a bigger house, a car, don't know, the player, that's your problem, your problem is you don't have any objectives, another way of distinguishing the men, the one with objectives and the one without, a guy's gotta have objectives in this life, I never distract myself, I am always, always thinking, remember you have an objective, you are here to achieve your objective, it's the only way to put up with this, today it's this woman, tomorrow it's someone else and then someone else, I've seen so many that I've started to think that everyone dies on the road, anyway this passes quickly, one day you're born and then another day you're dying, you might not even need as long as two days, if we don't have objectives we're screwed, when I start getting caught up in nonsense I just think about the farm and then everything is fine, guys like you, just going around with no objectives, have a problem because you have nothing to hold on to, the man with no objectives remained silent as did the one with objectives, they both have cold feet, they are both sleepy, hungry, they both want dry clothes, warmth, a bed to sleep in, a piece of bread, these men are truly alike, how long will it take them, either one of them might ask, don't know, the other would reply, it depends, the road is in bad shape, they may have been called to another accident, the men are quiet again, the rain drums on the car roof, it almost sounds like it's singing, says one of them, I don't think I ever saw so much rain, that woman must have had something urgent to do, if it wasn't urgent then she was crazy to be on the road on a night like this, she must have had something urgent to do

why do they talk about me in the past tense

I wouldn't be surprised if she didn't, says the sceptical one, there are lots of crazy people out there, soon I will be pulled out of the car and the sceptical one will be the first to smell the alcohol, didn't I tell you, the one thing we're not lacking is crazy people out there, smelling like that the only urgent thing she had to do was smashing herself to pieces, the sceptical one still doesn't know he'll be saying those words, the men talk about me in the past tense even though the future never seemed so clear to me, the man who plays lotto and has objectives and is sceptical adds, at least she killed herself on her own, the worst thing is when they take out some innocents with them, the sceptical one does not know he will say the things I know he will say,

bêtises, ma chérie, bêtises

I know everything there is to know in this time that is not the one happening, or the one that just happened, or the one that will happen, a flattened out time, entirely accessible like the roads on my maps, time finally charted like the lands in my map collection, places that only exist to await me, places that only exist for me to roam them, head down, suspended by the safety belt, in a moment in which I may no longer exist, in a moment that may no longer exist for me

one of the men looks at his watch, what good are clocks if they only count the time we no longer have, or the time that has passed, when the only thing that matters is how much time we have left, what we still have, from today everything will be different,

don't worry, there's nothing we can do

you never know

the other men are delayed, how alike one another these two men are, once again I can't tell them apart, the worst thing is writing up the incident reports, I don't like messing around with the times, I'm always worried it will cause a problem later on, and it may well do one day, one day someone, a siren, I'm sure I can hear a siren, I can see a recovery van approaching in the drop of water my eyes are fixed on, on its roof it has yellow lights like the ones at the junction of the four roads, a shower of fireflies, a white line, the road, from here I can see the road as if it were in one of my maps, a whole road, with its beginning and end, unlike the black line that swallowed me, from here I can be in many times at once,

bêtises, ma chérie, bêtises

the moment the phone rings in my home, when Dora meets Ângelo in the hospital waiting room, waiting for the doctor to give them news, Dora and Ângelo in a hospital waiting room just like me and Ângelo many years ago in another hospital waiting room waiting for the doctor to give us news about my father, our father, Ângelo the scarecrow wanting to say to me, I am also his son, and now wanting to say to Dora, I can be your father, your mother and I, I stopped him from talking that time, I made him say he was a friend of my father's, I invited him back to my house and when we entered the street he started acting funny, Ângelo had already picked up the habit of telling jokes,

if this is Paradise Street just imagine what hell is like

now it is Dora's turn to stop Ângelo from talking, Dora is still in the wrought iron bed with the birds and the flowers on the headboard, a curled up child's body, it won't be long

279

before the sun comes up on the paradise of Travessa do Paraíso, the storm calmed, the children play with a football, old women are hanging clothes on the drying lines, old men go back to their verandas and balconies to put down roots, it is the roots that prevent them from jumping, Alice's problem was not having roots, from her balcony Alice could only see the sea and the sky, sea and sky, sooner or later she would have felt compelled to be part of that green or that blue, sooner or later, the men who are going to pull me out are on the road, this night will finish like any other night and the new day will begin like any other day, the men coming to find me speed up, they do not pay heed to the signs by the roadside, keep your safety distance, one chevron, danger, two chevrons, safety, the men obviously never played hop-scotch like I did in the garden,

death is not a *passe-temps*, Violeta

how I hate my mother's habit of throwing around French words, she forced me to have lessons with Madame Santos who very soon gave up on me,

la pauvre, is so 'arrd for 'err, the *pauvre fille* will never speak French

that day I felt sorry for my mother, it is true the feeling did not last, the things that brought us together never lasted, a few hours, a few minutes, the day Madame Santos gave up on me my mother opened her handbag and smiled, she was in the habit of smiling when she was sad, a line of straight teeth, her lips outlined, a sweet smile

where is the *porte-monnaie*

for Madame Santos, Madame Santos who after a few years was left with no students, when she realised that nobody wanted to learn the most beautiful language in the world anymore

brainstorming, coffee break, the curse of English, the curse of English, *whatever*

Madame Santos convinced herself that pastries and cakes would never go out of fashion and would always be in demand, she practised her *crème brûlée,* her *bavaroises,* her *feuilletés,* my mother never knew that Madame Santos begged café owners to buy her pastries, that Madame Santos became old and poor and is still old and poor and begging for charity in the most beautiful language in the world, nobody listens to her, it is hardly surprising, poor people today are very different,

fashion is fickle

you no longer see those unsophisticated yokels or even those blacks who came from the colonies, Madame Santos cannot compete with the blonde poor that have come from the east, their skins so fair and two pieces of sky set in their eyes, the traditional poor don't stand a chance if such good-looking poor are coming in from the east,

if I had let Maria da Guia do as she pleased, what would have become of the poor creature's life

I have to agree with my mother, if the creature had done as she pleased now she wouldn't have the happiness of languishing in a cage, no more than five square metres, a hovel, because these people are only happy when they are constrained, were it not for my mother Maria da Guia would be one more among the poor because she is not blonde, she is not pretty, she is not cultured, like some of the poor you see nowadays, Maria da Guia is old, ugly and illiterate, like almost all of the poor you no longer see, if my mother had not intervened Maria da Guia would have become one more old and poor communist and today nobody wants to give them the time of day, even so, just being old and poor means that there is nobody to take pity on her and rub a bit of rouge on her cheeks,

un peu de rouge et voilá

the thing about the poor, like everyone else, is that some are more in demand than others, my mother for instance liked the healthier poor, Teresinha liked the sick poor or was it Maria do Céu who liked the sick poor, stupid Clarissa preferred the orphaned poor, but I never met anyone who liked the communist poor, in any case Maria da Guia was lucky to have been languishing in that hovel while the world changed so much that people had stopped using the most beautiful language in the world, had stopped buying Madame Santos' pastries, that the poor were now very different, the world changed but Maria da Guia does not need to worry about being the *dernier cri*,

fashion is fickle

if I went to the newspaper kiosk to look at some of the fashion magazines like the ones gathering mildew in the basement I'm sure the fashion advice for this season would be all about the poor from the east, pages and pages of the poor from the east, instead of the bell-bottom trousers and the shirt collars like airplane wings, fashion is truly fickle, that is what the buyers will say before throwing the magazines out, I'm losing time with nonsense and the men who are going to pull me out are getting near, they drive past another sign they don't read, maintain a safe distance, yellow hard hats painted on the road, one chevron, danger, two chevrons, safety, life is not more complicated than a game, like hopscotch, the game of hopscotch has

it's too late for you to understand the game

two or three rules and the rest is pure luck, maintain a safe distance, one chevron, danger, two chevrons, safety, a simple game with simple rules, the most important, accuracy, it's about handling the markers with skill, about the luck of handling the markers well, life is a simple game with a simple aim, to jump from year to year without stepping on the lines, that's another rule, never step on the line, if someone steps on the line there will always be someone ready to call foul,

the game only seems simple to you because you can't play it anymore

dirty snitch, get lost, go crying to Ângelo who snitched on my father because he was also his father, the men who are coming to find me do not think about the game that the road, or even better, that life presents them with, the ambulance lights cut through the storm, neon, the men are looking at the orange and white cats' eyes by the side of the road, the white line that divides the lanes, they do not know that they are always gambling with their lives, I see the road that only a moment ago I could picture as if on one of my maps, I had dozens of maps in my house, a habit like keeping birds, we learn the strangest things from our parents, Dora will throw out my maps, my entire collection into the rubbish bin with no hesitation, Dora

how do you come up with these things, Violeta

does not miss travelling with me, I miss travelling with Dora, I used to sit her on my lap and we would navigate on the clear blue waters of my paper maps, my Dora in the middle of the ocean, on the roads marked in many colours, like a rainbow, let's go this way, and my child laughed, she had not yet decided she hated me, she found comfort in my warm flesh, she did not yet think of the mound of flesh embracing her as an aberration, she had not yet learned to be ashamed of her monstrous mother, she knew only some essential things, I am hungry, I am thirsty, I am sleepy, I like your warm flesh, Dora was far from being the adversary she would become, which way are we going, I would ask, to the island of squirrels, the island of squirrels it is then, lands we knew nothing about, a flower, a landscape, a colour, Wilkes Land, places that served only to ignite my desire to leave, always the desire, never the consummation, at that point life was a succession of simple acts and Dora only knew simple things, every now and then Dora would rub out places with her thumb, my child's little thumb would destroy entire cities with my permission, Dora would raise her thumb and we would rebuild the destroyed cities, when she was tired of travelling over lands, rivers, seas, when she got tired of destroying cities, of rebuilding them, Dora would fall asleep on my lap, the little miscreant with the sweet breath, I wiped the beads of sweat off her neck, and nodded off, the most beautiful being I ever was, the tamest, I miss travelling through my maps with Dora, becoming intoxicated with her sweet breath, wetting my hands with her sweat, Dora who will be waking up shortly, my Dora going through a series of mechanical motions because she has forgotten the wisdom of maps, of the eyes of our creator, caught up in the gestures of days that are all the same, in certainties as absurd as the products she scans at the hypermarket, the men coming to find me see the fallen tree I passed not long ago, the tree branches waving, a whirlwind of leaves, the men drive past the tree and don't think about the sadness of trees that die standing while dreaming about the next spring, the men waiting in the car are still silent, all the talk about the lotto, about objectives, all the doubts and the scepticism have become unimportant because the men are tired and cold and sleepy, I wait, I don't mind, I always managed to entertain myself with anything, with the idea that I may have died or some other such silliness, inside the drop of water a strange light, blue, but it's a different blue from the blue of a summer sky, a light like the one in the room where my mother waited, how could I have forgotten the light

of all the mysteries I choose pain, which brings oblivion

in the room where my mother and a dozen other bodies waited, whenever I visited her the cruelty of that light would startle me but after a few blinks I became used to it, it usually took me as long as it took the nurse to confirm that the plastic overall she had given me would not fit me, in that room I was the only one not using a plastic overall, the nurse apologised,

one size only

I smiled, the nurse smiled, we smiled despite the bodies waiting in that room, despite the unbearable light, I reached my mother's bed which was next to a window I never saw open, I had to move the bed to get close, the space was too tight for me, I checked whether the bed next to my mother's still had the same occupant, and then the bed next to it, and the next, I openly looked out for the ones who had died, I placed my own personal wagers, who was going to die next, who was going to die after my mother, there can be no other thoughts in a room where ten or twelve moribund people are waiting, when I stood alongside my mother I felt the pointless urge to kiss her, embrace her,

bêtises, ma chérie, bêtises

but the lady volunteer, the doctor, the nurse all looked at me, and the urge disappeared, I leaned over and put my lips on my mother's forehead as if I had bumped into her in a café where we were both regulars, the indifferent kiss on her forehead was yet another wound in her body, I could have chosen to forgive her, or to avenge the anger that even now makes my heart race, I could have chosen to forget everything but I chose not to change what we had been,

when we turn our back on the past we lose the future

the lady volunteer would come up to me and tell me I could feed my mother, it's best if I don't, I replied assuredly, the eyes, the face of the lady volunteer seemed to lament my mother's fate, what kind of daughter refuses to feed her mother, the lady volunteer would take charge of feeding her a mush that my mother had difficulty swallowing, my mother could not escape the lady volunteer, or walk around from one side to the other as she did at the bumpkins' home, the lady volunteers are there to ensure that the moribund patients leave on their journey with a full stomach, it is always a journey, although nobody knows how long the journey takes, nobody says moribund any more, people talk about terminal patients, it is a skill to find words that do not hurt, my mother's thin arm attached to a bag of blood that shimmered by the headboard, the lady volunteer knew that the shimmering blood was useless to a moribund body, nothing could stop death, it became visible in that light, not in screams, the moribund are tame, desperation is for the living, I looked at the body that had belonged to my mother, that had served her an entire life, I looked at everything without understanding

the lips of the moribund are so ugly, don't you think, lady volunteer

how one could become that, my mother's legs attached to the bed by her ankles, so she would not hurt herself because her body had no-one to rule over it, my mother so distant from the light-yellow dress that suited her so well, instead a hospital gown covered in ink stamps concealing the tube

I've been wanting to tell you for some time that stamped hospital gowns are out of fashion

that connects my mother's bladder to the red-tinged plastic bag, stupid Clarissa giving herself airs because her son is a medic and walks around the hospital corridors with a stetho-scope, no, that was the revolutionary one who wears the camouflage uniform, it's Maria do Carmo whose son is a medic and walks around the hospital corridors with a stethoscope,

my friends had normal children who have normal jobs

my mother's body resting on a stamped hospital sheet, on the pillowcase some yellowed vomit, dark drops of blood, different from the shimmering blood in the bag,

whether it is far from or close to the end this body deserves the best

another stamped sheet covering her, a torn blanket also stamped,

fashion is fickle

the initials of the places it has been laundered, other hospitals that the bedlinen has been through, my mother not even noticing the stamps, with eyes so empty, almost like my newly born Dora's eyes, my mother's body degrading as conspicuously as my daughter's body grew, the same force, the same inevitability, causing the same perplexity to whoever is witnessing it, my mother existing only to carry the body that betrayed her, an ungrateful and rebellious servant, unlike Maria da Guia who learned who was kind to her, my mother's body was the first traitor who disregarded my mother's authority, my father, Ângelo, Ângelo's mother, stupid Clarissa, Maria da Guia's communist boyfriend, Alice's husband, the bumpkins, until she was betrayed by her body there was no-one my mother had not expelled or silenced, my mother powerless when faced with the only traitor that defeated her, the first unpleasant business she was unable to sort out because

there is nothing that silence won't kill

bodies always say a lot, they are indiscreet by nature, at the end of everything my mother's body,

of all the mysteries I choose that of bodies that are continually reborn

flower, tree, cloud, a grain of sand in the desert, the miracle of life offered to the cruellest of traitors, the only one who had a chance to redeem itself, it's laughter that saves us, I belong to a group of well-disposed beings, fat people have a reputation for being happy despite the weight they carry, despite the fewer years that statistics grant us, the diseases that hover around us, I belong to a group of well-disposed beings, a true mystery, the men who are on their way to find me drive past a factory unit, whatever happened to the word factory, tonight its lit-up rectangles seem false, smoke comes out of its chimney and curls up in the storm becoming a pretty fog, pretty as a picture, the factory workers are still busy, I did not know factory workers worked through the night, the workers do not know that the men are driving past on the road, that they are on their way to find what remains of me, no matter how much we think we know there are always things that escape us, things we don't know, the workers don't know that I always liked the idea of a factory, that I think of life as a factory, a giant factory in which all pieces can be easily substituted, Ângelo is right, nobody can correct the past because there is nothing to correct, life is independent of the will that animates it, my father's life happened as if Ângelo and his mother did not exist, my mother's life happened as if my father's life were different, my life happened as if I had not been born a freak, Dora's life still to be fulfilled, life happens as a mechanical and unconscious act, like breathing, nobody has a say in any-thing, we inhale and exhale while we still have time, the men drive past the factory that I passed not long ago, a few hours from now Denise and Betty will be wondering why I'm late, their phone numbers are in the diary that one of the men threw away, but I can't tell them I'll be late, an unfore-seen delay, nobody can read rain-soaked stains, nobody

   don't leave

can stop a life that has decided to end, I must tell Denise and Betty, I can't lose any more customers, I already lost the Princesa Beauty Salon, an Indian restaurant, the Rosa da Manhã, the pigeon and old poster sanctuary where the blue velvet sofa was boarded in, the blue velvet sofa from which I sprang up with unexpected agility, I always tried to make my body appear light to others but only now do I feel its lightness, Denise and Betty are waiting for me at the Princesa Beauty Salon, my refrains are always the same,

salespeople's refrains are always so tedious

for years I've been repeating the same facts, it's a poor performance, every human being has close to five million hairs, I was never able to say, we have close to five million hairs, I always left myself out of the picture, I always pretended that my enemies did not defeat me every day, an unpleasant matter, a salesperson must not, cannot have personal issues, good salespeople never talk about themselves, the entire surface of a human's skin is covered in hair except the palms of the hand and the soles of the feet, glabrous skin, I know everything I need to, I'm a good salesperson, the best, I survived the Princesa Beauty Salon, the Rosa da Manhã, the most beautiful language in the world falling into disuse, my parents, the house I sold today, Ângelo's revenge, Dora's shame, I never stopped to consider the deaths my life was made up of, is made up of, I never stopped to consider the details, it is the details that keep us attached, I met the majestic blue velvet sofa as well as the vulgarity of Denise in Lycra tights beneath her robe with chewing gum in her mouth, a ruminant with her hair tinted a reddish brown that does not suit her, Denise and the blue velvet sofa did not overlap in time, there was nothing to connect them apart from me, my existence, these mismatches are frequent, time is rarely accessible in its entirety, unless you happen to be in this strange head-down position, hanging by the seatbelt, in a time that may no longer be for me but still is for Denise, who not long from now will wonder why I am late and will drop her comb, or her scissors, she is always dropping things, she will complain about her varicose veins and about some damned spot on her face, about the Ukrainian fellow and all the ones that preceded him, time, which seems to be the same but is always another, which continues existing so that Betty who not long from now will not only wonder why I am late but will also fill the unlicensed beauty parlour in the unlicensed Villa Elizabete with the sickly scent of lemon, she will tell her customer about the wax's melting point, a wax just like the one left lying in the nearby shrubs, or that other formula lying near the puddle, resin, honey, time that seems to be the same but is individualised for each one of us, in the time that continues to exist for Betty there are documentaries on the cable TV that her husband has pirated, Betty learns that in ancient Greece priestesses placed hot ashes onto their skins to get rid of body hair, my enemy, the pain was so intense that the priestesses got drunk before going into battle, Betty continues to doubt what she hears, in this case, was it Greece or Egypt, Betty smiles, there's so much information that I get confused,

did you know that our skin is the human body's largest organ

Betty's time continues to pass in the unlicensed beauty parlour despite my not being there to talk about hair follicles, the precise composition of wax needed for a certain type of skin or a specific type of hair, azulene wax, beetroot sugar, resin, gum arabic, beeswax, essential cinnamon oil, in her time Betty will listen to another salesperson, not as good as me, inexperienced, lazy, my life is a battle against millions of enemies, I drove one, two hundred kilometres, as many as were necessary, I never considered the need to change, Ângelo was certain that, sooner or later, I would give up,

the future no longer belongs to us

defeated by laser clinics, by the increasingly dangerous road, by opportunistic customers,

the curse of laser

Ângelo does not know me, I am not easily defeated, I never gave up on anything, Ângelo told me many times to give up because he doesn't know that machines never stray from the purpose they were built for, when they are no longer necessary they top themselves, they never stray from their purpose, Ângelo does not know many things, it was because he does not know many things that he thought himself capable of taking revenge on my father, on me, on us, Ângelo showed up at the hospital the day my father decided to let his heart stop and die in a hurry,

these people always have the richest pickings

unlike my mother who died unhurriedly, they could not even agree on how to die, Ângelo pretended it was the first time we had spoken as if he had forgotten the most idiotic revenge that a bastard like him can dream up, for who other than a bastard might dream of impregnating his freakish half-sister, the men coming to find me are changing lanes, they are very close, the men in the car have given them the location, there can be no mistake, no misunderstanding that will keep me here for longer, the men find each other, there's nothing we can do, the siren is silent, only the lights are turning frantically, the men come down the slope with their torches, they reach the patch of ground where I landed, the torches are drawing open circles, so pretty, a rain of fireflies, get me out of here,

why does nobody hear me

get me out of here, I shout in the silence to which my body abandoned me, my body, the most cruel traitor I could have encountered, it defeats me at the first chance I give it, he is a good adversary, the best, I can do nothing against it, a man peers through the glass, a round face, bug-eyed, flat-nosed, if this is the last face I will ever see then the man has a duty to smile, that is what the human resources manager taught Dora, the last image of life, of what remains of my life,

a lost life is always sad

a smile is the least we can offer others

another man peers, a thinner face, preposterously blue eyes, a grimace revealing two missing teeth, one incisor and one canine, the man shakes his head,

just one second and boom, we end up like this

I always manage not to hear or not to see what I don't want to, against my will I hear and see these men who instead of smiling say nonsense and

she must weigh a ton

worry about their lives, about the lives of the ones they love, they use others' deaths to ponder their own, or those of the ones they love, the men begin the work of releasing me, they might take the opportunity to release the blue velvet sofa from the time in which it is trapped, the noise of a chainsaw, trees knocked down and the dream of spring definitely over, every now and then the men exchange words that mean nothing but might be offensive in the state I'm in, pass me the wrench, or this rain doesn't help one bit, the headlamps finally turn off, I repeat, dead, dead, dead, the word cannot hurt me anymore, all words stop hurting when repeated, dead, dead, I repeat, what to do with legs you cannot feel, gestures you cannot make, the voice that fails to reach any-one, nobody put a sign on the roadside,

in case of death immediately get rid of the memory of
your body

die at high speed

the men reach me, they free me, how long did it take them,
how much of the time that is probably not mine anymore,
how much of the time that is now my own, and what if now
I exist without time, one of the men says, the stretcher, he
does not hurry, there's nothing we can do, they are wrong,
I am resilient, it's a habit, I can resist anything, new feelings,
I don't like feeling anything different, being in new states, I
am certain that all things behave like my wax, feelings, the
simpler they are the more effective, life, the simpler it is
the more resistant, the men are going to put me on the
stretcher, I resist the fear of becoming just another number
in the blue-lit room where my mother waited,

number twenty-two needed urgent gastric care, seventeen went to get a CT scan, number fifteen passed away

I resist, I run over my maps to avoid seeing the light of the
waiting room where names disappear, our name, the first
thing we get and the first thing we lose, sometimes life
shows some coherence, when we start to live, our name,
when we start to die, a number, sometimes life makes no
sense, number seven had swollen ankles, number ten needs
a blood transfusion, sometimes life stands still like in that
waiting room

there is nothing that silence won't kill

where names disappear, and names carry everything away with them, no, names do not take away hope, the moribund have everything taken away from them apart from hope, I will recover, the moribund in that room have nothing left, a charitable soul should tell them that hope is a scam that delays their death, a terrible scam, perhaps the doctor, or the lady nurse, the lady volunteer,

we refer to them as terminal patients

since they are shielded from the senseless hope of the moribund, pardon me, the terminal patients, it sounds more chic, cosmopolitan, the idea of a dock, a point of arrival, a party, perhaps these people might warn patients that hope will only delay them on their journey,

I don't know what keeps them attached

they are taking me, I imagine it's to a party, after all I can be counted among the obese, a group known for its sunny disposition, the admirable chirpiness of the chubby,

welcome to the Chirpy Chubby Club, for those over one hundred kilos only

they are taking me, I imagine it's to a party, experts say that the fat compensate for their low self-esteem by putting on a show of fake happiness, what do experts say about the moribund, about the fat moribund, what can the experts know about such an impenetrable mystery, death kills those who catch sight of it, a lethal seductress, the men carry me with difficulty, my weight, the slippery mud, the rain prevents them from watching their step, my mother's mortified body, my father's body, light, easy to move, there is nothing experts can truly know about death, they did not ask my parents anything when they started to die, or Maria da Guia, you don't just die instantly, Maria da Guia, for instance, started dying when she was prevented from caring for senhora, senhora's sheets, senhora's food, senhora's aches and pains, when she was replaced by the lady volunteer, what funny titles these people have who fill the moribund with mashed baby food and cooked apples, in the hope, not hope because hope only hoodwinks the moribund, in the expectation that they will have a front row seat in Ângelo's performance, I mean in heaven, the lady volunteers are playing with dolls, a little more, just a little spoonful, these dolls are not quite as entertaining as the ones in the Princesa Beauty Salon, they have no secrets to tell and do not have heads covered in soap suds, the only tricks they know are how to be hooked up to beeping machines, how to be attached to bags of blood by the headboard, how to empty their bladders into plastic bags, let their lips become purple, whoever invented these dolls was clueless, had no idea what children like, or how children have fun, the men carry me on a stretcher with night closing in around us,

reeking of alcohol

why can't I get up and walk, a miracle I read about somewhere, not even a new kind of miracle, one made especially
for me,

she was partying

why can't I get up and stop them from leaving me in the
room with the bad lighting where my mother was made
to wait, at first my mother fixed her attention on the
stethoscopes leaning over her, the wristwatches moving her
around, the rings prodding her body, she fixed her attention
on anything that would keep her attached to the life that
was slipping away, a bubble, a blemish, a smile, anything
that prevented her from drifting away, when they get to
their destination the men who took me will tick the part of
the report that says dead on arrival, one of the men, or some
other man like them, will call Dora, yet another will fill out
the paperwork, full name, ID card number, date of birth,
date of death, place of birth, place of death, marital status,
last known address, parents' names, these people must be
sick of collecting boring information about the dead, of
having to notify people about someone's death, someone
else, the last person to add additional information, writes

how did I end up ending my life

road accident, casualty drove off road, inebriated, police
and next of kin notified, my body smashed to pieces, my

300

mother's body an old deposit for faulty organs, a junkyard, a few pieces, not many, in serviceable state, the white teeth, nice and straight, I will never be whole again, my mother was never whole again, the sum of faulty pieces, we are very sorry, they say to Dora, we are very sorry, and Dora thanks them, she has the habit of being thankful for everything, a docile child who never disagreed with her work colleagues and who never stopped smiling at her customers, an angel who does not want to save me, the men are carrying me on the stretcher,

pissed as a newt

they complain,

she weighs a ton

this bloody rain that won't stop

she was partying hard and then just went and killed herself on the road

the men exchange words that hardly add up to a conversation,

watch out for that tree stump, go to the left

lying on the stretcher I repeat once, twice, many times,

I want to fly up to the sky, I want to fly up the sky, I want to fly

lying on the stretcher I float, I stretch my hand towards Dora who is floating in the sea wearing the bathing suit with the flowers, I try to touch her but the flowers come loose and form waves that take her away, I had never seen a wave made of flowers, it's been so many years since Dora and I went to the beach, these days Dora usually goes with the artist, she goes everywhere with the artist

I told you his name is José, is it so hard to say José

who leaves messages for her every day, I love you, I'll wait for you, I love you too, I'm also waiting for you, the artist and Dora are convinced that they know what love is, that from this day forth they will never be without love, our only fear is the fear of strangers,

I have heard about love

of the unknown I am going towards, the artist and Dora believe themselves to be more complete, more perfect, they don't know that what unites them is their shared habit of contriving a feeling and then performing it repeatedly, I love you, I'll wait for you, when she heard about my accident Dora did not repeat any of the words she heard and she did not cry, if you want to smash yourself to pieces on the road that's up to you

nor did Ângelo, they are so alike, Dora did not cry because sculptures do not cry, Ângelo did not cry because scarecrows do not cry, Dora and Ângelo are so alike, when I saw Ângelo at the hospital,

I am also his son

I had not realised he was so like my father, the slumped shoulders, feet set apart, bug-eyed, too-long arms, the difference is that that Ângelo will never develop the habit of keeping birds like his father did, a scarecrow scares the birds away, nobody can stray from the purpose they were created for, the men cannot take me to the room with the moribund light, they cannot make me wear the stamped hospital gown,

one size only

cover me with a stamp-covered sheet, perhaps something can still be done, if I can still feel the cold rain falling on my face

where's your body at, Violeta, where's your body at

I am certain that something can still be done, I feel nothing, it's also true that fat people do not feel the cold as much, they are warmed by the flab that ends up exploding in their brains, their hearts, I am free of fear, the anxiety of being between life and death,

where's your head at, Violeta, where's your head at

I feel nothing, for some time now the road has been only a long straight stretch of tarmac, an airport runway, a ring of lights seen through the mantle covering me, the men covered me completely, a plastic bag, straps immobilising me, for some time now the road has been only a long straight stretch of road, the storm has let up, one of the men says, it's almost sunrise, silence again, another day is starting that will be like every other day that has passed, every other day yet to come, in a moment the alarm clock will wake up Dora, Ângelo wakes up later, he spends his mornings in the bed in which my father and his mother would lie down together,

bastards are just like that

Denise is cuddled in the arms of her Ukrainian fellow, dogs are so useful, Betty is dousing her body in lemon scent, she pulls her hair up with a rubber hairband and will wake up the pale children who always arrive in time for the future, the lorry driver is asleep embracing his wife in the lorry cabin, the café windows witness the servers' change of shift, if it is almost sunrise why am I covered in this dark mantle, a mantle darker than any night I have ever lived through, than any night others will live through what the earth

a splendour beyond the clouds, within the clouds, a blaze in
the sky disturbing its colour, the light leaping, fearless,

of all the mysteries I choose that of the untamed light that
every day defeats the darkness

a gesture that undresses the earth, running across balconies,
wings, hands, a gleam left on the camelias, acacias, and the
eyes so blind

three dead, eleven seriously injured and twenty-three
slightly injured

to the mornings that begin, to the numbers in the newspaper headlines, a provisional balance of the road accidents
caused by the storm alongside a graph of the week's average
temperatures, in centigrade, and rainfall, in millimetres per
square metre, a graph comparing this week with the same
week last year, the week beginning, three thousand two
hundred and seventeen accidents, twenty-two dead, seventy-
seven seriously injured, seven hundred and fifty-four slightly
injured, the graph shows that the number of dead decreased

a little, the number of seriously injured increased, the number of slightly injured diminished,

you can translate reality into numbers but that won't make you control it

on this day that is just beginning I make my debut in a set of numbers, I still don't know which category I belong in, nor do I know yet whether I can choose between casualty, dead, seriously injured, slightly injured, unscathed or whether that is the sole prerogative of the employee that the men handed me over to, the one responsible for the paperwork, it must be the employee that decides which category I belong in, better like that, in any case I don't mind being part of a number, I have been one my whole life, numbered among the obese, the literate, the single mothers, the self-employed, the car users, the smokers, the active tax payers, the agnostic, those who read less than a book a month, those who practise unsafe sex, those who have never left the country, those who do not keep pets, those who do no physical exercise, those who will eat anything, those who sleep on their backs, those who snore, I don't mind being part of a number, numbers confer some order to my existence, on this day that is just beginning I make my debut in a group of numbers and as part of a number I can be added to the child whose lungs were crushed by the family car's plate metal, the child is also part of a number that, like all other numbers, can be subtracted, the child's parents unscathed, death and life a series of random events, before becoming part of a number the child was travelling with the parents and asked them for a chocolate,

when we get home

the child smiled and thought about chocolate, children can waste a lot of time thinking about complicated things like chocolates, how long until we get home, the child asked, the parents said they were going slowly because of the storm, the child did not know what a storm was but if it had would not have been afraid because it did not know about the danger of being on the road, the child knew almost nothing, it was strapped into a child seat in the rear of the car having serious thoughts about a chocolate, asking if it could have one of the chocolates in the red wrapper, the parents laughed,

when we get home

and the child asked if it could have one of the chocolates with the biscuit, the parents pretended not to know what biscuit the child meant, the one with the biscuit is in a blue wrapper, the child explained, and the parents continued to pretend they did not know, the parents were playing with the child, they don't remember hearing the thump but they remember a terrible silence, the cruellest, most atrocious, most unjustified silence, the journey was over and the child had behaved but there is something wrong about this story, the child became part of a number that, like any other number, does not like chocolate, besides the child cannot say

to its parents, in its new state, that it does not need chocolates, the parents will spend the rest of their lives blaming
the road, the storm, the driver that rammed them, fate, the
number the child has become part of excludes some of
the other numbers the parents had dreamed of, the number
of children who will get a present next Christmas, who will
start school, who will go down park slides, who will learn
to ride a bicycle, the parents mourn the child who is now
excluded from the numbers he once belonged to, the
number of children who like chocolate, who go to the circus
at Christmas, who listen to a bed-time story,

reality beyond the realm of numbers is almost always
incomprehensible

me and the child are added to the boy who borrowed his
mother's car, I just have to get something from Dad's place,
his mother tried to dissuade him, not with this rain, but the
boy, I have to go, is it really that important, the boy said yes,
but in this weather, son, I don't think it's a good idea, please
I have to go, what can possibly be so urgent, the son did not
want to say, it's just something I have to do, the mother was
worried about the storm but picked up the car keys and gave
them to the boy, drive carefully, the son left the living room
whistling a song that plays often on the radio, the mother
sat down to correct her students' tests, already wearing his
windbreaker the son came back to kiss her goodbye, I'll be
back in a moment, and slammed the door shut behind him,
the mother heard the lift taking him down, turned back to

correcting tests, in this sonnet the poet is sad because his lover left him, the teacher underlines and scribbles in red, regretful, the teacher underlines the relevant verse,

if I could turn back

and continues marking, one test, two, three, a pile of corrected papers, another pile of papers yet to be corrected, the teacher is fed up with teaching the language of poets, days are too short for what she has to make of them, she lights a cigarette and starts to think that perhaps one day her husband, her son's father, the ex-husband, the only sweetheart she ever had, will write her a sonnet as regretful as the poet's, perhaps one day, the mother corrects tests, the son drives carefully to his father's house, a ten-minute journey, the boy is going to recover a photograph

how do you come up with those ideas, Violeta

of the girl he is in love with, it is the first time he's been in love, the mother finishes smoking her cigarette, she has a rule of not having more than five a day, she starts boiling water for a cup of tea, a cup of tea is comforting on a cold night like this, the son will want a hot chocolate, when the son comes back they will sit together and drink tea and hot chocolate and then go to bed, perhaps the son will tell her what he was looking for, the mother is still not used to her son keeping secrets, growing up, nineteen years old, she thinks, they grow so fast, at this moment the mother still does not know that her son is destined to never grow older than nineteen, to be nineteen forever, at this moment the mother does not know that her son just spent the last second of the time that his life comprised, a car driving the wrong way, two bright headlights dazzling him, nineteen years against a car driving the wrong way, at this moment the mother still does not know anything about the pain that will make her punch the wall with closed fists, shout, I killed him, it was me that killed him,

nineteen years lost to a car driving the wrong way

she will say, I killed our son, it was me that killed him, the ex-husband, the father of the boy tries to calm her down, it is not your fault, I will never forgive myself, nobody can help her, the woman looks at the man she thought she still loved but cannot feel anything, pain has taken over everything,

how do you come up with those ideas, Violeta

me, the child, the boy added up to another and then another until we have reached the number of the yearly tally, for now we are one of the numbers from the night of the storm

three dead, eleven seriously injured and twenty-three slightly injured

life and death as abstract and unreal as the numbers one, twenty, one thousand strangers saved, they mean the same as one, twenty, one thousand strangers murdered, nobody feels anything about numbers, numbers can be added, subtracted, divided and multiplied but cannot like choco-lates, cannot fall in love, cannot wage war against a million enemies,

bêtises, ma chérie, bêtises

the sun is rising and through the badly closed shutter of Dora's room seven slivers of light are filtering softly onto the birds and flowers in the iron bed, seven slivers of light scratching at the day without waking my child from the night in which she still sleeps, the radio presenter coming to life in the radio-alarm on the nightstand

a significant improvement in the weather from this after-noon, some early fog patches throughout the morning with some frost forming in the north

awakens the most perfect part of me, this day began like any other, Dora opens her eyes and spreads her sleepiness around the room, she yawns to expel her dreams, what did my child dream about this night, if indeed she did dream, nights are getting shorter, Dora's sleepy eyes wander around the room,

my eyes fixed on a drop of water as it clings

Dora stretches out her arm and presses the button that switches off the radio presenter, last night's storm caused three, then she pushes off her blankets, Dora sits on the edge of the bed, stands up, there is no particular will in any of these acts because they are repeated daily and repetition can dispense with will, Dora puts on a robe, fastens the robe's belt, steps into her slippers, half a dozen short steps to the toilet, she enters, sits on the lavatory, urinates, pulls open the shower curtains, flushes, lifts a leg and enters the cold bath, a chill runs through her and makes her blonde body hair stand up, peach fuzz, she runs the shower, there is a noise that sounds like the phone ringing but is drowned out by the running water, nobody calls this early, hot water sliding down her thin body, small, almost a child's, she is holding the showerhead against her chest, head against the wall, the mirror fogged up, a sprawling haze, Dora reaches for the soap and it slips away, a bell that sounds like the phone ringing, Dora lathers herself and lets the warm water strike her body, when she is done she once again puts her head against the wall, the pleasure of warm flesh, of pinkened skin, again the noise that sounds like the phone ringing,

pick up the phone, Dora

these men need to know that the smell of alcohol is a small detail that they mustn't get too hung up on, like the semen from the lorry driver at the service station, the screaming bright pink nails, the garish dress, the high-heel shoes, the men need to know that there are other details about my life, pick up the phone, Dora, tell these men that this night was no different from any other, I was travelling for business,

I stopped at a service station, Denise and Betty are waiting for me, I am a good saleswoman, the best, pick up the phone before I, before the men

say the word Ângelo, because words hurt less when they are spoken

hang up, the too-hot water, the stirred flesh, Dora is now certain that the phone is ringing but is enjoying the water streaming down her body, she thinks, if it's important they'll call back, it must be nothing, a mistake, somebody called another number and it came through here, phone numbers have to travel along such intricate paths that it is only normal that some might get lost, Dora turns off the shower, her skin reddened instead of the usual whiteness I created, blood running more quickly, heart racing, the packed suitcase in the bedroom, the most perfect part of me determined to leave,

I'm leaving home tomorrow

my child's voice no longer hurts me, maybe one of the advantages of the day having started without me, the sun is rising ouside Ângelo's two basement rooms, on the road I was driving down, on the house I took my revenge against, on Denise's bedroom, on Villa Elizabete, on the service station, on the meeting room where I signed the deeds yesterday, on my wrecked car, on the empty ground where I landed, of all the mysteries I choose that of light

and the light is never the same, seven slivers of light through the badly closed shutter on Travessa do Paraíso, a glimmer on Ângelo's awning, the dazzle of headlamps on the road, bright spots piercing the cracked roof tiles of the house I just sold, a bird singing outside Denise's window, the smell of soap at Villa Elizabete, the noise of the café at the service station, pale yellow light on the polished tabletop where I signed the deeds, the sheen of my car's twisted metal, the desolation of the empty ground where I landed, light is never the same

and yet light, only light flooding over everything

on this day that might have started without me, I was always late for my own future, this time it is not just a delay, it is something more serious, I must hurry up if I want to be on time for a day I can still be part of, I have to catch up with the time that life is made of, Dora picks up the phone,

dirty snitch

Ângelo with a handkerchief over the transmitter to disguise his voice

your time has come, now you'll pay for everything

threatening my father who also happened to be his father, life is filled with absurdity, Ângelo with two hands clutching the handset, leaning over by the jade elephant with its trunk turned towards the door for good luck, Ângelo determined to avenge the young boy who spent hours standing at the end of the street hating us, the boy who said how are you senhor whenever my father entered the hovel where he lived, and then, always polite, I'm calling my mother, Ângelo's father who died the morning he wore his black shiny tailcoat, with his shoes gleaming, Ângelo's father dead next to a young woman dressed as a bride, Ângelo holding his mother's hand and wearing an itchy woollen jumper, asking, only moments before his father died, who that lady was dressed in white and standing next to his father, Ângelo's mother crouching, in her eyes two embers of rage, that man is not your father, your father died, Ângelo cried like any boy would cry when he finds out his father is dead, Ângelo cried for the death of a father who was wearing his shiny black tailcoat while standing alongside a very pretty lady wearing a tulle veil on the grass on a sunny morning, Ângelo's newly dead father acting as if he'd forgotten he knew the boy,

the dead are almost all forgotten

Ângelo started to hate the pretty lady dressed in white with a long veil standing on the grass, a tiara with fake diamonds on her head, Cinderella shoes, at that precise moment he started his habit of hating us,

that man does not know you, never forget that you don't know him either tell them you know me

it's funny how all habits have an origin that may even appear irrelevant, like the streets filled with red carnations, or stupid Clarissa's son appearing on television in camouflage uniform, all habits have an origin that we sometimes forget, when did the boys first start inviting me down to a basement, when did the other girls run away from the infectious disease that my reputation seemed to have become, Ângelo developed the habit of hating us the day his father died which is why

you cannot correct the past but you can redress it, full stop

he denounced my father to the revolutionaries,

that man who forgot to acknowledge me the day he was dressed in a tailcoat is a snitch

Ângelo pointed his finger at my father one afternoon when the sky was the colour of the sky and the flowers were the colour of flowers, Ângelo was still a good-looking boy, far from the scarecrow hired to provide entertainment for dances at social clubs, old folks' outings, children's birthdays, that perfect afternoon my parents

tell them you know me

were once again surrounded like the day of their wedding, revolutionary guests, same thing, only people, many, coming too close, becoming unpleasant, not knowing how to behave, perhaps that is why my mother did not notice how much the boy looked like the bridegroom, the long arms, the enormous hands, scarecrows, or how much the leader of the revolutionary gang looked like her husband,

these people will make anything up to save their skins

when my father raised his head to see Ângelo he had the look of a loser, the mob started dispersing, my mother looked at Ângelo, at me, Ângelo and I were both standing on the same side,

nobody can distinguish a bastard from a freak

Ângelo shoved my father with his hands, he had already tried to kick him but had failed to connect with my father's body as it toppled over without anyone touching it, my mother not losing her composure, a lady

always *chic, très chic*

who confronted the revolutionaries, I am sure there must be a mistake, we are not the people you are looking for,

the freak and the bastard, united, will never be

no-one like our children to hurt us

my parents were free of the people mobbing them and Ângelo lost forever the chance to be an angel that saved them, if Ângelo had listened to my father's plea,

tell them you know me

this man has never done any harm to anyone, only to me

by freeing him from the mob my mother made the bastard forever miss out on the chance to be an angel that saved them, my mother would not have been able to tolerate a revolutionary saviour, a communist maid, a black grand-daughter, my mother was always convinced that there is an order to all things, or a nature to all things, as she would say it, bastards are vengeful and cannot be angels, angels have to be white, maids are not clever enough to be commu-nists or anything else, despite the mob having dissolved my mother clung to my father, keeping the promise

in sickness and in health, in joy and in sorrow, mobbed or free to go, as long as we both shall live

that she made on the day that Ângelo witnessed his father's death, my mother's hand so elegant with her fingernails painted in pearl-coloured polish, a lady must never paint her fingernails in garish pink, no, it wasn't only that, a lady must not be afraid of a gang of thugs even when they are disguised as revolutionaries,

let's go, Baltazar, it looks like these people don't know
what they want

my mother acting as if the revolutionaries did not know what
they wanted to do about the revolution, I mean, about their
hostages, my mother acting as if she did not know what to
do with my father who implored the leader of the revolutionaries,

tell them who I am

who did not know what to do about the boy that looked so
much like the bridegroom that entered the church on the
day of her wedding, the young man that now looked so much
like her husband, suddenly my mother knew she had to
pull my father away and they had to start walking, Ângelo
did not wave as he did that morning when the newlyweds
left in a black car, he stood there dreaming up revenges, of
all the revenges he chose the cruellest, the one he is still
performing today

I understand everything that happened, it could not have
been different

because it is revenge that keeps him attached to life, he
cannot abandon his two miserable rooms so he will always
remember that he has something to do, he spends hours
standing at the end of our street, denounce his father to the
revolutionaries, harass his father and the wife, knock up

the freak sister, the two miserable basement rooms serve to remind him that he has something to do, Dora picks up the phone, an unknown man's voice might unsettle my child but so many people call to conduct phone surveys, there is so much deceit, the man confirms my name, my car's licence plate, simple questions that Dora replies to while wrapped up in the bathroom towel, very simple questions that do not frighten Dora, if the questions were harder Dora might be nervous but they are easier than the questions in any television contest, my name, my address, my car's licence plate,

she was in an accident last night

Dora gathers all the little yellow papers left lying around the house and none of the messages says anything about being in an accident, the last message I wrote, please buy some bread, the penultimate one, call electrician, the one before that, stop at cobbler, no message that said, have car accident, the man's voice crashes into Dora's silence, deep lament, none of the little yellow papers said, don't forget deep lament, to lament me deeply, the man's voice insisting on something that sounds like

someone to identify the body

a request, a formality, the man's voice strident when compared to the silence that Dora is keeping because she can't imagine there is nothing that silence won't kill

how to acknowledge that the body that gave birth to her is dead, that the flesh it is made of is now rotting, that the blood running in its veins stopped, Dora is ashen, the man's voice coming from the place where my body is kept, the body's bulk, this is a difficulty that murderers come up against in police novels, a body's bulk is difficult to hide, getting rid of it requires serious effort,

everything you touch dies

it was a moment of carelessness, we cannot guarantee that we will never hurt ourselves,

everything you touch dies

sooner or later a moment of carelessness like when Alice was looking at the bird-filled sky, carelessness, the man's voice in the place where my body is being kept and Dora walking around the house not knowing where to stop, a lump in the throat, Dora wrapped in her bath towel without shedding a single tear, the man's voice tripping up with opening hours, if that doesn't suit just come whenever you can, an unpleasant matter that Dora's silence cannot solve,

bêtises, ma chérie, bêtises

there's nothing we can do

my child's pain wanders around the house without knowing how to find its way back to the body that trembles with cold, a thin body, almost child-like and wrapped in a bath towel, she walks past the half-open door to my bedroom, lies down on my bed, is there anything we can help with, asks the man's voice at the other end of the line, Dora pictures me in the place where my body is being kept, she pleads for mercy from the pain that is sitting in the place on the sofa that I used to sit on, a pain that squeezes her throat and prevents her from asking where the accident happened, what time, Dora's silence tangled up with the details that are also part of death, the man's voice, a deep lament, and Dora's silence seeking the hatred it was accustomed to, the shame, anything to replace the pain that won't let her breathe, Dora knows from her grandparents' deaths that those who outlive the ones they love also die a little, it is possible to die little by little and slowly, death may not be in a hurry, Dora sits up on the bed where I will never lie down again and wants to cry to be freed of the heaviness pressing on her chest, inside her chest, claws scratching her heart, the most perfect part of me can hear me and doesn't know

you were born to give me the certainty that there was someone able to hurt me

how to live her first day of freedom, a whole life spent serving one specific need and suddenly my child's life is left without justification, freedom can be frightening, Dora is merely an easily replaceable uniform at the hypermarket checkout, despite Dora's absence the hypermarket works normally without anyone noting any difference no matter how small, the same light, too white, the loud music, too loud, nothing different in the vegetables, the baby nappies, the cleaning products, the charcuterie, the frozen items, nothing different other than

manager to checkout counter number ten, please

Dora's absence, which nobody notices since another woman with the same uniform and the same smile has replaced her,

so alike one another, you can't even tell them apart by their uniforms

another woman has replaced Dora who is lying on my bed anticipating the fear of finding me, blue-tinged skin, my hair pulled back in a strange hairdo,

nothing like the classic hairdos, *ma chérie*

hands crossed over my chest, no, at the moment my arms are still stretched alongside my body, Dora is lying on my bed when the artist rings the doorbell,

José, is it so hard to say José

when José rings the doorbell, Dora thinks it is a neighbour trying to say something, a problem with the intercom,

advertising, the postman, always so many reasons for someone to be ringing the doorbell that Dora opens the door,
when she sees the artist her heart, still hurting a moment
ago, beats faster, so this is the jolt that people always talk
about, this contentment that seems so inappropriate in the
circumstances,

I have heard about love

is anything wrong, he was worried, you didn't go to work,
you're not answering your phone, and you come to the door
wrapped in a towel and didn't even ask who it was, you
shouldn't do that, what if it was a burglar, Dora steps back,
the artist

José, is it so hard

falls quiet, the happiness in Dora's heart vanishes slowly, she
has to say that, she has to say, my mother, how do you say
it, the artist waits, I woke up feeling indisposed, my child
was always a good liar, a gift she was born with, but I feel
better now, and José,

you heard me say José

did something happen, nothing, no, nothing happened,
Dora unable to hear the words forming inside her, waking
up unwell but now feeling better, a bad dream, I just need
to rest a little, Dora stunned in the absence I have become,

unable to stop reading the last message I wrote, please buy bread, the bread I like is still being sold at the bakery, the kitchen table where I kept it is in the same place, if everything remains the same why does Dora not go and buy bread, why doesn't she leave it on the kitchen table, never upturned because it's bad luck, if nothing has changed why is Dora not able to buy bread, not today and not ever again, the irony of the meaningless things for which we will be remembered, the bread I like, a written message, my child's agony, the most perfect part of me, or the most perfect part of what I was, trying hard not to cry in front of

this time I went too far

the artist who wonders why she is indisposed, my child did well to put the pain she is feeling into the category of ailments that pass quickly,

of all the mysteries I choose that of pain, which brings oblivion

my child always knew how to play, a good adversary, the best, pretending her pain is an ailment that will pass quickly, even if she can feel the unusual violence of the pain that she innocently thought she had tamed after her grandparents' death, even if she feels the terrible pain my child resists, a good daughter, the best, are you sure you are OK, I only need to sleep and wake up again, better to speak tonight, I can stay here in the living room while you sleep, no, please don't stay, Dora leads him to the door, don't worry, I'll be fine, a quick kiss on the lips and the artist walks out, goes down the staircase, Dora opens the door, no, she will not call out for him, the artist looks back at her from the bottom of the staircase, Dora asks, do you notice anything different about me, the artists does not understand, Dora explains, in my face, my body, anything, the artist looks at her from downstairs,

I am forever too far away

a mortal looking at an angel that is distant as only angels can be, the artist does not know what to reply, don't worry, we'll speak tonight, when she is alone Dora sits on the sofa, my death is invisible in the most perfect part of me, and for the first time she looks carefully at the painting I bought a few years ago in a Chinese shop, the mountains so green, the sky so blue, on one side a button to start some tinny music and on top another button to switch on a little bulb that lights it up, when I brought it home Dora could not stop squealing that

how do you come up with these things, Violeta

this was obvious proof of my bad taste, she refused to help me hang that horrible thing on the wall, and now Dora looks for me in the Chinese landscape, she takes my place on the sofa, she nestles in the hollow my body carved out over the years, looks at the oddly green mountains beneath an oddly blue sky, she tries to like what I liked,

maybe we won't die as long as someone still feels what
we do

she does not want to calm herself, Dora notices for the first
time the comically disproportionate horses' necks, the unin-
tentionally crossed-eyed Chinese woman, things that might
make her want to laugh,

maybe we won't die as long as someone laughs with us

my adversary defeats me with all the things I am no longer
able to feel, with all the things I am no longer able to do, this
time there is no stalemate, my adversary has defeated me,
I should feel the defeat of the final fight, I should feel the
bitter taste of defeat, nothing, I feel nothing, Dora defeated
me, finally an uncontested winner in one of our contests,
Dora gets up from the sofa, feels light-headed, for a few
seconds she leans against a table, she has to get ready to go
to the place where I am waiting for her to certify what I
was, our own flesh is sure to have some certainties about us,
when she says my name

the name of a flower that is also a colour

a man points the way to the room where I am waiting for
her, I don't mind waiting, I was always able to entertain
myself with anything, like the idea of being dead or some
other such silliness, another man greets her after she has
gone through many doors, corridors, the paths that take us

to others are always long and confusing, we get easily lost in them, another man brings her to me, Dora looks at my body, stunned, it is not my mother, I don't know this tender body, discreet, the body that belonged to my mother was overblown, immoderate, Dora's faint voice says to the man,

it's her

get me out of here, get me out of here, the man helps Dora who is stumbling, poor child,

look at the state I'm in

my mother lying on a hospital bed in a nursing home, not yet in the room with the unbearable light, tell me if I deserve this,

be quiet, mother

how can I be sure that I'm not confusing my stories, mixing my conversations,

reeking of alcohol

I can't even distinguish the men who are helping Dora, is this the one who brought her to me or is he the one who pointed her down the corridors, if these men are indistinguishable I cannot hold on to a distinct final image of my life like the human resources manager taught Dora, if these men do not cooperate it is difficult for me to be persuaded to come back to life, Dora thinks of the secrets that will remain forever hidden in the body she has just left behind,

my father

details that are irrelevant to our history, in our history there is only one truly important fact, do you hear me, Dora, are you able to hear me, you were born so I could experience love, you were born to save me from myself, that is the only secret you need to discover

bêtises, ma chérie, bêtises

a secret is always a misunderstanding

because secrets cannot be unveiled, just to think that my father wanted to share with me his little secret, the work of a lifetime thrown away in a moment of desperation, I told him to be quiet, I could not let him throw away an entire life, I even wonder whether your grandfather was OK in the head, I wouldn't be surprised at all to know that he had gone crazy,

come here, little birdie

you are so stubborn, I have told you so many times, your father picked up that habit as he might have picked up any other disease,

the most perfect part of me instead of becoming a single being, a part

don't change the subject, I have the right to know who my father is

don't think about this now because suffering stokes what is worst in us, suffering makes us worse than we ever thought we might be, it is finished, everything is finished

full stop, or better, a gelled asterisk

be quiet, Ângelo

Ângelo

it's a theory, a theory like any other

I'm not interested in theories

be quiet, Dora

everything is a theory

life is a theory with no thesis

how do you come up with these things, Violeta

we never were one single thing, we were incompatible parts, the bastard and the freak

I recognised the bastard from seeing him standing at the end of our road, you were the first one I saw among the gang of thugs that wanted to mug us, your father never knew or never wanted to know that I too spent hours standing outside the two miserable rooms hating you, forgiveness is not in my hands, even if I had let your father tell me his little secret I could not have forgiven him, your father loved that creature and the bastard like I never thought him capable of loving, a habit, nothing more than one of the many habits that hurt me,

the refrains in our histories are so tedious

you should not ask questions when bodies are quietened forever, Dora identifies my body, she bends over me and cries, I also cried when the midwife separated us, quietly at first but then out loud, louder, when the midwife cut the umbilical chord

never again one whole being

and I heard Dora cry, the only thing I felt was her death in me, that is why I cried, nobody had warned me that all lives are born from a death, I was not prepared

also nobody ever warned me that all lives are born for a death

to feel so alone, I have never felt as alone as on the day when the most perfect part of me was pulled from within me, after crying on top of me Dora walks away held up by one of the men, stumbling,

look at that poor daughter lost in grief

when she is alone she picks up her mobile phone and calls the artist, she has to speak to the artists before it is too late,

there is nothing that silence won't kill

Dora wants to tell the artist that she cannot exchange her life for nothing, that the flesh I made her from cannot be transformed into stone because lifeless bodies are terrifying, Dora walks out of the building and dials the artist's number, she wants the artist to listen to her before it's too late,

come find me because I'm alone

at the other end, is that you, Dora, I can't hear you, Dora remains quiet without saying any of the things she has been thinking about, now that she is certain there is somebody who will respond to her call, who will call her, she hangs up and cries again, quietly at first, but then out loud, louder, Dora bent over my body, now cold for the first time, seeking my flesh, now fully surrendered, seeking my eyes, forever closed, seeking my words, forever silenced, seeking me, forever dead, Dora bent over me crying loudly like the day when she was born, like the day when the sentence I condemned us to, the sentence we were both condemned to, was served

compassion is the only thing we can offer others,

my sympathies

thank you, many thanks, a handshake, a hug, a quick kiss on the cheek, it depends on the person, on the intimacy, on the circumstances of the greeting, gestures retain some surprises unlike words that repeat themselves in the same refrains, my condolences, she was still so young, my commiserations, we will miss her, she did not deserve to go so soon, poor thing, nobody really hears what they say, what is said, words

bêtises, ma chérie, bêtises

in a confused jumble that vanishes into the walls of the mortuary chapel, yellowing, the chapel walls are so ugly, words blend into a murmur that moves away from the flame of the candles flickering next to the coffin, Napoleon model, suggested by the funeral director, I prefer undertaker, a name that suits the profession much better, who is always changing the words, high quality wood, as promised by the same funeral director, aggrieved words stabbing the crucified Christ's lanced flank, the Virgin's exposed heart, give us the suffering of others and deliver us from our own, amen

I don't understand why people come to watch such a poor performance, the décor is terrible despite the Napoleon model proposed by the funeral director, the protagonist is always and will forever be quiet, I don't understand why there should be spectators for this sort of show, if Ângelo performed some magic that actually worked or if, for a change, he told a good joke,

in the end the heart was so weak, so weak that instead of beating it got beaten up

perhaps Ângelo should perform at wakes, fear causes laughter, nervous guffaws that bounce against the yellowed walls, the supporting actors have practised their air of sorrow at other performances, the hugs they almost mean, the supporting actors are very professional, they save the show from being the fiasco that the leading actor condemns it to,

the dead are all forgotten

the supporting actors talk about the future, nothing makes the future as urgent as a death interrupting it, they insist on the duty to carry on,

drive on the right and with caution, the living wish you a pleasant journey the refrains of duty are so tedious, I mean, the refrains of a wake

for this show Ângelo should have worn his satin suit and the frilly shirt instead of this unflattering black suit, he looks even more bug-eyed, his arms look even longer, if he was never able to show up in the right place at the right time then he certainly wasn't going to start doing it today, a day like any other, Ângelo showed up at my house carrying a bunch of lilies, as soon as the door opened he made a tasteless little joke,

I came to check if you needed anything

I don't need anything, the advantage of being in this state is that you never again need anything

Dora thanked him and said she didn't need anything

I haven't stopped thinking about your fight at the restaurant yesterday, your words have been going round my head all night long, even though I am used to you and her having arguments

there is nothing worse than a scarecrow that thinks of itself as a mediator, I was worried yesterday, as if he could foresee that the worst would happen, Ângelo never understood that every argument between Dora and me made us closer, a scarecrow unable to undertake the revenges he plotted, a scarecrow scared by a harmless threat,

I'm leaving home tomorrow

your mother just says those things but she loves you, after all she was the one who brought you to life, you are flesh of her flesh, blood of her blood, nothing can change that,

Baltazar, anyone in your family with a knack for spouting nonsense

the tumour grew inside my mother, flesh of my mother's flesh, blood of my mother's blood, the doctors, dozens of doctors that my mother went to see in hope, hope, the trap that no moribund can escape,

I'm leaving your life tomorrow, *ma chérie*, I'm leaving your life tomorrow

the tumour, which was flesh of my mother's flesh, blood of my mother's blood, killed her in the end, nothing and no-one can alter that, in any case I never thought so many would come to watch such a poor performance, they don't stop coming, the man who just came in tightly hugs another and then another, he would hug everyone there if only they would let him, the proximity of death has the magic power of making people ridiculous, if these men ran into each other anywhere else they would not be hugging like this, they would not have these expressions that are meant to be grief-stricken but are only risible, they would not be telling stories, it is appropriate though not entirely *chic, très chic* to be telling stories that the dead person was part of,

she wanted to go to Paris, the last time I saw her she said
she wanted to go to Paris

but it is not appropriate to rejoice about the things that the
dead person was unable to achieve while still alive, the living
only do that to make the time they have left seem more
important, anyway it is a form of malice that the dead no
longer care about, the dead are so indifferent,

the living are so tedious

from this strange position time appears to me as I had never
imagined it before, crickets are chirping in my ears, chirp
chirp, eyes blinded by a drop of light, Dora crying, the card-
playing companions letting out a stream of trivialities, the
death of people we know, of people we don't know, serves
only to distract us from our own death, the time of the living
acquires a greater importance, the acts of the living, even
the most trifling, become inordinately special,

three down, victim of a car accident, seven letters

penultimate letter is t

I try to dispel the silence that all lives are made of, I speak
very loudly, almost a shout, I am frightened, I don't know
any animal more frightened, to defeat the silence I cling
on to my fear, at this point only fear can save me from this
blizzard of hands, faces and flowers, the noise of cellophane
paper irritates me, an unpleasant noise,

three down, victim of a prolonged illness, seven letters

penultimate letter is t

Violeta

Celeste

Dora sleeps on the iron bed with birds and flowers on the headboard certain that she hates me, the hypermarket uniform is on the back of a chair, not a single wrinkle, the seven slivers of light have not yet reached the badly closed shutter, morning has not yet started in Dora's bedroom, Maria da Guia is constantly skulking near my mother's coffin, a dog whimpering for its departed owner,

    does senhora need anything

Maria da Guia without the uniform that distinguishes her from the other maids, I don't scold her only because there are no other maids, if there were it would be a problem, they are all so alike, the same skin tone, the same oily sheen, the smell of soap, eyes lowered as if in a silent protest that will never leave their lips, wide hips, strong arms, calloused hands, if there were other maids it would be hard to tell them apart,

    when we are given one life we don't know how to live another, menina these people only do what they shouldn't, everything these people do is wrong, when we are given one life we move straight away into another, without looking back at the life we left behind, without thinking about the life that awaits us, Maria da Guia could make some *petits fours* for these people who are so exhausted from pretending to be sad, I don't know how she would serve them in this overcrowded chapel, in any case it would have been a nice thing to do, a gesture that would have spoken well of any maid, Maria da Guia did not make the *petits fours* because she cannot do anything without receiving a direct order, serve the drinks in that tray, when you're done bring the platter with the veal *canapés*, Maria da Guia never did anything she had not been ordered to do, someone must have told her to put on those sad eyes, Dora, or Ângelo, or Denise, I will have to find out who gave her that order,

do you need anything, menina

where's your head at, Maria da Guia, it is not me you need to ask, it's my mother, maybe senhora needs something, a magazine, the eyeglasses she left in her bedside table drawer, it is not like my mother to forget everything, she prepared for our trips to stay with the bumpkins long beforehand so she would not forget anything, the *nécessaire* filled with face creams,

in this place even the air burns the skin, I would not be surprised if someone told me this is where hell is the suitcase full of dresses that impressed the bumpkins, a bag filled with shoes, matching handbags, the jewellery box with real pearls, the perfume that sweetened the smell of the house in a losing battle against the stench of the pigswill, the wine barrels, the oil, my mother, pretty and elegant, proof that the bumpkins had done well to reject Ângelo's mother, when they prevented my father from chasing after her, the bumpkins did what they had to do, in fact

we didn't make all those sacrifices to see you married to a maid

the bastard himself acknowledges it, my father was not going to throw away the life he had ahead of him just because he had knocked up a maid, creatures like her learn that skill early on in life, Ângelo's father who had fallen for the world's oldest trap was moved when he saw his son, were it not for the bumpkins Ângelo's father would have thrown away the life he had ahead of him, there is no shadow of a doubt that the bumpkins did the right thing when they chased the tramp away and refused to even look at the bastard, like they did not look at the litters of puppies and kittens that they drowned in the well, the bumpkins could not run the risk of becoming attached, the bumpkins did everything right but could not stop the bastard from growing up with revenge in his blood, the bastard took advantage of the first opportunity he had and then it was my father's turn to understand, the bastard was not going to throw away the life he had ahead of him with a revenge to carry out, my father understood the dozens of anonymous phone calls, the bundles of letters with cut-out newspaper type, the denunciation to the revolutionary committee, there was not a single revenge that the bastard put into place that my father did not understand, it was all a matter of opportunity, he did not do it maliciously, the problem was having had the opportunity,

knock up his freak sister

stupid Clarissa, who came to offer my mother tears she did not need, she too had never imagined that her stupid son would become so important but the opportunity came up and he took it, the bastard and stupid Clarissa's son could have been friends, besides not wasting an opportunity they have other things in common, they both bought the poster of the blonde boy putting a red carnation in a machine gun barrel, both sang about the seagull that flew, flew, after some time, just enough, the reasonable amount, they ripped the posters off their walls and forgot about the song's lyrics,

revolutions are fleeting

every now and then stupid Clarissa puts a handkerchief to her eyes, she has taken part in many such performances and is always well behaved, there is nothing to say, her handkerchief smells of lavender, all those afternoons playing cards with the smell of lavender from stupid Clarissa's handkerchief, stupid Clarissa taking on more airs than ever because her son is now appearing on the television almost every day, he is a *full-time politician* and *part-time opinion maker*, jobs titles are getting stranger every day,

once there was a chameleon that changed so much, so much, so much that by the time anyone saw him he had become a dinosaur

and the curse of English, if only people still used the most beautiful language in the world, stupid Clarissa's son has got rid of his beard and his camouflage uniform,

fashion is fickle

now he appears on the television in a suit and tie and is exactly like all others who appeared on the television in a suit and tie just like before he was exactly like all others who appeared with beards and in camouflage uniform, the only thing that drives stupid Clarissa's son

you can only tell maids apart by their uniforms, if it weren't for the uniforms it would be a problem

is to be the same as others, it was thanks to that concern that he became a much sought-after *opinion maker*, stupid Clarissa's son an *opinion maker* or even better an *opinion killer* because opinions can only be had but not made, on television stupid Clarissa's son always says half a dozen words in English to appear more competent, *chic, très chic*

and to justify his high living standard, stupid Clarissa's son is so important that he now even features in some of the scandals reported in newspapers,

soon, very soon, nobody will remember anything

stupid Clarissa as proud of her son as she is of the *pacemaker* that they put into her in a private clinic, she thinks her son and her *pacemaker* the best in the world, stupid Clarissa still weeping anyway because envy is the worst thing of all,

in the old days there were fewer envies, fewer envious people,

and because she has not understood that this country is so ungrateful to those who serve it, even the most loyal like her son, stupid Clarissa who came to my mother's funeral to test, once again, her *pacemaker*'s efficacy and who can watch the spectacle with no worries because the device ensures that her heart will beat normally, stupid Clarissa spared from feeling things irregularly, a normalised pulse that in Maria da Guia's opinion will end up killing her from boredom, Maria da Guia is not an *opinion killer* only because nobody pays her for the half dozen truths she serves up to those who will listen,

if we don't die of one thing we'll die of another

she is only a maid and the voice of a maid never made it very far and much less to heaven, not even the maids' heaven if such a thing exists, a small rented room, no more than five square metres because these creatures feel uncomfortable in large spaces,

soon, very soon, *chacun à sa place*

soon, very soon, nobody will remember stupid Clarissa's revolutionary son, stupid Clarissa's politician son, stupid Clarissa's *opinion maker* son, soon, very soon, nobody will remember anything, it took some time, quite a lot, for Maria da Guia

nobody can escape the place they belong in

to understand the place she belonged to, some time, quite a lot, and she gave up on the communist boyfriend, some time, immense, a lifetime, and she forgot about the communist boyfriend, some time, and Maria da Guia still doesn't know if she did the right thing, these creatures are never sure about anything, every now and then Maria da Guia thinks she could have risked becoming one of the old fashioned poor, like the old, or blacks, or gypsies, or bumpkins, fashion is implacable, Maria da Guia remained forever in the place she belongs to and is waiting for something she can't quite identify since

when we are given one life we can't have another

the wish to die is not allowed, Maria da Guia does not know the wish to rest her body forever, the wish to end her life, that's why

> God gives it to us, God takes it away, menina, everything else is the work of sinner souls that will wander in Purgatory forever

she continues to put up with a body that only ever served for working, she does it in pursuit of a duty that makes her happy, even if sometimes she stumbles upon the life she might have had, even then Maria da Guia is happy, she understood that life is no more than time that always passes, a simple thought because she never had much of an imagination, she always told me the same story, so I could see that she was an unimaginative creature,

> once upon a time there was a woman who gave the world her eight children

when Maria da Guia was in a good mood she would embellish the story with cemetery gates opening on their own at midnight, or with thirteen black cats announcing the death of the villagers, sometimes in a moment of carelessness she would put herself into the story, I was the sixth child, after me there were still two others,

> eight children all alive, my mother would say that she was blessed in not having lost any one of them but that could only mean she was cursed

when she put herself in the story she became very cautious, the menina cannot tell her mother that I am telling you this, Maria da Guia must have known the woman in the story very well because she always described her in the same way, without changing a word, very tall and strong, a black shawl wrapped around her shoulders, black eyes, blacker than burnt wood,

once upon a time there was a woman, very tall and strong, who gave the world her eight children

if your mother had not liked me my mother would have given me to another house, by that point there were only five of us because the three eldest had been given away, the woman's skin was harder than a piece of leather, her hands as big as spades, and on her feet were wooden clogs as noisy as an oxcart,

all children belong to the world, I don't understand the story

and did she have any warts, I asked, trying to imagine the witch that Maria da Guia was talking about, no, she did not have any warts, or a broom to fly around like in the stories the menina reads in books, this woman had eight children and not even a piece of bread to give them, so she had to get rid of them,

that woman did what all women have done since the world began she killed them, I asked, trying to dramatise the story, it depends on what the menina means by killing them, when the woman chose a child to give away that child knew it no longer belonged to the house, it would never belong again, never again, what does never again mean,

I also gave the world the only daughter I had

if the menina is always asking questions I can't get to the end of the story, the woman had a daughter who was very well behaved and who liked her parents and her siblings, and because she was so well behaved the girl never thought that one day it would be her turn, she was convinced that her mother was going to keep her until her old age, it was normal for mothers to keep a daughter to look after them in their old age, one day, the girl had gone to the village fountain, the mother called out to her, the girl left the buckets and ran towards the mother, perhaps the mother needed something, she was in a hurry and didn't notice the old women, everyone knew that it was bad luck to cross paths with the old women, very bad luck, when she was in a garrulous mood Maria da Guia would talk about these old women who muttered rotten curses to give bad luck to everyone who passed them by, the girl was in a hurry and ran into them, the old women were angry, perhaps that is where the bad luck started, even today the girl can't be sure, sometimes Maria da Guia replaced the old women with a cripple who spent his day lying down on a pallet outside a tavern downing glasses of wine, lying on the pallet all day long covered in flies and waiting for the tavern keeper to remember to entertain his customers, the tavern keeper would take a piece of rock-hard bread and give it to the cripple who would start bleeding from the mouth, the cripple would placate his hunger with the piece of hard bread that hurt his mouth and the tavern keeper's customers had fun with that, they had to be entertained somehow, Maria da Guia might add small variations to the story but always arrived at the same conclusion, of all the things I learned in life, menina, of all the things I learned in life the only thing I never forgot is that cruelty is a bottomless well, this conclusion and the woman with the eight children were the only things that remained the same in the story that Maria da Guia would tell, the old women, the cripple, the cemetery gates, the black cats, were always changing, which annoyed me, Maria da Guia would become visibly moved when she told the part about the mother wiping her face and the girl's hands with a handkerchief and telling her to put on her best clothes, the girl realised her turn had come and started crying, the mother came closer, the wooden clogs were even noisier and her voice was loud as thunder, if you cry in front of those people I'll give you a proper hiding, I'll thrash you so hard you won't be able to move for days, the girl did not cry anymore and did not ask to stay, she could have promised not to annoy the old women, or never again to speak to the cripple at the tavern, she could have promised but she kept quiet instead and her mother said, I'm giving you what nobody gave me, if you stay here you'll be just one more mangy girl crawling with children and with headlice, I'm giving you what nobody gave me, a warm place to sleep and enough food to eat,

and the world welcomed my only daughter

Maria da Guia would take her time over the telling of this part, which made me impatient, I would ask about the thirteen cats, this time the cats are not in the story, Maria da Guia would say, I want the part with the cats, if you don't tell me the part with the cats I'll tell my mother you're telling me the story, Maria da Guia would get fretful, the menina is a naughty girl, the menina is a very naughty girl, if you carry on like that you'll end up in hell,

and my only daughter is still happy today

I did not want to cause Maria da Guia any trouble but I always complained to my mother, cruelty is a bottomless well,

in the end the bastard and the freak are cut from the same cloth

snitch, dirty snitch

and because of my complaining my mother would sternly scold Maria da Guia, for a while the creature would stop telling me story but after a while she would resume her habit habits are so hard to break

of talking about the mother and the eight children, if
Maria da Guia does not stop skulking near the coffin I will
complain about her and my mother will scold her, maids
when properly trained can stand for hours at a time, I might
have even welcomed a story, perhaps it would have distracted
me from the card-playing companions, from Alice's husband
hand in hand with his mixed-race children, no, they did
not come to the wake, or perhaps they did and nobody saw
them, it's been a while since we stopped seeing them in the
cafés, the bakeries, the streets, all the places where they no
longer belong, if Maria da Guia could tell the story again
I would pretend not to hear the rejoicing of the living,
the murmur of self-satisfaction, if I paid any attention they
would hurt me, the mumbling of the living that says, my time
has not come yet, the time of the ones we love has not come
yet, if I cherished them they would hurt me, chirrup-chirrup,
crickets, it can't be crickets, if I cherished them, I won't
run that risk, I took their measure a long time ago and that
is the measure I use, that is why we are alike, I too feel
the fear that makes their steps uncertain and their mouths
dry, the fear that makes them come to Christ begging him
to spare them, fools, sooner or later their time will come
and when it does they will not be able to expect more
compassion than the amount they were able to give,

you cannot give what you don't have

there are small differences, tears, for instance, not all of them as easily produced for merely physiological reasons, stupid Clarissa always puts on a good performance at every wake, she can cry well, she can fake sadness well, it's a knack, everyone present knows that when their time comes they will be served the same measure of compassion, that is what worries them, only that, if Maria da Guia would tell me the story again instead of skulking near the coffin,

do you need anything, menina

Ângelo won't stop asking Dora if she is OK, Dora always says she is OK and that she doesn't need anything, how can my child say she is OK when next to my coffin is a heart-shaped floral wreath that Denise ordered together with Betty, Lilita and half a dozen others whose names I can't read, my customers all chipping in for this heart-shaped wreath of roses and orchids with a card and a message chosen by the florist

as we pay our final respects we express our sincerest condolences to the family

from one of the many messages for occasions such as this, there are also messages for births, weddings, silver and gold anniversaries, get well wishes, christenings, there are messages for every occasion where flowers are offered, when she saw Denise struggling the florist rummaged around in her drawer, I have a choice of words that always do nicely, she likes to say do nicely, she was picking out scraps of paper, these are for weddings, on the day of this happy event we express our sincerest wishes for, this is one of the more popular ones, people usually like this one, look, this one is for a girl's christening, one of these days I need to organise all of this, ah, here we are, the ones we are looking for are always the last ones, whenever a customer's own words do nicely I always ask their permission and copy them, this was written by a doctor for the death of a friend who was also a doctor, the florist read the text with such feeling that she made Denise laugh, it's nerves, nervous laughter, Denise apologised, but it sounds good, as we pay our final respects we express,

how do you come up with these things, Violeta

it is one of my favourites, in fact the doctor writes some very lovely things, for a wedding he wrote something that makes me want to cry, so have you picked the little flowers you want, the florist likes saying everything is little, Denise looked at the buckets filled with flowers, bunches of daisies, white lilies, carnations, flowers are so pretty,

of all the mysteries I choose that of flowers that die at the height of their beauty

Denise might notice how pretty the flowers are if she were not so worried about choosing them, I really have no idea, the florist helped, roses, for a lady some little roses always do nicely,

and what flowers are appropriate for a freak

if it were a gentleman carnations would be better, or these white lilies, and Denise, these orchids are so pretty, they are pretty but as you can imagine they're also a little pricier, and Denise, well you only die once, this time both Denise and the florist laughed, nervous laughter, surely it is nervous laughter, the florist says, even if we don't laugh about these things we'll all still die one day, you are right, a good florist, the best, next to the coffin a heart-shaped wreath made of roses and orchids with a card bearing the words that the florist copied from a doctor who wrote them for a friend who was also a doctor, on my chest the calla lilies that Dora bought at another florist, incompetent, such an incompetent florist that she had no idea what flowers were appropriate and

where is my father, why hasn't he shown up

let Dora buy half a dozen wilting calla lilies, let her write on a little piece of paper, like the little yellow papers I use for my messages,

the lilies in our garden were prettier, but now I can only offer you these where the hell is my father

I wonder what type of person this florist is who suggests a message like that, someone as rancorous as that florist should not be allowed to exist, she should be made to shut down, you never know what a rancorous florist might get up to, Dora's flowers on my chest and over my face Ângelo's bunch of lilies,

what is the bastard doing here

wrapped in cellophane, a card made of good quality paper, a few words, and at the end, eternal sorrow,

how do you write a condolences card

another unfunny joke, he can't help it even at a wake

in permanent ink

if Ângelo were not so worried about Dora he would realise that the joke has not gone down well, nobody laughed, it is still not the right kind of performance for Ângelo, he did not write what he should have written on the card, for instance, from the bastard who never forgave you, Ângelo should have written that not to be funny but to be honest for once in his life, the truth is the best thing we can offer others, not laughter, Ângelo could have used the opportunity to give me the truth, and besides a few words written from the heart always do nicely as Denise's florist said, so a bunch of lilies and a card on my face, and on the rest of my body more flowers, from neighbours, acquaintances, flowers piled on the good quality wood, the Imperial model,

if my father doesn't show up it might mean he is

a classic and elegant model, for my mother I chose the Napoleon that suited her so well, I'm confused, wasn't it the light-yellow dress that suited her so well, and for my father, I forget what model I chose for my father, maybe the Imperial model, this time we didn't need the fashion magazines that my mother

classic lines never go out of style, *chérie*, there is nothing like classic lines

and the seamstress used to thumb through, a small catalogue, laminated, horrible, my mother and the seamstress always thumbed through the magazines but always ended up agreeing on a cache-cœur and a straight skirt, in a dark colour, not black, because girls shouldn't wear black, and besides black is an ugly colour, I hate black, the seamstress used to say, it is the hardest colour to work with, the fashion magazine remained in the attic and the buyers laughed at them, my mother saying, what if we did this one, and the seamstress, have you thought what those pleats will look like on her body, she'll seem twice the size, I'm not a miracle-maker, if I were I'd be a saint instead of a dressmaker, at least my back did not hurt, my mother was resigned to the tragedy of having brought into the world a creature that never wanted to wear the *dernier cri* of the Paris magazines, perhaps the Imperial model is the *dernier cri* in this collection, the funeral director promised me that it was a nice model, why did he speak to Dora and not to me

it is so difficult to let go of what keeps us here

where are you, Father

how life carries on

Ângelo and Dora are sitting in a café, the waiter picks up the plates left by the previous customers, Dora asks him to please also take away the plate used as an ashtray, the waiter, who looks like he is annoyed, does as Dora has asked but seems bewildered, every table has a plate used as an ashtray and nobody has asked for them to be taken away, Dora turns to Ângelo for support but he tells another joke,

two dinosaurs are eating traffic lights and then one says to the other, careful, that one there is still green

it's his fifth joke and they haven't been sitting for long, with every joke Dora fulfils her duty to laugh, truth is not the best thing we can offer others, if Ângelo refuses to acknowledge he's not cut out to be a comedian there's nothing to be done, Dora and Ângelo agreed to meet in this café, an ugly place with white half-tiled walls, scuffed plastic tabletops, unmatched chairs with ripped upholstery, dirty floor, paper, crumbs, cigarette butts, Dora looks around,

this café was always so sad

Ângelo says, in the affectionate tone he uses with her ever since, ever since

what you mean is that this café was always a bit grimy

he's got it into his head that now it is he who knows what Dora is really trying to say, since he's started to know everything about my child because he watches her at the hypermarket checkout scanning the barcode for a blanket 150 × 200 cm, 100% cotton temperature compensation fabric moisture-wicking breathable non-shrink machine-washable up to 60°C dryer-safe, for non-slip socks cushioned Turkish fabric elastic seams for perfect fit sizes 35 to 46 various colours and patterns, for delicious Norwegian smoked salmon 5–7 slices 100 g, for dog treats 100 dried strips with vitamin A, D and E for clean and healthy teeth reduces plaque strengthens gums trains chewing muscles, for a planter box with 4 wheels 79 × 38 × 34 sturdy and decorative, Ângelo who has got a lot of nonsense into his head since I, since I

say the word, say the word so it stops hurting, so it loses its meaning

have been far away, Ângelo is convinced that he knows what Dora wants from life as she sits there in her ridiculous uniform mopping up the water from a bag of fish that split open on the conveyor belt, if I said I am OK that's just what I meant, says my child without getting annoyed, she never gets annoyed with Ângelo when he corrects her, if I said this place is sad I meant to say it's sad, she does not get annoyed like she got annoyed with me even when Ângelo lurks in the aisles with the very white light, my child sees Ângelo the scarecrow and smiles, waves at him, sometimes Ângelo watches the girls in roller-skates without knowing that Dora wanted to be an ice-skater, and a doctor, and a petrol station attendant, she wanted to be everything and ended up becoming a cashier at the hypermarket, with the expectation of being promoted to cashier supervisor, how can Ângelo be convinced that he knows what my child means to say when he knows nothing about her, he met Dora the day he went to the hospital, the day my father, or his father, or our father, words complicate life to the point

I'm your half-brother

that our siblings come in halves, since then Ângelo has remained close by,

whole days spent standing at the end of our street hating us, I mean, looking after us

I always thought of Ângelo as a gift I offered Dora the day her grandfather died, to avoid seeing her cry I offered my child a man who was like her grandfather but younger, when my child saw the present I brought her she was very happy, she had never had a scarecrow before, sorry, I mean an uncle, I always thought of Ângelo as a present that I offered Dora the day she lost her grandfather, an old and tattered doll, today my child is taking a day off from the family buying veal rolls in the three-for-two offer, from the woman who arranges her groceries in plastic bags while the husband pulls a car magazine out of the magazine display to verify the price of the car he left in the car park, space F 78, second floor, the two siblings arguing over the strawberry chewing gum, today Dora has the day off and can meet with my half-brother, her half-uncle, for a week Ângelo has been insisting on the meeting, scarecrows can be so persistent, a whole life spent insisting on a meeting or chasing away birds, they don't care as long as they can repeat their days, tomorrow Dora will be back at the hypermarket and the secrets she gleans from families' purchases, as if the attendants at the Princesa Beauty Salon would allow any family to have any secrets,

tell me a secret, keep me awake, don't let this life come to an end

as if the attendants at the Princesa Beauty Salon had not already stolen everyone's secrets, even the one Ângelo wants to tell Dora, poor Ângelo unable to do anything right, the same lack of self-awareness that trips him up when he is on stage, when he sits at this café with Dora,

can someone from DIY section come to checkout 37, someone from DIY to checkout 37 you were born so that I could know the love that I had only ever heard about

since I have been, since I have been far away Dora hears voices inside her head, if only the crickets could move into Dora's ears, chirrup-chirrup, I am certain that Dora would prefer to hear crickets singing, chirrup-chirrup, if Ângelo were not so oblivious he would realise that Dora is miles away from him, from the café, entangled with the voices in her head, if he were not so oblivious he would not mind the silence that has grown between them,

there is nothing that silence won't kill

he would not try to draw my child's attention away from the man at the next table, tapping the tabletop rhythmically with his fingers, he would not talk about the rain that continues to fall, the storm has not becalmed the sky that still looms threateningly over the earth, Alice, on the other side of the world,

the worst thing is someone getting an idea into their head

she also jumped into the sky at two-fifteen when the temperature on earth was thirty-five degrees, a driver passing by heard the body's thump and when he got home he talked about it with his wife and the following day had forgotten about it, Dora is looking at the man at the next table and the drops of water on the windows, the wind threads the drops into a trickle, the window is covered with thousands of watery streaks, the man has not stopped drumming on the tabletop with his fingers, he is impatient, waiting for someone, Dora tries to guess who it is that is running late, through the café door she sees a man crossing the street in such a hurry that a car honks its horn at him, she thinks that is who the man is waiting for but quickly concludes he isn't because the other man just walks off, now Dora notices a man taking shelter in a shop entrance, an old woman fastening the coat of a child she is holding by the hand, seen like that people are very funny, fish in a fish tank, Dora says quietly to Ângelo, the man sitting there is tired of waiting, I'm glad you weren't late, I don't like waiting, Ângelo looks at the man as if he were trying to find something, like how to wait for a better moment to say what he has to say, Dora asks, did you have a performance yesterday, I did and it went really well, Ângelo starts telling her about the performance but Dora interrupts,

you said you wanted to tell me something

Ângelo smiles awkwardly, yesterday's show was, Dora leans forward, I'm curious, but Ângelo continues talking about how performances should start earlier, it's tiring having to go to bed so late, it's the only downside of the career he chose, Ângelo might point to his audiences' disapproval as a downside had he not been so deluded about his performances always going very well, and he is right, applause and heckles take the same time to be forgotten, a woman enters the café and smiles at the man at the next table, Dora says, he was waiting for that woman, the woman who arrived is wearing a grey coat that suits this rainy day and she smells of expensive perfume, the woman greets the man discreetly, as if she should not be there, and then she sits down and slowly removes her fine leather gloves pulling them off by the fingers, Dora notices the woman's hands, very thin hands, almost waxen, a small diamond on the right hand ring finger, the hands the woman puts on the table seem false, that man and that woman behave like lovers, they are worried that their eyes will betray them, Dora notices the woman's lips are the colour of pomegranate seeds, she has never seen anyone with lips the colour of pomegranate seeds, the woman has a measured voice and pronounces words in a very particular way, I was late because of the rain, a pause, I don't like these days at all, another pause, these days are horrible, have you seen how long it's been raining non-stop, and they say it'll go on, the man shrugs his shoulders, the man is so strange, I don't mind, I think I even prefer these days to the blue-skied days, the blue-skied days baffle me, the man does not hear the woman who is saying, this morning I went for a swim, swimming does me good, the woman seems used to the man not listening to her, the man points at the street and says something that Dora cannot hear because of the loud laughter from a group of boys sitting at a table at the end of the café, one of the boys is wearing a T-shirt that says, *have a nice day*, Dora's attention returns to the couple, it feels like I'm among clouds, like I'm part of the clouds

the pool ceiling is transparent, I just float on my back looking at the sky

birds never rest in the sky, the beating of their wings tires them out, takes them somewhere else, the birds only come to rest when a hand takes them to their final sky, my father's hand

Dora doesn't always hear what the man is saying, a low voice, the words curling, the opposite of the woman, I often dream I am flying, it's a common dream but I know people who have never dreamed they can fly, in fact there are people who don't dream, they only sleep, it must be very sad,

bêtises, ma chérie, bêtises

Ângelo touches Dora's arm to get her attention, what do you want to drink, Dora smiles, I get distracted by other people's conversations, my child does not know how dangerous it can be to smile at a bastard with revenge running through his veins,

the worst thing is someone getting an idea into their head

Ângelo calls the waiter who hasn't smiled once since Ângelo and Dora have been there, the waiter is not angry but likes to appear angry, it is a habit he developed, Ângelo asks for some toast and tea, Dora asks for a beer, which surprises Ângelo, a surprised scarecrow is so comical, a beer, I didn't know you liked beer, Dora, we know so little about one another, we all know so little about others, and with this weather, I don't think a beer would be nice on a day like this, Ângelo can be so tedious, the weather makes no difference, Ângelo keeps quiet, he was always a weak adversary, Dora confirms her order, a beer, the waiter scribbles something on a notepad and shouts through a half-door that opens onto the kitchen counter, one toast, and then he walks away, Ângelo and Dora met at this café because they have to talk but Dora is still paying attention to the couple at the next table, she can entertain herself with anything, with the lives of others, the voices inside her head, anything, Ângelo starts talking about the performance again, a monologue interrupted only by the duty Dora feels to laugh at every joke, Dora goes back to the couple at the next table, the lives of others always seem more interesting than our own, other people's houses always seem tidier than our own, for a few seconds Dora thinks that other people's hatreds are always more reprehensible, that other people's loves are always more ridiculous, Dora has time because Ângelo insists on his boring monologue, Ângelo has not yet decided how to say your mother made up lots of lies about me, I'm worried that you believe them

the things that a scarecrow worries about

what he needs to say, Dora cannot make out whether the man at the next table is paying attention to the woman, the woman says, I hate the cold, I am so unhappy on days like these, the man speaks a little louder and Dora is able to hear him, the cold doesn't bother me, people are more decent, I like the hygiene of cold weather, the woman looks surprised, hygiene, the woman looks more beautiful when she is surprised, people cover up more, sweat less, smell better, I like the hygiene of cold weather, the woman is irritated by the man, stop talking nonsense, hygiene and decency, I only see people feeling hassled, the woman looks almost ugly when she is irritated, she lights a cigarette and exhales the smoke quickly, I shouldn't have come, I don't have the time, I thought of cancelling but since I hadn't seen you in such a long time, I hadn't heard from you, these days make me crazy, if I could I would stay in bed until, the woman stops abruptly,

do you have something to tell me

Dora is surprised to hear from the woman's mouth the very same question she asked Ângelo just a few minutes ago, the man also has something he wants to say to the woman, maybe that is why he seems impatient, Dora says, I thought he wanted to leave but he has something he needs to tell her, Ângelo replies tersely, we always have things we need to say to others, and Dora, I also have something to tell you, I hope you are not upset with me, the man at the next table talks about a bed and breakfast, about the bed and breakfast owner, things that Dora is sure are meant only to hide what the man does not want to say, don't worry, I am incapable of being upset with you, I will never be upset with you, Ângelo promises,

nothing like a child to hurt us

the woman at the next table stubs out her cigarette on the plate that serves as an ashtray, she rubs her hands,

I've had a bad premonition

the man coughs, whatever he is hiding seems serious, it is so easy to hide things from others, Dora hid from Ângelo her decision to leave our home, to leave with the artist, she doesn't know how to say to Ângelo that

I'm leaving your life tomorrow

she is leaving with the artist, that Ângelo's lonely and miserable life will not stop her from leaving, don't think I'm going to throw away the life I have ahead of me for your sake, words can be very unpleasant, Ângelo also doesn't know how to say that I made up things about him, things that might make someone laugh if they weren't also so serious, the thing is that your mother, I can't let Ângelo say what Dora is not willing to hear, Ângelo can construct whatever truth he wants as long as it is in both their interests, Dora will accept Ângelo's story if he leaves out certain details, for instance, that his plan was easy to execute because her grandfather, my cowardly father, felt so guilty that he forgave him everything,

tell them you know me

these people will make anything up to save their skins

because I, her mother, the freak half-sister, was a slut, there was not a single boy I had not been with,

a black returnee, even with a black returnee

the menina is a naughty girl, the menina is a very naughty girl, if you carry on like that you'll end up in hell

Ângelo cannot say, it was easy to fulfil my revenge because they were all so lonely they were pitiful, they were all so vulnerable, it was easy to execute my plan because unhappiness was like a serious disease in them, they were at everyone's mercy, Ângelo has to construct a truth that Dora will accept, the man at the next table should also invent something nice to tell the woman, truth has the advantage of being malleable to our will, the waiter brings the beer, the tea and the toast, Dora fills her glass, Ângelo says, I'm really surprised, I have never seen you drink, Dora takes her first sip, she is always so elegant, the blue jacket suits her so well, her blonde hair falling down her back, the greyish eyes, the woman at the next table asks, unexpectedly loud, how long ago since you've been with someone, if they are lovers as Dora believed then what sense can that question make, others are always a mystery, the woman continues, you never loved me but I always considered that to be your shortcoming, the woman pauses and then continues in a firmer voice, if that is true then I forgive you, but if I find that you betrayed me I am capable of killing you,

I have heard about love

I am serious, I have never been so serious about anything in my life, Dora is moved, she had never heard anyone talking like that, Dora likes the unutterable phrases from some of the novels she reads, the woman must have read her lines in some old novel, pity those who choose to copy someone else's life, the man does not respond, Dora thinks this might not be the first time he has heard the threat, Ângelo dips his toast in the tea and eats it with satisfaction, Dora tells him off without hesitation,

the way we eat distinguishes us from animals

a bastard is never anything more than a bastard, *ma pauvre chérie*

369

and Ângelo says something he can't get out of his head, you remind me more and more of your mother, I hadn't realised you were so alike, it's strange how I never noticed

the most perfect part of me

the most imperfect part of Dora

it's very remarkable, it looks like you and your mother somehow became one after she, you are so alike, the same gestures, the same way of saying things, I don't remember you being so alike, Dora is still paying attention to the woman at the next table who insists, are you sure you have nothing to say to me, the man is rattled by the woman's inquisitiveness and keeps his eyes on the café table, close to the waxen hands, how can he get the idea out of the woman's head, you're not dressed warmly enough, you'll catch a cold, you have to find someone to take care of you, when the woman finishes saying that the apprehension in the man's eyes vanishes, Dora drinks her beer and looks at the couple, she is no longer interested in the watery streaks on the windows, in Ângelo dipping his toast in the tea, that woman who is worried that the man will catch a cold is the same one who only a moment ago said she was capable of killing, Dora tries to put together everything she knows about that couple to find out what keeps them together, what pulls them apart, in this café, anywhere, then again nobody knows what keeps her together with or apart from Ângelo, the woman looks affectionately at the man, for now she has given up on discovering what he is hiding, perhaps it is best, the truth is useless, Dora can also do without what Ângelo has to say to her, two tables in a café and four strangers united by something as unnecessary as the truth, the two strangers behaving like lovers but who aren't, Dora and Ângelo behaving like adversaries but who aren't, at the next table the woman says, you're a lost cause, you're really a lost cause and the man lights another cigarette, they smoke a lot, the plate that serves as an ashtray, and which they have not asked to be taken away, is filled with cigarette butts, the waiter approaches, can I get you anything, he says, a beer, a tea and some toast, they placed the same order we did, says Dora, Ângelo shrugs his shoulders, indifferent, he wants the full attention of the most perfect part of me, my child, an angel that has not saved him yet, that does not intend to save him, now the woman is talking about a swimming pool that has been covered because of the rain, I always need to be close to water, the woman says, I need water to temper my heart, Dora smiles, later she will tell the artist about a woman sitting at the next table in a café who needs water to temper her heart, and about a man, her companion, who responded, you didn't need the water before, remember, although you won't admit it, the truth is that you changed, the woman becomes restless, nobody changes, get it in your head that nobody changes, the woman is wrong, anything is enough to change us, Dora had no intention to leave with the artist, Ângelo never wanted to share our secrets, anything is enough to turn us into others, do you think we were happy, the woman asks, such difficult questions should never be asked, the man pushes his chair back to cross his legs, I don't think it makes any sense to talk about that now, Dora wants the man to say that they were happy but the man says, perhaps we were happy but happiness is never what we imagine it to be, Dora would like Ângelo to say that he and I were happy, everyone deserves to hear what they would like to, if the past has no use then let's turn it into something we want,

there was never a secret in your father's life

I was the most sought-after girl at the matinées, all the boys wanted to be with me

my father never developed the habit of keeping birds

the name of a flower that is also a colour, never a monster

the menina is a very good girl, if you keep it up you'll go straight to heaven

tomorrow I'll stay with you forever

remaking the past costs nothing, it is a matter of patience, the woman, whose lips are the colour of pomegranate seeds, picks up her fine leather gloves, gets ready to leave but does not get up, looks at the man, at the plate that serves as an ashtray, at the café's white tiles, Dora looks away, she suspects the woman wants to leave because she feels she is being watched, the lovers, those who behave like lovers, do not like to be watched, or overheard, my child looks away from the next table and turns to Ângelo, say whatever you have to say,

do what needs to be done even if later they regret it

Dora should not incite Ângelo to hurt her, pain is not for them, it never was, they like one another without the need to hurt one another,

I don't know how to say this

Ângelo did not rehearse this conversation, perhaps that is why it will go well since when he rehearses his performances they always go badly, Ângelo cannot decide where to begin and all stories need a beginning, I don't know what your mother told you, anyway, I think you should know, I mean, it's important that you know what really happened, Dora remains impassive,

when they tell us a story we always hear another one

Ângelo is a stuttering scarecrow, it is so absurd I don't even know where to start, I met your mother the day I went to the hospital, the day I also met you, it was only then that I met your mother, Dora blows away some breadcrumbs on the table, Ângelo looks around despondently, I don't know why we agreed to meet in this café, I never liked this café, cafés are almost all the same, you were saying that you only met me the day my father

I don't know what your mother told you but I'm afraid that, Dora frowns lightly as she always does when she does not like something, my child's gestures remain the same, they mean the same things, Ângelo loses the nerve to continue,

I never told her anything special, I told her that her grandfather had a child with another woman and so she had a half-uncle, I never told her about the revenges you plotted

now it is the woman at the next table who looks over with curiosity, your mother invented a lot of lies and then started believing what she made up, Dora is waiting silently for Ângelo to finish, your grandfather, Dora interrupts him, have you noticed that you never say my father, you always say your grandfather, when you spoke to my mother you always referred to him as your father, Ângelo stutters, it doesn't come naturally but it doesn't mean anything, Dora is angry, an angel ignoring its own wings, do you want to hear a story my mother told me,

once upon a sunny morning

I never told you stories, it was Maria da Guia who would tell the story of the woman when she wasn't selling waxing products my mother would take one of my grandmother's recipe books and would start making food as though she were preparing a party for many people,

> with or without the guests my life, every life, deserves to be a party

one of those mornings my mother was sticking cloves into an onion, the sun puddled over the floor tiles in the kitchen, the kitchen that was so beautiful but looked even more beautiful on sunny mornings, I was looking at my mother, I liked her a lot,

> with or without the pretence my death, every death, deserves to be a tragedy

my grandmother was already ill, Maria da Guia took care of her, my grandfather was back from pruning the strawberry tree, or pulling out the weeds that took over everything, none of this is relevant, I just mention it because that's how I remember it, my mother was piercing an onion with the tip of a knife and then sticking in the cloves,

> start again, once upon a sunny morning

I think that succession of gestures calmed my mother, it was spring, the garden was filled with swaying poppies,

poppies had invaded the garden,

my mother finished sticking cloves into the onion, she showed it to me, do you know what this is, Dora, an onion, I replied without hesitation,

the cats roamed happily at our feet

and my mother smiled, no, it is a hedgehog, and she smiled again, when my mother smiled two dimples appeared on her cheeks,

the sky was the colour of the sky

then my mother said my name in a soft voice, Dora, listen to what I'm going to teach you, Dora,

the flowers were the colour of flowers

people are like hedgehogs, when they get close they always end up getting hurt, they can't help it, they don't do it out of malice but wouldn't know how to do it differently,

the story you are going to tell is the one about the gang of thugs that wanted to mug us

my mother, on a sunny morning, not yet knowing that we too were fated to be alone forever, when she finished cooking we went travelling through the maps as she often did but I think we did not go on the same journey, my mother opened a map, I think we both chose the destination but we didn't leave together, this is not important but memories are like this, a cascade of unrelated facts, while Ângelo listened he turned the teacup around on the saucer, he is so tedious, Dora notices the woman at the next table overhearing her but doesn't lower her voice, all stories are looking for their ideal audiences, perhaps the stranger is the ideal audience for the story Dora is telling,

at a café table the story of a man and a woman behaving like lovers

Ângelo leaves the teacup, he joins his hands on the table, I don't want to hurt you, I want you to understand that the terrible things you were told about me cause me great distress,

at a café table the story of a man and a child not behaving like father and daughter

it is true that I often came by your grandparents' house, it is possible that your mother saw me there, when I was very young, just a boy, I was enraged, your grandfather grew too fond of the idea of us being a family, he hurt us, he didn't do it out of malice, he just couldn't help it, when I was a boy I used to come by your grandparents' house and, Dora interrupts, I don't want to know any more about this story, I don't want to hear it again, the past cannot be corrected, full stop

stories never come to the end, they never have an end

Ângelo hides his unease by gesturing with his head, swallowing more quickly, he was always a weak adversary and the excessive affection he feels for my child weakens him further, when the waiter brings the bill the woman at the next table mechanically opens her handbag, pulls out a note and puts it on the table, a toast, Dora proposes, it's bad luck to toast with tea, Ângelo is obsessed by good and bad luck, the jade elephant always has its trunk turned towards the door, Dora signals to the waiter with her hand, impolite,

the most imperfect part of Dora

two beers, I'm not sure beer will go down well, I just had tea, Dora does not change the order, she doesn't care if Ângelo does not want beer, I'm sure you have other things to tell me, I'm sure, Ângelo is getting more nervous, he stutters, I only want you to know what really happened, Ângelo's nervousness does not stir my child who seems determined to get hurt, to hurt Ângelo, they recklessly became too close, the waiter, who likes to appear angry, brings two beers and two glasses on a tray, the woman at the next table looks away, for the sake of discretion, for no reason, Dora fills the glasses and raises hers, to a story that is not the least bit interesting, and never was

I did not know my child could be so cruel, Dora speaks loudly, very loudly, and

to the story of a son who never forgave his father, a common story, as old as the world

she laughs, a spasm shakes her, an angel that lost its wings and fell, she looks at Ângelo with rage, a dry fury, you can do nothing about what has happened, the little revenges you keep yourself entertained with are useless,

a story even weaker than the jokes performed by a scarecrow

Ângelo folds a paper napkin, runs his finger along the edges, the same gestures with which he straightens the bedspread every morning so the frilly edges fall straight, Ângelo is very nervous, he had not foreseen Dora getting angry, he is a weak adversary, we always spared him our fights, Dora is waiting for Ângelo to admit defeat but scarecrows are persistent, a whole life scaring birds away, or trying to make people laugh, they don't mind which as long as they can remain standing and repeating every day,

silence

not a single voice, a beating of wings

silence

Ângelo musters his nerve, I want you to know that I did not denounce your grandfather, I did not write anonymous letters, I did not make threatening phone calls, I did not have him mobbed, it is all a lie, a big lie, your grandfather did not go kooky because of me, if I call him father, if I understand him, that is my business only, you need to know that I did none of the things your mother accuses me of, that's all you need to know,

you wanted to make your freak half-sister pregnant

cruelty is a bottomless well, those who fall into it immediately lose their footing, the menina is still very young, be careful not to drown

Ângelo goes quiet, Dora is about to say, the problem lies with you, your father did not want you as a son and I don't want you as a father, the problem lies with you, some incapacity, some defect, everyone knows that bastards are incomplete beings,

nobody wants you

everyone knows, Dora is about to say this but hesitates, it is so easy to defeat an adversary as weak as Ângelo that the fight is not interesting, Ângelo does not take advantage of his adversary's hesitation, he has become convinced that Dora wants a father so much that she will accept anything, even a scarecrow, he does not know, he could not know, that Dora likes to dream about her father and hopes he will never appear so she can keep on dreaming about him, that is the only point of dreams, that they endure, that they last forever, Dora a child lying on the grass, her blonde hair spread out on the floor, the luminous body beneath the soft spring sunshine, the stray kittens walking over my child who is asking

is my father coming to see me

her grandparents about her father, the grandparents don't know how to reply, nobody knows how far angels will go in search of a father, one of these days your father is coming to find you and will take you on a big outing, the grandparents felt an obligation to protect the dreams of the angel that saved them, my child, her whole life spent dreaming about her father, praying that her father did not show up and ruin her dream, worried that she would never again have such a beautiful dream, and now a scarecrow wants to destroy everything in one fell swoop, he is capable of stealing her dream, my child resists, she is a good protector of dreams, the best, Ângelo

I still don't know what you wanted to say to me, I don't have much time

understands that Dora wants to leave, that he doesn't have much time, he understands everything ever since he experienced the revenge of understanding, the old men who heckled him in yesterday's performance, the children who pelted him with pieces of cake last Saturday, Ângelo understands everything, to gain some time he folds another paper napkin, it is the fourth one he folds in exactly the same way, Dora feels nothing for the scarecrow who set up a meeting to tell her a truth

I am not your father

I am your father

that Dora has no use for, Ângelo puts his hand over Dora's, he wants to make peace, such a pitifully weak adversary, Ângelo's hand on Dora's, I am sure your mother did not do it out of spite, I understand why your mother, Dora lets out a loud laugh, stop understanding, Ângelo pulls his hand away, don't talk so loud, stop drinking, Dora manages to hate Ângelo, an impossibility given the blood that runs through her veins, the flesh she is made of, Dora asks Ângelo if he feels ashamed of her, the woman at the next table would like Ângelo to say no, Ângelo is not ashamed of Dora, it is always ourselves that we are ashamed of, never others, Ângelo with his eyes on the folded paper napkin, I am sure on Ângelo's bedside table there is a book with the underlined phrase, it is always ourselves that we are ashamed of

Ângelo wasted another opportunity, Dora taunts him, if only that were true, my child is a survivor of shame, she survived the shame of a cheap whore, a snitch, an ignorant *coquette*, a scarecrow, my child has survived all forms of shame, Ângelo realises there is nothing more he can do, it is too late for him to save his truth, Ângelo's truth will die like

my sympathies

mine, my mother's, my father's, none of these truths matched, one story can be told in so many ways, Ângelo's mother, for example, told this story as if she had loved my father and had thrown her life away for him, Ângelo's mother's truth is almost interesting in dramatic terms, the only problem is that those kinds of stories are no longer in fashion,

fashion is fickle, there's nothing we can do

Ângelo gives up and

and you, do you have anything to tell me

changes the topic, Ângelo had imagined a story with a happy ending, for instance, a father reunited with a daughter, he doesn't know what to do with this wounded story that life is weaving for him, Dora replies with

I'm leaving

no compassion, I'm leaving, that's what I had to tell you, a few hours later, not many, nobody will remember the meeting of the scarecrow with an angel in this sad café, some time later, not much, nobody will remember anything, not even the woman at the next table who is listening attentively, a few hours and it will be as if this meeting had never happened,

I'm leaving

too much noise in the café, or in Ângelo's head, it is the noise of Ângelo's heart beating rapidly, stupid Clarissa might lend him her *pacemaker*, with one of those devices maybe Ângelo would not mind Dora going away,

don't leave

nor would he try to stop her, Dora laughs, my child can be so crass, who are you to say that, Dora has her life ahead of her, she is not going to throw it away because of a scarecrow, I can do whatever I want, Ângelo cannot talk, pain is robbing him of words, I can do whatever I want, Dora insists, that is what life is for, nothing else, Ângelo lowers his head,

if you want to ruin your future that's up to you

if Dora could tell Ângelo that she loves him despite the hurt the meeting would go better, some words are very hard to say, sometimes what we feel for others becomes complicated to the point of seeming unrecognisable, if Dora could recognise the love she has for Ângelo, if Dora could, while sitting in this grimy café next to a couple of strangers, recognise the love she has for Ângelo and tell him, nothing to it, but the past cannot be corrected, full stop, a story cannot be told twice in the same way, Maria da Guia knew only one story and never told it the same way twice, Dora puts her hands on the table and turns her face away with annoyance, the gesture is *chic, très chic*, the same indifference with which her grandmother

it looks like the bastard got tired of lurking near the house, it looks like he finally understood his place

talked about the bastard, a shout from the boys' table makes Dora and Ângelo look, as does the couple at the next table, one of the boys has a sheet of paper in his hands and his friends in unison ask him to read it, the boy with the sheet of paper in his hands clears his throat, the friends go quiet, the boy starts reading a declaration of love and

don't leave

they all laugh, guffaws amplified by the white-tiled wall, the dirty floor, the rain, Dora looks at the group of boys, especially the one reading the letter

air mail, *par avion*

who laughs and reads at the same time, one of the friends puts on a girly voice with squeaky shouts, don't leave, Dora empties the beer bottle and with a hand gesture, *ordinaire, très ordinaire*, orders another, raises her glass,

to my journey

Ângelo does not want to raise his glass, or drink beer, he feels embarrassed, about himself, about the most unknown part of him, but he ends up making a toast, to your journey even if I still don't know where

the most important thing is the journey, the destination does not matter

it will take you, Ângelo is good at pretending, let's drink to the desire to leave, Dora objects, no, I want to drink to the fulfilment of all our desires, Ângelo is about to leave the table, he does not want Dora to drink any more, the waiter brings another beer, Dora quickly pours it into her glass and raises it again,

to Ângelo, my dear uncle

she adds, loudly, almost as loud as that friend of the letter reader who continues to let out little shrieks, stay with me, please, don't leave, I can't live without you,

to my dear uncle who sooner or later will stop understanding everything

Ângelo scolds her, stop it, my child, an angel condemned to
this life, expelled from the paradise she had lived in, Ângelo
apologises, such a pitifully weak adversary, he raises his glass
and clinks it against Dora's, to your journey, Ângelo is very
scared, for instance, of losing Dora, of birds pecking his
body, nobody knows a scarecrow's fears, to my journey, says
Dora who never again wants to wake up with the presenter's
voice coming out of her radio alarm, repeat the gestures
she goes through every morning, take the bus, put on her
ridiculous uniform that suits her so badly, the roll of coins
for change, reply to one of her colleagues who is complaining about the rain, water is good to temper the heart,

where do you get the nerve to leave

this one is easy to answer, very easy, poor scarecrow

I'd need courage to stay, to leave I only need the desire,
or the need, depending on how you see it

the woman at the next table gets up and gives the man a
quick kiss on the cheek, she firmly fastens her raincoat and
walks out of the café without looking back once, Dora
watches the grey raincoat and the elegant steps disappear
down the street protected under an umbrella with coloured
panels, the man gets up soon after and leaves the café in a

hurry, walks in the opposite direction without sheltering from the rain, Dora raises her glass again, she proposes a toast to lovers, corrects herself, to the false lovers that feed off their own pain and to the true lovers that feed off the pain of others, tell me, Ângelo, which kind was your mother,

you are going too far

my child cannot imagine what too far might be, everything is so close to her, the words with which she hurts Ângelo, the sadness of the café, the artist, my voice, the desire to leave, her grandparents, the house she will never enter again, the dream of a big outing with her father, the products she scans at the hypermarket checkout, the managers, the girls on roller-skates, Dora gets up suddenly, walks towards the counter, I'm going to pay, Ângelo runs behind her, today is the day to settle accounts, to pay everything I owe, Dora says

you are going too far

before tripping, the boys at the table at the end laugh, nothing as pathetic as a stumbling angel, its wings hitting everything, Dora smiles at the boys, at first just a movement of the lips, then, involuntarily, deep laughter, waves of sound that shake her, Dora grabs the arm of the angry-looking waiter,

why the long face

Ângelo apologises, leave it, let's go home, Dora thrusts a
note towards the waiter, keep the change, she allows herself
to be pulled out of the café by Ângelo, it won't be long before
the house on Travessa do Paraíso is shut down, before everything begins the slow work of rotting, my clothes, my maps,
my furniture, the painting of the unreal mountains, some
time from now, not much, my house

pourri, completely *pourri*

a giant rat's nest that the lady from the estate agents was
afraid to enter, in this state it will be difficult to sell, people
get put off, Ângelo is apologising profusely, he is funny in
that role, blue bug eyes, faltering words, if he acted this well
in his performances I am sure everyone would laugh and
applaud, they leave the café, it is very cold, Ângelo opens
the umbrella and pulls Dora towards him, shelters her from
the rain,

if we see each other again

the world has an end, but human cruelty is endless

they walk towards the car that Dora parked nearby, Ângelo
says he will drive, and my child does not argue, they continue
in silence, they look out at the city beneath the rain, Dora
asks, into how many parts can a father's brain split, Ângelo
does not reply, you were the one who taught me, remember,
it depends on how hard you hit it, Ângelo does not laugh,

he is thinking about another joke, a father can do nothing for a child, a child can do nothing for a father, a good joke, the best in this type of performance, poor as life

I drive through the light

I drive through the light, gently, the road is narrow, winding, the sunlit tarmac dazzles me, I continue, on the right, the slope, covered with flowers that are the colour of flowers, on the left, trees that have the shape of trees and keep in their branches birds' secrets, in the sky, which is the colour of the sky, clipped wings, forever free of hands that grip them,

little bird, come here, little bird,

I move on, a field of poppies in the morning breeze, electricity pylons on the roadside, giants on their way to the fair, cotton candy, Ferris wheel, the gypsies deciphering fates, I drive through the light, I am on a journey, at the café, at the bakery, at the hair salon, everywhere, a single subject,

spring is here

a single topic of conversation, the air making flowers crazy and animals restless, the warmth awakening the flesh, from today nothing will be different, nothing will ever be different, an exchange of words, this season is terrible for allergies, I look for a cassette tape in the glove compartment, I stretch my hand to the right, the sun pounding on the car's plate metal, unbridled gleam, a fury that the trees placate, a dance of shadow and light,

of all the mysteries I choose that of light, this light

I squint, I need time to get used to this transparent light,

not white like the light in the room where people wait for death

of all the mysteries I choose that of shadow, this shadow,

the sun, the warmth feels good on my legs, on my hands, life feels good on my body, spring is back and

we can do nothing against the force of nature, against life that continues

brought with it the light from the world's beginning, it is difficult to breathe, pain in my chest, a single subject, a good day to travel, my body follows my hand with ease, the dexterity of angels despite the wings, the dexterity of bodies despite the flesh, I drive past a house at the side of the road, a front pergola with a pink bougainvillea, a dog barking by the gate, I could have been happy in this house, I was always happy in other people's lives, I pass the house with the bougainvillea, I leave behind the happiness that might live there if it were not already living in my heart, I find the tape, I put it into the tape player and press rewind, inside the car the chirping of birds suspended in the sky, on tree branches, a single subject of conversation at the service station I stopped at recently,

that one looks like a bride

an exchange of words, I had never seen anyone dressed all in white like that, not even a conversation, these days you see all sorts of things, my luggage is in the boot, he is waiting for me,

I'm impatient to reach you

always, everywhere, at all times, an understanding, he is waiting for me at the inn by the sea, I move on, I am not afraid of

a solitary inn, abandoned next to the sea

anything, not even love, my eyes brimming with happiness, on my skin the scars left by all my dreams, from today nothing will be different, ahead of me the sea with its never-changing time, my song playing eternally,

how do you come up with these things, how do you come up with these things an abandoned inn by the sea, I will lie down over the noise of the waves and offer my smile, the mindless air that suits me so well,

I am in such a hurry

he is waiting for me at the inn by the sea, I never travelled without someone waiting for me, I cannot be late, a leaf sticks to the windscreen, I can take it wherever I want to, I move on through the light that the morning is devouring, from today nothing will be different, the wound in the heart forever,

a hurry that hurts

I am attentive to the road, I don't know it from the maps, I had never seen it, a new route, the hands of the one who awaits me burn my skin, I run my fingers over the small grooves that his fingernails left on me, on my whole body,

I will never belong to myself again

I no longer have a place within me, the morning crashes impetuously through the car windows, six blasts of light stunning me, it is 14:37 on the dashboard clock, it is 14:37 out there in the world, accounts settled with life, a road sign advertises a junction up ahead, four roads all appropriately numbered, four destinations, I soften, I cannot desist now from losing myself with the one who awaits me

it is so easy to let go of everything that attaches us

bêtises, ma chérie, bêtises

I move on, tree boughs block the sight of the road, the enchanted forests in fairy tales, I overtake a man on a bicycle, I wave at him, the man smiles, I drive through a tunnel carved out of the tree trunks, branches and leaves, the sky replaced by earth, under the earth's shade

the position I'm in, head-down

the tarmac is a stormy sky unfurling ahead of me, I move on, I am going down a road that continues stretching towards the light, a convex world

a drop of water that won't fall

with me inside it, I move on, a force compelling and sus-pending me, expanding time, for the first time free of gravity, for the first time this happiness that prevents me from gesturing, it would be so easy to be like this forever, in a moment I'll be at the inn and in his arms, losing sight of the silver water, he calls to me from the bedroom window, says my name,

the name of a flower that is also a colour

an inn devoured by the sea

a fright that the heart does not forget, a blessing that the eyes cannot remake, the waves at our feet, the lace-like foam, murmurs, I close my eyes for just a moment, no morning will steal this lovely dream from me, my life a jolt in the universe's ongoing dream, I close my eyes for just a moment, a peaceful dream, here inside, here where I am, whatever happens nothing happens

suddenly

Casa do Campo Grande and other places,
August 2001 to October 2004

DULCE MARIA CARDOSO spent her childhood in Luanda, Angola, and returned to Portugal following the Angolan War of Independence in 1975. She studied law at the University of Lisbon and worked as a lawyer before becoming a full-time writer. Her first novel, *Campo de Sangue*, won the Grand Prize Acontece de Romance, *O Chão dos Pardais* won the Portuguese Pen Club Award and *Violeta among the Stars* won the EU Prize for Literature.

ÁNGEL GURRÍA-QUINTANA is a journalist and literary translator from Spanish and Portuguese. He writes regularly for the books pages of the *Financial Times*, and his translations include the anthology *Other Carnivals: Short Stories from Brazil* and *The Return*, by Dulce Maria Cardoso.